IT

It did take calm and precision, but it wasn't sniping. They were all moving, the terrain shifted and there was nothing to call a baseline. He rapped out bursts and kept them low.

Overhead, Colonel Wiesinger was trying to snipe. The bullets snapped over Kyle's head. They didn't hit anything. Moving platform to moving target was a tough shot. It was something Kyle wouldn't attempt, and he had a hell of a lot more practice than Wiesinger.

He and Wade had each fired a half-dozen bursts before the first motorbike went down. Two others collided with it and the rest gave up in a slewing, swerving tangle.

"Well, that was royally screwed up," Wade said, going to a fallen terrorist.

"That's because we're playing this like cowboys," Weisinger said. "Damn it, from now on I will be the voice of reason."

"Can it," Kyle said, anger welling over. "We got the target. We'll get the intel. All that, despite you falling asleep on watch."

Wade wasn't going to get in the middle. He went to the wounded terrorist and lashed him into a pretzel.

Kyle watched the rear. He didn't give a rat's ass what the colonel did now . . .

Books by Michael Z. Williamson

CONFIRMED KILL
TARGETS OF OPPORTUNITY
THE SCOPE OF JUSTICE

MICHAEL Z. WILLIAMSON

CONFIRMED KILL

AVON BOOKS
An Imprint of HarperCollinsPublishers

AVON BOOKS
An Imprint of HarperCollins*Publishers*
10 East 53rd Street
New York, New York 10022-5299

Copyright © 2005 by Bill Fawcett & Associates
ISBN-13: 978-0-06-056526-8
ISBN-10: 0-06-056526-8
www.avonbooks.com

First Avon Books paperback printing: September 2005

Avon Trademark Reg. U.S. Pat. Off. and in Other Countries, Marca Registrada, Hecho en U.S.A.
HarperCollins® is a registered trademark of HarperCollins Publishers Inc.

Printed in the U.S.A.

10 9 8 7 6 5 4 3 2 1

To Morgen Kirby,
for bad puns, worse jokes,
and a disgustingly delightful acronym

CONFIRMED
KILL

SERGEANT FIRST CLASS KYLE MONROE TRIED
to think about other things than an impending parachute jump.

It wasn't that he didn't like jumping. He did—though he preferred "admin jumps" to maintain proficiency, or an occasional civilian free fall, to a combat jump over hostile territory. At least he assumed so. He'd made over a hundred jumps. He'd been in more than enough combat, too, but this was the first time he'd jumped in to meet it. It was also the first time he'd done a free fall military jump outside of the High Altitude, Low Opening course he'd been rushed through in a few days. HALO was supposed to be a four-week school. He'd done it in nine days. Officially, that was impossible.

That was the Army. There was never time to do it right. But there was always time to do it again after screwing it up the first time . . . if they could replace him.

Of course, they'd also have to replace his buddy and spotter, recently promoted Sergeant First Class Wade Curtis, sitting next to him. Replacing the third member of their team, Colonel Joseph Melville Wiesinger, who was sitting across from them, wouldn't be hard and would be a very good idea, Kyle thought. He had no idea why the man was along, except to grandstand and try to hog glory. That was typical of this type of officer, and likely the only reason he had come. It wasn't as if Wiesenger had a lot of depth to him.

The C-141 wasn't the most comfortable craft to ride in, though there were a lot worse. Still, the inside was all metal and harsh. The steel frame had an aluminum skin, with tracks and padeyes for pallets on the deck. Harnesses and webbing hung here and there. The latrine was much like a Porta Potti, tucked under the cockpit. They were pressurized for now, but it was still cold. The USAF jumpmaster and flight engineer wandered through periodically to check the craft, and they were happy to share the huge cauldron of coffee they had with the three soldiers.

The problem was that Kyle and Wade tried to avoid caffeine because it affected their nerves. As snipers, they needed to be and wanted to be as steady as possible. While the coffee would warm them, it was contraindicated.

Wiesinger was theoretically a sniper, too. He was drinking coffee by the gallon. Kyle studied him again. The man looked very unmilitary, as did Kyle and Wade. The two NCOs had learned to do that as camouflage, to blend in. It was often useful to look like grubby bums rather than soldiers. In Wiesinger's case, he was simply a slob, in uniform or out—overweight, shaggy-haired, and with little regard for his uniform or civilian clothes. Kyle grimaced. Amazing how fast things went to hell every time.

As usual, it had started out with a good idea . . .

Kyle had previously been an instructor at the U.S. Army Sniper School. He'd been pulled out for two temporary duty missions to stalk and kill terrorists, first in Pakistan, then in Romania. Following that, it had been decided—and he concurred—to reassign him to avoid damaging the class schedule again and again. Wade Curtis had changed units twice in that time, from 10th Mountain Division to 3rd Infantry Division, and he'd also been given orders. The two of them were now assigned to an innocuous numbered detachment at Fort Meade that sounded like an administrative position. That put them closer to their boss General Robash, made deployments a lot easier, and let them use the range at Aberdeen Proving Ground for practice, as well as get some face-to-face practice time with the outrageously highly paid professionals from Blackwater Security, whom State Department hired to guard foreign leaders against terrorists and rebels.

Those worthies had even tried to recruit him. He'd been offered $300,000 a year plus expenses, based on his experience. He'd thought long and hard before turning that down. Perhaps when he was ready to retire in a few years . . .

Though honestly, it was more likely he'd be forced out with High Year of Tenure than voluntarily retire. He couldn't say why, except that the Army was his life and he was a patriot. Why else would he let them send him to exotic, distant lands to meet exciting, unusual people and kill them?

Unless he was a masochist?

He'd come into his office one cool, crisp morning, feeling very comfortable and confident, and found Wade and General Robash already talking. The general nodded and indicated a chair. Kyle would have stood otherwise, out of respect, even though he knew the general was casual about such things.

"We have another one?" he asked, sitting easily in his Army standard swivel chair.

"Indonesia," Wade said. "All-expense-paid tropical vacation. Gorgeous Balinese dancers, equatorial sunshine, fine crafts and artifacts . . ."

"Kraits, saltwater crocodiles, and Jemaah Islamiyah terrorists," Robash had finished. Even when he sprawled, he looked professional.

"Endangered species." Wade grinned. It was a

cheerful grin, but not one to reassure potential enemies. Wade was a hair over six feet, a coffee-skinned black man with rock-solid, lean muscles and the quiet confidence of a man who didn't need to prove how good he was.

"Not endangered enough," Robash said, his expression half smile, half grimace. The general was broad and bulky with a gravelly, resonant voice that rarely needed a microphone. He'd aged a bit over the last two years, directing the two snipers and possibly other units—they didn't need to know—to hunt down, dig out and exterminate terrorist leaders and bombers. The massive activity in the Middle East was proof it was working. The enemy was getting desperate as real professionals closed off avenue after avenue, closing inexorably in on what would be a bloody finale.

Then it would have to start all over again. Old enemies changed and evolved; new ones were created. But as long as there'd been civilization, there'd been those who hated it and wanted to tear it down. It was job security for those who defended it. A security many of them would be happy to do without.

"Good," Kyle said. He took professional pride in his part. He and Wade would never be known in any history book, but the results were their trophy.

"Good," Robash agreed. Not that there had been any doubt the two snipers would take the mission. Kyle was vaguely aware that he could refuse if he didn't like the op, and either other arrangements would be made, the op would be changed to suit him, or, if the general or others didn't like his reasons, he could be replaced. But so far, as rough and violent as things had been, he and Wade had come out okay, and the terrorists had become usually nameless statistics in unmarked graves.

Dead, along with two close friends of Kyle's. Old news now, but still a cold part of his soul. Jeremy, his spotter in Bosnia, before all this, and Nasima, their local guide in Pakistan, a stunning and brilliant young Pashtun who'd been their translator before things went to hell and she got shot during their escape.

Kyle wouldn't turn down a mission lightly. His friends were worth a hundred terrorists each, easily. The score wasn't even close, though revenge didn't enter into it other than as a faint glimmer in back. As he'd told his last target right before shooting him, any scumbag can hate things and blow them up. It takes a real man to leave others alone. Kyle had nothing against Muslims, he'd met too many good ones. And that made him despise the bad ones even more, for tarnishing the image of his friends and allies.

"So, what's the mission?" he asked, making it official.

"Aceh."

"Ahchay?" He had to look at the map Robash

was fingering on the table. A province of Indonesia at the far west end of Sumatra.

"Aceh. It damned near floats on oil, and could be the next Brunei. The sultan of Brunei was the richest man on Earth until Bill Gates came along, so you can imagine the political stakes. Most of the nations on Earth aren't even in the same universe as that kind of money, and Indonesia doesn't want to let it go. Jemaah Islamiyah is linked to al Qaeda, of course. They blew up the nightclub in Bali, have attacked other targets including hotels, and are now moving after Indonesian and corporate interests. They figure the civil war in Aceh and the antigovernment insurgents are good support for them. This group, the 'Fist of God,' are sadistic sons of bitches who like to be more discriminating. They choose very visible targets on an individual basis."

He continued, "There have been more ambushes, which are symptomatic and not really our problem. There have been a handful of hostages taken, and all killed in that gruesome hack-through-the-neck-with-a-rusty-saw method these pigfuckers have taken up. Those are our problem. Last month a ship was intercepted on the way in, with a large amount of explosives. Read: 'several tons.' Intel and traffic indicates they're planning something big. It might be in Jakarta, it might be in Singapore just to play hell with things, or it might move up into India or Pakistan or across to the Gulf. There are a lot of routes out of there.

"Much like Pakistan, we have a decently friendly government which is full of leaks. They have some decent intel and forces, but they can't get in close without being exposed. So we made our offer, and with the recommendations of Pakistan and Romania, they agreed. You gentlemen are getting quite the reputation." He flashed a thin, cruel smile.

"What's the target?" Kyle asked.

"We have no names, but we're working on them. We want you to take out the so-called brains behind either the explosives smuggling or the executions. There's an excellent chance they're one and the same. The first means you stop the source of those explosives you were dealing with in Romania. The second means you save civilian lives."

"Sounds good," Kyle said. "What's our terrain?"

"Jungle, mountain scrub, and some smaller urban areas," Robash said, indicating on the map. It was large enough to show crude features but not details.

"SR twenty-fives and M fours, at an initial guess," he said.

"Makes sense," Wade said. "That gives us range and concealment and some grenades for support."

The Knight's Armament SR25 was an updated version of the Armalite AR10—the predecessor to the M16 and AR15. It was in 7.62 × 51mm caliber, the Winchester .308 that was the standard for Western snipers and many deer hunters. It had been in production for decades, but had only recently been accepted into the military.

It had come about during operations in Afghanistan, where, for the first time since World War II, there was sufficient range to justify a larger caliber round. The M16's 5.56mm cartridge was great up to 300 meters—far better than many shooters gave it credit for. But at long ranges, size does matter. Old M14s from the 1950s had been hurriedly pressed into service, and they served well. But it was a sixty-year-old platform lacking a lot of modern modular features. The SR25 shared a trigger group and operating mechanism with the M16 and M4; could accept different upper assemblies and barrels, and different stocks, grips, sights, scopes, and bipods; and was inhumanly accurate—as accurate as the men who used it, for precise killshots on enemy leaders, support personnel . . . or terrorists.

The SR25s would mate well with M4 carbines that the two were so familiar with. Those had short barrels, collapsible stocks for ease of carry and for adjusting length of pull to match clothing and armor. They could and would be fitted with 40mm grenade launchers to provide additional firepower and some combination of night vision scopes or EOTech's holographic sights for quick targeting. An Aimpoint model was the standard issue, but both men preferred the EOTech.

They were given some leeway on their missions, because General Robash understood the need for a certain amount of individuality, and trusted their judgment. Unlike movie snipers, the two men were highly technical professionals, able to gather intelligence silently, select a target, determine the range and trajectory, and take it out, whether "it" was a generator, a facility to be illuminated with incendiaries for a passing Air Force jet to demolish, or a terrorist surrounded by sentries and sure of his immortality. They didn't boast, didn't show off, and when they parted ways with the manual it was for a good reason.

"The first thing is to get you gentlemen to HALO School," Robash said. "It's remote enough the easiest insertion is just to drop you in to our allies. Saves security issues at airports and we don't need to smuggle the weapons and gear in, like last time." For their mission in Romania, they'd flown commercial, met with CIA and State Department personnel, and transferred weapons around clandestinely. It was certainly doable, but there was no need to expend the political effort and money if they could just slip in, or in this case, drop in.

"Has to be HALO?" Wade asked. It wasn't asked out of fear, just out of curiosity.

"Yup," Robash nodded. "We've got scheduled flights going through that airspace from the

Philippines. You just bail out as they fly over. No one will even know."

"I like that part of it," Wade agreed.

"And we can just carry all the gear with us this time," Kyle said. "Why does that sound too easy?"

"Oh, don't worry about it," Wade said. "I'm sure something else will screw up, just to keep us feeling at home."

"That's what I like about you, Wade," Kyle said. "You're so optimistic."

"Yeah, something will get FUBAR'd," Robash said. Fucked Up Beyond All Recognition. "But we're going to try to stall it as long as possible. And I've got messages at my office and State ready to drop, if something happens. Unlike Pakistan, you'll be within range of a whole battalion of Indonesian special forces—the Kopassus. They hate terrorists, and the only reason they're not doing this now is because there's one or two leaks no one can track down. But the unit as a whole is clean."

"Nice to have backup," Kyle said. "Though frankly, I'm tired of getting into situations where we need to be bailed out." It had nothing to do with sharing credit. Kyle was fine with that, and certainly didn't mind letting other soldiers play when it came to shooting bad guys. But when things got to that level, it always sucked to be him. His wounds had been minor, so far. But he'd lost two friends and come within three tenths of an inch and a hundredth of a second of dying last time, being saved by a perfectly placed shot from Wade. If you bet your life, sooner or later you lost.

"Hey, practice makes perfect. Third time's a charm. Proper Planning Prevents Previous Piss-Poor Performance. I've got all the clichés we need to get through this," Wade said.

They all chuckled.

"Okay, so we HALO in, ruck our gear, we're meeting an ally?"

"Yes," Robash said. "And most of them speak at least some English. Reduces the burden."

"Oh, this is too good so far. Please give me some bad news."

"Very well, ninety percent of the people you'll meet will as soon kill you as look at you."

"See?" Wade said. "Don't you feel better now?"

"Right." Kyle nodded to Wade. "Why is that, sir?" he asked, turning back.

"Aceh is riddled with anti-Indonesian sentiment. They're all Muslims of one type or another. Some few in charge support the government because they're siphoning enough money. The rest feel put upon. Some are rebels, some are allies with the terrorists, some are having tribal feuds. And now you're going to give them a reason to hate Americans directly, not just intellectually."

"Got it. So, discreet, make nice, don't offend

any sensibilities, don't hit on the local women, be model advisors?" he guessed.

"Pretty much."

"And then drop some tangos quick and wave politely as we leave. How are we leaving if not with a battalion of Kopassus?"

"We're figuring you walk to the beach, call by cell and transponder, and the SEALs pick you up in a boat."

"And then we puke all the way home," Wade said. "Sorry, but my skin looks horrible when I turn green."

Kyle looked over his spotter's coffee-colored skin and said, "I'd figure it'd just add to the camouflage."

"Yeah. Oh, I'll do it. But I *do* get seasick in a hurry."

"Sorry about that," Robash said. "But you'll only be aboard ship a few hours to Singapore, then you'll just fly back on another Air Force jet. No need to entrust your gear to anyone."

"Yeah, that's not bad, really," Wade agreed. "Kyle?"

"Sure. I assume you have a detailed plan for us, sir?"

"I've got a rough itinerary and outline. You take care of the rest of it, and Colonel Wiesinger will handle the logistics."

"Yes, sir," Kyle said, frowning slightly at that. Wiesinger was very by the book, and had been a royal pain a time or two.

"But the first thing on the schedule is to get you gentlemen to HALO School, fast. Can you leave Wednesday?"

"Two days? Yeah, I guess. Good thing we're both unattached. Mostly." He had a semi-regular girlfriend, but he didn't need to worry about plans for departure. They had their own homes and accounts and just got together for fun.

"The Army greatly appreciates your dedication to the cause of freedom by not getting married." Robash smiled.

"Hell," Wade said, " 'marriage' and 'freedom' are kinda mutually exclusive, anyway."

"Tell me about it," Robash said, flashing the ring on his finger. "Sometimes I think it's on my testicles. But you gentlemen pack, I'll work on the fragorder and arrange for the movement orders for all of this. See you soon, and good luck."

"Roger that, sir," they both said automatically.

2

WHEN THE PHONE RANG AT 0600, KYLE was just getting ready for the duty day. He was out of the shower, toweling his longish-by-Army-standards hair, and naked.

"Monroe," he answered.

"Sergeant Monroe, Colonel Wiesinger. The general is in hospital."

"What? Sir?" It was a shock he wasn't ready for, this early in the day.

"We're not sure," the colonel said. He sounded worried. But there was an undertone of . . . eagerness? "Likely a heart attack is my guess. He's been transported. I don't have any other intel yet."

"Roger that, sir. If there's anything I can do to help, do let me know."

"Will do, soldier. Carry on."

"Yes, sir." Kyle hung up slowly, thinking that

was an odd phrase to use. It was too cliché. Almost as if Wiesinger hadn't had enough practice dealing with troops.

Just what was his background anyway?

The phone rang again. It was Wade.   .

"You hear?" he asked.

"Just now. Shit, pal, that sucks personally and professionally."

"Yeah, tell me."

"Listen, what do we know about Wiesinger?"

"Nothing, really. Want me to dig?"

"If you would."

"No problem. See you at the shop in an hour?"

"Right." Sighing, Kyle turned to get dressed.

Wade was very good with intel. Kyle was better at politics, though at times like this he realized he was a rank amateur compared to the men, mostly officers, who spent their careers at desks figuring out where the bodies were filed. The proper innocuous paperwork could kill a career or make it. He had a battlefield grasp that matched his knowledge of first aid, but he was not a surgeon.

Of course, Wiesinger might be more butcher than surgeon. But he undoubtedly had friends to have gotten as far as he had. It was a game Kyle didn't want to play. He drove mindlessly, parked, and got out. He unlocked the office, which was in an old but clean WWII building that was drafty in winter and had humid spots in summer. But it was discreet and private and theirs alone. He sat down and started on paperwork.

Wade had his cell phone to his ear as he strode in only a few minutes later. "I appreciate it, Sergeant Major. Yes, I will do so. You've been more than helpful . . . Sure, if he wants some range time, send him down, that's what we're here for. Thanks. Bye." He clicked it closed. "Are we secure?" he asked.

"I don't think we're bugged and he's not here," Kyle said.

"Good. Well, I found out an amazing amount, my friend."

"Yes?" Kyle prompted, figuring he wasn't going to like this.

"Colonel Joseph Melville Wiesinger is the son of Brigadier General Joe Wiesinger, retired."

"Never heard of him," Kyle admitted, brow furrowed.

"Exactly. He was an administrative general in the Pentagon."

"So he was nobody." One-star generals were a dime a dozen at the Pentagon

"Right. But he had enough pull to get his boy in through ROTC. He's not Academy."

"Didn't think so. Academy grads can be assholes, but they typically know what they're talking about even if they do quote the book. He just has the book."

"Yup. He was a staff officer from Day One. Logistics mostly."

"Hell, nothing wrong with logistics," Kyle said. "You can't fight a war without them."

"Right," Wade agreed. "But he wasn't an issuing officer. He was a procedure-and-documentation wonk."

"Ah, I see."

"Right," Wade said. "He's done nothing but sort papers, except for a year each, commanding an infantry platoon and company."

"One year?"

"One year, just to fill the box. And his year as CO was nineteen eighty-nine. He wasn't in Panama or Kuwait. Nothing close to combat. But he had to be a commander to make major in time. And as a major and light colonel at the Pentagon he was obviously a staff officer. And now he's a colonel detached from the Pentagon with half intel and half operations designators. So he's had a career full of nothing but pretty uniforms and neat stacks of papers."

The phone rang and Kyle snagged it. The normal Army greeting rolled off his tongue. "Sergeant First Class Monroe, this is not a secure line, how may I help you, sir or ma'am?"

"Sergeant Monroe, Colonel Wiesinger."

"Ah, yes, sir?" he said, switching mental gears.

"Nothing new on the general, but he's in critical care and is breathing and does have a heartbeat. I don't know more about it than that."

"Good to know, sir."

"Agreed. He's got a hell of a job here and I've

got some pretty big shoes to fill. It occurs to me I don't know as much about this operation as I need to, in case of ongoing problems."

"Well, anything we can do to help, we're at your disposal, sir," Kyle said. It was good when officers admitted they didn't know everything.

"Glad to hear it. Please calculate me into your travel arrangements. I'm coming along to get a firsthand look at how this is done."

"Ah," Kyle said, and then followed it with the only possible answer. "Yes, sir. I'm on it."

"Good. See you tomorrow for the flight to Bragg."

"Roger that, sir."

After they hung up, he turned to Wade. "He's coming along."

Wade got his first joke off quick. "He sleeps with you." He didn't even look up from his desk.

"Oh, fuck me, how do we stop this?" Kyle ran his hands through his hair and rubbed his eyes. Suddenly he was tired again.

"I'm not sure anything you say will change his mind," Wade said. Considering, he added, "You might try just loading him down with details and stuff that's intimidating."

"I could," Kyle agreed. "But no, I think we've just got to bite this one." He sighed again. "He is a sniper, right?"

"On paper . . . but he went through the course during the Clinton Years."

"Oh." For a long time, the sniper school had

been audit only. Once selected by his home unit, an existing infantryman attended the course for credit and then returned. It wasn't until later that the course became pass/fail.

Before that, candidates had been required to have both small-arms expert qualification and a maximum score on the Army Physical Fitness Test. Most commanders were good about selecting only those soldiers they felt could handle the job intellectually and morally. Then there was selection within the sniper teams for those who could handle the realities of it in the face-to-not-face conditions of battle.

But there were ways to pencil-whip qualifications and call favors to get any school slot. It didn't take much of a stretch of imagination to think Wiesinger was one of those. He certainly didn't have the physique to suggest great fitness, and his quick temper alone would contraindicate letting him handle any task requiring patience.

"And he wants to come along," Kyle said.

"Hey, it's good that he realizes he's behind the curve," Wade said.

"Yeah, though realizing it ten years ago would have been better."

"No doubt. Still. It can't be all bad."

"You are so cheerful, my friend," Kyle said. "No, it's not all bad. But the bad it can be is still plenty bad."

"Hey, we're in the Army to be screwed over. It's the Army's job to provide the screwing."

"Yeah. But just once I'd like Vaseline." He sighed and stretched. "Dammit, I've got to make lists and calls. There's only one good part to this," he said.

"Oh?"

"We're so short on time he'll pretty well have to approve what I call."

HALO School was at least fun. "Fun," of course, assumed the attendee liked waking up early, PT-ing a few miles, loading up with a ruck and parachute, then jumping into free space.

"How can you jump out of a perfectly good aircraft?" was the standard question from those who would never consider it to be fun. The stock answers were, "Two perfectly good parachutes on my back" and "It's not a perfectly good aircraft, it's a U.S. Air Force aircraft."

Physicals were necessary, as well as dental X-rays, presumably because the lack of pressure at altitude might loosen fillings. The two reported to Fort Bragg and were weighed, as always, to ensure fitness. While some soldiers always pushed their weight limit, Kyle and Wade had 20 pounds of leeway each and muscle tone that made it a mere formality. They were close enough in size to be buddied together and were assigned an instructor, a man ironically named Sergeant Storm. He was intense, and both blocky and short at five foot eight.

In a couple of days, they were rammed through

the physics of ram-air parachutes, repacking and emergency procedures, and were hung in training harnesses to practice. It was a fairly simple procedure for them, just strenuous and intense enough to not be boring without being a strain. Wiesinger was slightly taller and a bit heavier. They didn't see him much except in the evenings. The reports on Robash were that he was in hospital, critical but stable, and would be out of the picture for several weeks at least.

Then they moved to the Vertical Wind Tunnel, and practiced the rudiments of steering in free fall. It was easy enough for Kyle. He'd made a number of civilian skydives and knew the mechanics. It wasn't appreciably harder for Wade. He followed the guidelines and picked up on proper arch, bending to steer, recovering from a tumble and other moves. It was fun all around as students from all services watched the fan-generated wind blow each others' faces out of shape and billow up the loose, training jumpsuits that caught the 150 mph air to keep them aloft against gravity. Wiesinger had one advantage: he fell like a brick. Even cranked up, the buffeting winds couldn't tumble him.

Their fourth evening, Wiesinger looked them up. "News, gentlemen," he said.

"Yes, sir?"

"General Robash is in Walter Reed. It was a heart attack, but they think there may also have been a minor stroke. They're looking at angio-plasty."

"Thank you, sir," Wade said. "Damn, I hope he's okay."

"Yeah, he's a fine officer and a good man to serve under. Anything we can do for his family?" Kyle asked. He was anxious. Losing Robash would mean a new commander, new ways of doing things . . . and Wiesinger might be the one to assume that post.

"Nothing yet," Wiesinger said. To his credit, the inevitable excitement and thrill he was getting from being in charge for the time being wasn't shining through. He really was concerned about his boss. "I'll let you know."

Kyle was worried, and it wasn't just having to deal with Wiesinger. It was that he really respected Robash as a good officer and a friend, as much as one could be friends with a general. And professionally, the good working relationship they'd built would change drastically if anyone else took over. Stability wasn't a realistic expectation in the military, but catastrophic changes were rough.

From Benning they transferred to Yuma Proving Ground, Arizona, and jumped daily. Ten thousand feet with no gear under a 370-square-foot MC-4 canopy was even easier than a civilian jump. But the altitude increased each time, and more gear was added. The rig's mass limit was

360 pounds of jumper and equipment. The three of them were going to not only bend but torture that limit on their insertion. They worked up to altitudes that required oxygen, and even higher. Twenty-five thousand feet was the standard maximum altitude, but they did a jump at 30K and another at 35K, the weather outside the plane being positively arctic. Tears could freeze, skin could get frostbitten. Insulated jumpsuits were necessary, to be discarded after landing.

The word came down that Robash was recovering slowly and would require surgery, but would most likely survive. His military career was still very much up in the air.

"Frankly," Kyle said, "if Wiesinger takes over, I'm going to have to slip out to another assignment. I just don't know if I can work with him."

"Yeah, I know what you mean," Wade nodded. "The slot calls for a general, though. They'll have to assign someone to it."

"Unless they promote Wiesinger into it."

"I was avoiding that possibility."

The school was a good one. It was a no-bullshit, all-fact-and-practice session that both snipers appreciated. They were confident of their ability to perform the jumps in question when they were done, and didn't feel any time had been wasted. They thanked Sergeant Storm profusely.

"Glad to hear I'm doing my job well," he said. "If you have any suggestions, by all means give appropriate feedback on the end-of-course questionnaire."

Because of the speed they'd rushed through the course, there was no graduation party. Their class was only the three of them. They outprocessed quickly and departed.

By the time they returned to Washington, there was more information. Wiesinger had his cell phone out as soon as they hit the terminal. "Angioplasty didn't work," he told them. "He's got two fully blocked arteries. Surgery on Wednesday."

"Damn. Prognosis, sir?"

"Oh, he should be fine," the colonel said. "He was doing his morning four-mile run when he collapsed. So as long as nothing happens during surgery, he's plenty healthy enough to recover, I understand. Meantime, I've got to run this."

"Yes, sir," Kyle said. There wasn't much he could say, and he wasn't going to make a scene over the issue.

Instead, he got to work on prepping for the mission.

Wiesinger basically left that to him, which was good and bad. Autonomy wasn't a bad thing for a professional, but it did help to have feedback from one's teammates.

"Who carries which rifle?" he asked Wade.

"Take two of each? SR25s for shooting, M4s

for support. Means one spare rifle we have to lug, but allows us the option of one shooter and two support, or two shooters and one support."

"Good enough. I hate carrying extra weight, but flexible firepower is a good thing. Any idea what our local guides will have?"

"No," Wade said, shuffling through a printout stack. "That's not mentioned. Not much about them at all."

"Yeah, we keep getting that. I'd really like to know more about these people when we can."

"Indonesia uses a variation on the FNC. Insurgents may have that, or AKs, or M sixteens, or some Singaporean clone with no license fees paid."

"Okay, I'll keep that in mind," Kyle said. Wade had all kinds of information stuffed into his mind. "Is there an FNC we can examine for familiarization?"

"Not officially, no. But Sergeant Major Lewis has a troop who owns a civvy semi-auto version imported in the nineteen eighties we can shoot and take apart on the range. Different trigger group, but same teardown and characteristics."

"God Bless the Second Amendment," Kyle said. "Though it's a hell of a world when the Army has to call civvies for intel on weapons."

"C'est la guerre."

Beyond the technical information was the political situation. Kyle picked up another stack and looked at what background they had.

The Bali club attack on 12 October, 2002, had been blamed on the Al-Qaeda-linked Jemaah Islamiyah network that operated throughout Southeast Asia. The network's commander, Riduan Isamuddin Hambali, had been captured in Thailand and handed over to U.S. custody. But someone else had taken over. As with all the linked groups, they were getting desperate. Propaganda said they were surviving and coming out in revenge. Many Americans even believed that. But the fact was that Kyle, Wade, other operations, and world opinion were hurting them badly. And as the smarter leaders were killed, the less experienced and less stable often moved into positions of authority. It was the vortices at the tail of a large storm. But such vortices often produced tornadoes.

"I'm just amazed at the extent of these operations of theirs," Kyle said.

"Well, hell, look at their backing," Wade said. "Bin Laden has or had two hundred and fifty million dollars, four wives, fifteen children, several large chunks of stock in major corporations, insurance on projects at the World Trade Center that *made* him money when the planes crashed. He's loaded, and so are his buddies."

"Yeah," Kyle said, "Two hundred and fifty mil, four wives, fifteen children, a private resort and he calls Americans 'excessive.' Sure wish I could be as modest as him." He kept reading.

One of the problems they faced was that the

United States and Indonesia were treading delicately toward improved relations, after Indonesian Army atrocities in East Timor in 1999. And if they were discovered, it would be a slap in the face. Once again, shooting a terrorist was only one small part of the mission.

"This just sucks, buddy," Kyle said. "We'll be teaming up with insurgents against another group of insurgents, both of whom are fighting a government we want to be friendly with who is officially on our side. All are filled with snakes, and all are fighting other factions at the same time. You're black, I'm white, it's half industrialized and half jungle, full of billions of American dollars, millions of terrorist rupiah, millions of black market yen, dong, dollars, pounds, and whatever."

"Yes, and there are Dutch personnel with the oil companies, and mixed Malay and Chinese Indonesians who are Muslim, Christian, and Hindu."

"And a population way too high to make sneaking in the woods safe for any length of time," Kyle added. Alarm bells were sounding in his head, and part of him really wanted to bail on this one. But he couldn't. Not only would Wiesinger be an asshole over it, he owed it to Robash to finish what they'd started.

And he owed it to himself and Wade to maintain their reputation. Not to mention the civilians who were being abducted, tortured, killed, and possibly raped.

"So it's a challenge," he said. "We could ask Delta Force to handle it."

Wade snickered. "They're trying to remain unseen. And they were likely smart enough to not accept this one. Or else they're using us to see how not to do it."

"You are so reassuring," Kyle said with a shake of his head. "But hell, if we quit when it looked ugly, we wouldn't be here."

"Yeah, and I wouldn't be hearing the stories about you in the bar two weeks ago."

"Ah, hell, what now?" Kyle asked. "And never you mind the stories."

"Heh . . . I'll assume she's a lady. Will she be waiting when you get back?"

"That's a question I haven't even looked at yet."

Nor was he sure how. "Janie, I'm going to fly halfway around the world to skulk in the jungle and kill some asshole who likes to hack people's heads off and blow up wage slaves and schoolkids. Will you miss me?"

Somehow, that didn't work, even if he could discuss it.

"The Army is sending me halfway around the world. I can't tell you where or why, and I may come back with holes in me again, or not at all."

No, that wasn't much better.

"Good luck with it," Wade said.

"Thanks," Kyle said.

Sighing, he leaned back over his desk to other issues.

It was up to Kyle to inventory every damned thing they would take. It called for computer and book searches for National Stock Numbers, prices for items not on hand, weighing everything to ensure it would all fit under the 360-pound total mass allowance for these parachutes.

"Man, I've got a problem here," Kyle said.

"Yes?" Wade looked up from his console, where he was sifting reports on Indonesia.

"Wiesinger is seventy-two inches tall. Allowed one hundred ninety-five pounds. He claims two hundred ten and to make tape for body fat index."

"Okay."

"There is no way that bastard is under two twenty."

Wade looked thoughtful. "I'd say you're right."

"Well, he insists he's two ten. I can pack him a hundred and fifty pounds of gear. But if he's two thirty, that'll be twenty over. He goes splat. I've never seen the paperwork to do for a dead colonel. Pretty sure I don't want to. If I leave that twenty out of the calculations, it could be twenty pounds of ammo we need and don't have."

"Sucks to be you, pal. Split the difference? Pack him at two twenty? Ten pounds shouldn't break the chute. Actually, I'd assume the engineers put fifty pounds of leeway in there. He'll descend faster, but likely not fast enough to rip fabric or go in."

"Hmmm . . ." Kyle considered. "I might want to call Para-Flite and ask them to give me a no BS max."

"Then figure that for Wiesinger at two thirty and us at our weight minus three pounds for safety? Still means a risk, but a calculable one."

"Yeah. Thanks. I appreciate it."

"No problem. Glad to help keep us alive."

Kyle was still gritting his teeth at the thought of Wiesinger coming along. Wade and he worked well as a team. Adding in a third who hadn't trained with them was a bad idea no matter how you looked at it.

But he didn't get a vote. And he was the one who had to deal with Wiesinger the next day. That conversation wasn't fun.

Wiesinger called in and said, "I've been looking over your list, Sergeant Monroe. Hell of a long list you've got here."

"Sometimes, sir, yes." Kyle was tense. There were things on that list he didn't mind one way or the other. There were some he would argue to keep. There were some he'd consider a court martial over.

"I'll authorize you to take your forty-five," Wiesinger said, "since it's a military pattern and caliber. But you will carry ball ammunition only, none of that custom stuff. I don't want to see any silencers or other doodads, and Uncle Sam sure as hell isn't paying if you lose it."

"That's fine, sir, thank you," Kyle agreed. He hadn't expected even that much cooperation. Maybe Wiesinger was just a bit stodgy and wouldn't be in the way, rather than turning out to be the tin-plated asshole he'd come across as in the past.

"You can take the knives. I don't have a problem with that, though why you want to carry all that crap is beyond me. But as long as you have your issue gear, have at it."

"Yes, sir," he said. Two for two so far. And he carried "all that crap" because it had saved his life more than once.

"SR25s, suppressors, and all related gear, that's fine. I haven't shot that one yet, but I'm told it's good and you'd know."

"It is, sir. Thanks." That meant he'd have to get Wiesinger out on the range for some practice time.

"Aimpoints if you want them. That's the standard, and the EOTech has not been tested as thoroughly."

"Got it, sir." He and Wade had their own EOTech sights anyway. They'd take them as civilian luggage. And there were rave reviews coming out of Iraq. Part of him realized there wasn't *that* much difference, and he was doing it just because he'd been told not to. His independent streak got him in trouble at times.

"Please put together an appropriate list for me. Basic gear, an M4 and a standard M9 bayonet. I'll work on our travel arrangements and finances."

"Got it, sir. It'll be ready."

"Good. Don't worry about any pre-mission briefings. We'll deal with that in theater."

"We're not consulting our usual experts, sir?" he asked, confused.

"No, we're going to dispense with that and work through local assets and phrase books this time," Wiesinger said.

"Sir? Why not learn some basics? It's been very helpful in the past," Wade asked.

"According to your after-action reviews, it hasn't mattered squat," Wiesinger snapped. "Either you had translation books with you or a native. I don't see any need to risk OPSEC by dealing with civilians."

Kyle was aghast. He wasn't sure what clearance Mr. Gober, the ethnologist who advised them on languages had, but he knew the man was utterly reliable, never knew their actual destination, and was no threat at all to OPerational SECurity. To not utilize a resource seemed to invite trouble later. It was impossible to have too much intel.

"What about a cultural brief?" he asked.

"That's what the Internet is for. It's not as if we're trying to blend in and assimilate like Special Forces. We're just going in to take a shot and get back out."

Wade seemed composed. Kyle was ready to throttle this idiot. The problems they'd had on the two previous missions all came down to a *lack* of intel on their part, and Wiesinger proposed to jump in blind.

But the basis of the military was order and discipline. There was nothing they could do. Any appeal would stop at Wiesinger, unless it went farther up to a command level. The answer from there Kyle didn't need to hear—it would be to follow orders from the officer leading the mission, unless they could prove his doctrine was unsound . . . which would take longer than the time available and likely be fruitless.

"Understood, sir," Kyle said. "We'll do it the way you suggest." *Officially, anyway, you fat clown*, he added to himself. He hung up and sighed. It was sometimes harder to fight the chain of command than the enemy. You could at least shoot at the enemy.

That afternoon, they drove to Aberdeen Proving Ground to shoot. While Meade had a 600-meter known distance range, it was on land controlled by the Department of the Interior, and standard ball ammo was not allowed—only special environmentally safe rounds. As they needed to train with the ammunition they'd use, another facility was desirable.

The time they spent at the range was useful, but quiet. They adjusted sights, practiced correcting for wind, and made slow, methodical shots. They were quite capable of longer distances, but the range they had was sufficient to maintain proficiency and technique.

It was seventy rounds each into it before Kyle said, "I'm happy. Let's go to the office and talk."

"Okay. And clean weapons?"

"Yes. It's meditative."

"So it is. But only for a select few."

The vehicle assigned for their use didn't get much of a workout. They drove it to and from the range, because military weapons couldn't be transported in civilian vehicles, officially, and they used it for occasional supply runs. Otherwise, they found their own vehicles much more comfortable. Kyle was silent for the drive, and Wade followed his lead.

Once inside the office, papers spread on the floor, weapons cleared and stripped—a process that took them less than a minute apiece—Wade finally raised the specter.

"Kyle, you're really not in your happy place regarding all this, are you?" He managed the sarcasm without sounding goofy. Quite a trick.

"No, but I'm working on some ways to improve that."

"Oh?" Wade prodded.

"We can't consult Mister Gober regarding a mission. However, I've developed an interest in Indonesia. It has a fascinating history, a varied culture and could be strategically important in the future. As far as language goes, Mister Gober is the best man I can think of to talk to. Let's look him up."

"It does sound like a fascinating place, and I think we should. Perhaps we'll even vacation there, too." Wade was grinning.

"And luckily for us, he's based out of the D.C. area. I gather he does a lot of consulting on this type of thing, and I heard him mention a paper for Georgetown."

"Meet where?"

Kyle considered. While public would be less likely to be connected to any activity, that was in part because communications security sucked in the open, where any casual passerby or anyone with a parabolic mike could hear them.

"My place," he said. "Shouldn't arouse suspicion to do it once."

3

BILL GOBER WAS A LITTLE THINNER THAN
last time they'd met him. he was still portly
and cheerful, but seemed to be more lively. His
shirt and slacks were as casual as always, and the
case and backpack he carried were stuffed with a
laptop, disks, and books. He studied languages,
and seemed to have a stack of references on the
most obscure ones—Dari and Pashto for Pakistan, and no doubt something for here. Last
time, he'd briefed them on Romanian.

"Good morning," he said.

"Morning, Mister Gober," Kyle replied.
"Coffee?"

"Please," he agreed. "Some cream, some
sugar. Languages?"

"That will be fine," Wade agreed. "Some familiar, some gobbledygook."

"That should be easy enough," he agreed as he

sat. Kyle had moved his coffee table closer to one chair. It wasn't as if he ever used it for anything other than piles of reference material anyway.

"So, you mentioned Indonesia, and you specified Aceh. That's a rather contentious area."

"So we've heard," Kyle agreed.

"Well, the national language is Bahasa, and most people will speak it. However, Aceh also has the language of Aceh or Atjeh, with eight dialects. Officially, it's Austronesian, Malayo-Polynesian, Western Malayo-Polynesian, Sundic, Malayic, Achinese-Chamic, Achinese. It's actually distantly related to the languages of Madagascar and Hawaii. It's fascinating to track the development of languages across such a large area.

"Anyway, about three million people speak that. Actually, a phrase book should suffice, and some basic Bahasa, and some Dutch, as a lot of people still speak some Dutch."

"Dutch?" Kyle asked. He knew they were involved in the oil industry.

"Yeah," Wade said, "that was the Dutch East Indies until some bright boy decided to make it all one nation."

"Correct," Gober said. "There are fifty-two languages in Sumatra alone, and a total of seven hundred and thirty-one for the whole nation, of which five are extinct or nearly so. It's a very mixed area with a lot of cultural clashes."

"Sounds like," Kyle said. Seven hundred languages. Damn. "Do you have phrase books for Achinese and Bahasa?"

"No, but I can acquire some. Many military and technical words are actually English."

"Well, this isn't a military mission," Kyle said.

"Yes, but I assume you will be talking shop?"

Gober was obviously curious as to why they were pretending not to be running a mission. But he didn't ask, and was simply offering the information he thought they could use. Kyle had to respect that, and was disgusted at the situation. The man was no security threat at all, and yet they were ordered to treat him as such.

"We might talk shop with some Indonesian military people, yes. Actually, we might talk about oil, too. There's a lot of jobs opening up out there." That left the hint that he was looking for security or mercenary work after his enlistment was up. That should be all the misdirection needed.

Not, he thought, that Wiesinger would give a crap. He'd be pissed about them "breaching security" and "going outside the approved sources."

Not that Kyle gave a crap what Wiesinger thought. Which, he reflected, was one hell of a way to start a mission.

"Very well, I'll put together some common phrases for military and industry. I can send you online links to recommended phrase books you can buy. Will email work?"

"Yeah, it's not as if it's a military secret or anything, we just don't want any unfriendlies learning that U.S. personnel are coming, even off duty. My email should be fine." He hoped that explanation would cover any potential allegations that Gober had been informed about the mission. As far as Kyle knew, Gober had never been informed about any mission, only that "troops are deploying to somewhere and need a brief on languages."

"Okay, then here's what I have on Bahasa," Gober said, pulling out a couple of burned CDs and a thick book. "Face price on the book. I can let you have the CDs for free; they're public-domain sources. They're dictionaries and basic grammar, the book is a proper style manual. And these," he said as he pulled out four more slim, bright books.

"Those are children's books," Wade observed.

"Yes, with simple words and bright pictures that are easy to remember. An excellent way to learn some rudimentary vocabulary. And this is a CD of a speech, which is transcribed in Bahasa and phonetic English to display with the audio. It will help with aural recognition and inflection and accent."

"That's incredibly helpful. Thank you," Kyle said. They were loaded for bear, if they could find the time to review it.

"You're very welcome. I appreciate the business, and let me know how things go if you can."

"Once we return, we will."

"Good. And if you ever have a mission in Indonesia, you'll be prepared."

Was that a hint that he suspected more than he was being told? Kyle didn't let anything show. But he was amused at the potential irony.

"Well, anything's possible with all the training we do. I don't think we're sharing tips with Indonesia yet, but things are improving."

"Excellent. Keep me informed on General Robash's progress if you can. He's a good man."

"Will do, and thank you, sir." They all rose. Gober hefted his backpack and they escorted him to the door.

Once the ethnologist left, Wade said, "Look through the stuff now?"

"Sure, why not?" Kyle agreed. "At least a quick overview."

Wade brought out his laptop and plugged in. A quick connection with a LAN cable and they were ready to share data. They started downloading from the CDs.

"Wow, this is weird," Kyle said.

"What?"

"The number of words that are straight English. I see 'white paper,' 'telkom,' 'konstruksi,' 'elektronika,' 'transportasi.' "

"Lots of those could be from Dutch," Wade said. "But yes, that does help. Quite a few tech words."

They continued reading. Several minutes later, Kyle did a double take.

"Wait a minute," he said.

"Yeah, I saw that," Wade replied. "So it's not just me?"

"I don't think so," Kyle said.

The phrase on the screen in front of him was, "Prajurit itu tidak kompeten." *That officer is not very competent.*

Below that was, "Kolonel itu telah berbuat salah." *The colonel made a mistake.*

Beyond that were comments about engineering or artillery errors. But those two phrases together seemed to be telling.

"Gober knows," Kyle said.

"So it seems," Wade agreed. He was smiling a tight-lipped smile. "Which explains why he came over on less than twenty-four hours' notice, without needing to prep. He was ready."

"Doesn't help much," Kyle said. "But it's nice to have the support."

"I wonder if Robash had already contacted him and Wiesinger cancelled?"

"Could be. But why? It seems like he's trying to cover all bases himself."

"I think that's exactly it. Cut the budget, keep the cards real close to the chest, keep all the credit within the unit, and proclaim his genius."

"Great. A glory seeker." Kyle had several decorations and a couple of wounds from his missions. He'd never made the papers or even the military press. He didn't care. They were all on the same team, and as long as the mission was accomplished, everyone knew who'd done what.

"Let's break for lunch." He needed to unwind his brain for a few minutes.

"Suits."

After that, they needed to research the area. There was far too much wealth of information online, and as usual, half of it was dated, unsupported opinion, or flat-out worthless crap. Confirming data from at least two primary sources was more work than finding the intel.

Aceh certainly had a colorful history and present.

Aceh was as rich in oil as they'd been told: 1.5 million barrels per day. Natural gas production was 38 percent of the world's total. Other products of Aceh included iron, gold, platinum, molybdenum, tin, rubber, coffee, tea, and tropical timber. The locals were unhappy because all the income was taken away to Jakarta and they were left at the bottom end of the economic scale. Typical government thievery.

There were several factions for independence— GAM, Gerakan Acheh Merdeka, also known as the Acheh Sumatra National Liberation Front (ASNLF). "Acheh" as opposed to "Aceh." Apparently, the spelling difference was a point for them, which said something. Kyle wasn't sure what, but if they couldn't agree on a spelling in English, it wasn't likely they could agree on much else. GAM/ASNLF was split into at least two factions, one of which was negotiating with the government, the other which decried that and called them traitors.

There was also Hizb ut-Tahrir (HUT), the Islamic Party of Liberation, which claimed to not support terrorism but wanted a return to the Caliphate and hated the Saud family. However, there were indications that their condemnation of terrorism ended with the press release.

"I need a dance card for this," Kyle said.

"Yeah, tell me about it. Who's on first?"

"I dunno."

"Third base."

"I don't give a damn," Kyle replied, grinning. "Okay, actually, I do. You taking notes?"

"Yeah. Can we get a degree in international relations in lieu of attending class, just on the research we're doing?"

"It would seem fair. But I doubt they'll do it."

"Right. We probably have the wrong political viewpoint for college, too," Wade observed.

"Because we think that the way to solve this is to identify the trash and take it out?"

"Got it in one." It served as a mini break and to help them remember the dry data they'd just digested. Both men did it without conscious effort, and resumed silence again at once.

There were a number of prominent women figures in Aceh's military history. There had been an Admiral Keumalahajati in the late 16th century.

There had been four queens who successively ruled the latter half of the 17th. Guerilla commanders in the Dutch Colonial War era included Cut Nya' Dhien, Cut Meutia, Pocut Baren, and Pocut Mirah Inteun. During the 1945–49 fighting, the women of the "Revolution of 45" in Aceh not only served as service staff and medics (the Pasukan Bulan Sabit), but also involved themselves actively in fighting in groups such as Pocut Baren Regiment.

Women as troops and leaders certainly didn't sound very Muslim to Kyle. He said so.

"I dunno," Wade said. "This is all new territory to me."

GAM had had members trained in Libya. "I notice an ongoing pattern in all this," Kyle said.

"Oh, you do?" Wade asked sarcastically. It seemed as if every problem surrounding Muslim terrorism came back to Syria, Iraq, Libya, rural Pakistan, or extreme factions in Saudi Arabia. "I think if we took out about a hundred people worldwide, the whole problem would go away."

"Yeah, but they'll never let us do it, we wouldn't be able to find a lot of them, and it'd be suicide to go through their suicide squads to get to them."

"Yeah, why don't so-called suicide squads just kill themselves? I'll send the ammo."

"Heard it before," Kyle said. He did smile, though. "Wish it worked that way."

"So they have Muslim extremist women soldiers toting AKs and trained in Pentjak Silat and other lethal hand-to-hand techniques," Wade said. "Just what I want for a date on Saturday night."

"Reading this, I see why they're upset, actually," Kyle said. "They beat the Dutch six times over eighty years, costing the Dutch one hundred *thousand* troops. And then here: 'On twenty-seven December, nineteen forty-nine, seven years after withdrawing from Acheh, the Dutch signed a treaty with the newly fabricated "Republic of Indonesia" on the island of Java to transfer their "sovereignty" of Acheh to Indonesia, without referendum of the people, and against all the UN principles of decolonization.'"

"And the fight with Indonesia was on." Wade nodded.

"Yeah. They transferred title of an area they didn't control and only owned on paper to someone else. Damn. Why did the Achinese have to side with the goddamn tangos? I could support these people."

"The point is they have," Wade said. It was an unneeded reminder.

"Yup. So we get to do the dirty work."

"So, the Free Acheh Movement has wide support from the local population. The Indonesian government sent the special forces, called Kopassus, to hunt down members of the movement. Aceh was declared as a Military Operational Area. There are allegations of atrocities that rank

pretty high on the filthometer. The Achinese estimate twenty-five thousand casualties in custody
and in 'secret concentration camps,' which is one
I really wonder about, but they believe it, so it fu-
els the fire."

"What do we know about our allies?" Wade
asked.

"They're a separatist faction, but they're one
that is trying to negotiate with the government.
Of course, that means the nutcases want them
dead, too, for betraying their vision of independence, conquering Java and imposing a New
Muslim Order."

"What? Most of them can't think like that."
Wade had studied a lot of sociology. He didn't
believe stereotypes easily.

"No, most of them just want to be left alone
and get the money going to Jakarta. But a few percent are just nuts." And if it weren't for the nuts,
Kyle and Wade would be out of their current job.

"Forward that link to me. I've got to read up."

"Will do . . . sent."

"Got it, thanks." It was odd, Kyle reflected, to
keep swapping messages with a person a few
feet away.

The two pored over the language, maps, cultural pages with things such as recipes and holi-
days. The more familiar one was with an area
intellectually, the more easily and quickly one
could acclimate. That was a huge plus when trying to be discreet.

They were closing up the office at 1600 hours when Wade said, "We really should go visit the general before we leave."

"I agree," Kyle said. He felt guilty about not having done so, even with duty interfering, and he did feel friendly toward the boss who gave him such excellent support. "What are visitation hours?"

"Until nineteen hundred, I believe."

"Hit him now, dinner en route?"

"Works for me. Be good to see how he's doing."

Robash had been transferred to Walter Reed. It took a few minutes to find his location, an hour to drive through traffic, munching fast food on the way, and twenty minutes to get through security levels. Fortunately, senior NCOs visiting general officers was a very common and reasonable occurrence, and they were let through without too much hassle.

Robash looked comfortable, but tired and in pain. He also looked a little less bulky than he had. He hadn't been fat, he'd been *big*, but now he was just another patient in a bed, with a few wires and tubes.

"Good evening, sir," they said.

"Gentlemen. It's good to see you." His voice was even more gravelly than usual, with a croak to it.

"How are you feeling, sir?" Kyle asked.

"Like I lost both canopies and hit the ground."

"Sounds like fun. You look okay."

"Bullshit. I look like hell," he said. "But I'll live." His voice was definite when he said it.

"That's what we want to hear."

"Good. I didn't die on you. You're not allowed to die on me. How goes the prep?"

Kyle said, "HALO trained, lists made, orders on hand. Getting there."

"Good. How's Colonel Wiesinger doing?"

"Fine, sir," Kyle said. "We'll be ready on schedule."

"Don't bullshit me, son," Robash said, sounding stronger. "What's your opinion as an SFC?"

So much for not stressing him. Kyle met Wade's eyes, then looked back.

"We are managing, sir. He's more of a micromanager than I like, but I won't let him push me where it's not safe, and I won't argue with him otherwise." He blushed, because he was doing exactly that.

"Yeah, listen, move in close for a moment, will you?" His voice was strong but quiet.

They leaned in and listened.

"Look guys, BS aside, I know you don't warm to Colonel Wiesinger much," he whispered. "But he's the officer we've got. He can administrate, he understands the subject, and he knows where to get resources. Work with him, don't just pretend, and try not to let him rub you the wrong way. He's abrasive, but he's not bad."

"Roger that, sir," Wade said. Kyle was a moment behind. He suspected from what he'd encountered that Wiesinger's competence was all behind a desk. Yes, one needed that, depended on that to get the job done, but it went better when the officer had a grasp of how things operated in the field. The book existed for a reason. At the same time, the book was a guideline that didn't cover all situations and didn't apply to some situations it did cover.

"Anyway, I need to rest now. Good luck and good hunting. Rangers Lead the Way."

"Will do, sir," Kyle said.

They stood and left, shaking hands as they did. Robash's grip was weak, but Kyle could still feel the strength under it. That by itself reassured him the general would recover.

Kyle showered quickly and threw on a shirt and slacks. He was already late. Janie would probably understand him visiting the general, but he'd also been wrapped up in work and busy with HALO. It wasn't as if he could ignore her and expect her to hang around. They'd been dating for just over a month. And she was a nice girl. He wouldn't mind having her around for a while.

He drove fast, and was at her apartment by eight. She came walking briskly down off the steps, denying him the opportunity to knock on the door. He still got out and held the truck door for her, though. It might be old-fashioned, but the rules of etiquette and gentlemanly conduct had been drilled into him from an early age, and the Army encouraged polite behavior. It was a big plus for him in the social arena. He ushered her in, careful of her long satin skirt. He worried about lint. The truck wasn't as clean as it could be; he'd been on the range. Black satin fabric would show a lot. Her blouse was opened enough to show some cleavage, so he figured she wasn't too mad at him. If she wasn't happy, she had no problem letting him know.

"Where have you been?" she asked as she got in. She was upset and worried rather than angry. And he had called ahead.

"I'm sorry, Janie," he said, meaning it. Damn, she looked good, and it was great having someone to talk to about things other than shop. "General Robash is still in hospital. I had to go visit."

"He's your commander?" she asked.

"Well . . ." How to explain it? "He's in charge of our operations. I respect him a lot. I'm worried about how things will change if he can't recover. Can I leave it at that? I don't want to talk shop."

She softened. "Sure. I guess I thought you were ignoring me. Let's eat?" she hinted.

"I'll have to eat light, Wade and I grabbed a bite between the shop and the hospital." He pulled onto I-295. He was relieved. He didn't want her mad two days before he left.

"Good," she said. "Then I won't feel jealous of you plowing through enough food for three of me. You must work out a hell of a lot to eat like that."

"Sometimes," he said. "In the field I might hit six thousand calories a day. And you look fine, really. Eat what you want." Women were exasperating with their obsessions about diet and weight. She looked good and he didn't understand her worry.

She smiled. "Kyle, I plan on making love to you before you take off again. You don't have to sweet talk me." Then she gave him a sidelong glance.

"You know I'm leaving?" he asked, suspicious and worried at the same time.

"I assume if the Army sent you to a parachuting school and you're spending long hours with checklists and research that you're about to leave. Right?" She smiled again. It was coy, indulgent, mischievous, and exasperated all at the same time.

"Uh, yes. I just try not to let people know, as professional paranoia, and I don't like questions about it, because I can't answer them."

"You teach sniping, right?"

"Yes," he admitted. It had come up in conversation.

"So I assume you're teaching either our people or someone allied, out in the field. You're going to Iraq? Afghanistan?"

"Janie, I can't say. I'm sorry."

"Dammit . . ." She looked frustrated. "Okay, I guess I understand that. It must be hard on families. Is that why you got divorced?"

"Part of it. A big part," he admitted. Yes, it

was hard to have a social life, with people worried that you might not return. Some spouses could adapt to that. Others couldn't. He was also very wrapped up in his work and not as sociable as some other men.

"Tell me when you'll be back, at least," she begged. She leaned far back and stretched, and he could see her curves. She was in good shape herself. He'd met her at a gym.

"If I knew . . . but I don't. At least three weeks. Hopefully not much more than that. I've left instructions for them to tell you if there's a problem."

"If you're dead or crippled, you mean," she said. "Sorry, that was harsh. I appreciate you thinking of me. But, Kyle, there's something I want." She leaned over and whispered something in his ear that made him flush in anticipation. "And again when you come back. So come back? Please?"

"Hon, I want to come back anyway. But I'll be really careful." He reached over and took her hand.

"Good," she said gripping back. "I've seen your dress uniform. Don't get another Purple Heart. And I'll have a steak tonight. Hot and naked. Then you the same way." She smiled again and it was anything but coy. It looked like the smile of a wolf.

In the office the next morning, still tired and elated from a long night in bed with Janie, Kyle printed out a checklist and started packing rucks. He had three, with duplicate items for each and personalized gear. Both Wiesinger and Wade had brought in spare uniforms and toiletries tightly rolled in plastic bags. He started with "personal items" and checked them off the list. After that, it was ammunition, MREs in case local food wasn't available immediately, water, maps, and compasses, all the essential military gear that is rarely thought of by civilians but must be carried. Batteries for radios, phones, sights, and accessories were on the list aplenty. Interceptor body armor was quite heavy, so Kyle had substituted police-weight vests that wouldn't stop a rifle bullet but should slow it enough to reduce the wound. They'd stop most fragments and pistol calibers, and likely knives as well. But he'd taken enough fire to want something over his vital organs.

Beyond those he had his and Wade's pistols. Wade still took an issue M9 Beretta. Kyle had his gorgeous but slightly dinged Ed Brown that was as exotic as one could get. But it had saved his life at least twice by being available and flawlessly reliable. He'd thought of taking his Colt Mustang, too. It was pocket sized and had saved his life in Bosnia and Pakistan. He hadn't carried it since. It didn't weigh much, but they were on a tight chart. Besides, they weren't likely to be in town much and in the field he'd just as soon have a few extra magazines of .45

They had knives, Wiesinger had an M9 bayonet, Wade a Ka-Bar, Kyle his high-end Gerber. Pocket tools. Flashlights with infrared and red filters, both little Mini Maglites and the blindingly bright SureFires, which could be used to stun people.

As he reached the end of that list, he dragged over a duffel bag and another, handwritten list.

"So what's in the bag?"

"All the stuff Wiesinger told me not to take."

"Oh?"

"And ammo. Standard seven point six two NATO ball."

"Don't we have enough of that?" Wade asked.

"We have US issue, that incredibly solid stuff that just bores holes. I have old 'West German' issue that will shatter at the cannelure when it tumbles. But it is NATO spec, so no one can nail us for war crimes."

"You're a sick and twisted individual. I'm proud to call you 'friend.' "

"Yeah. Funny story about this stuff. The Germans and Swedes complained about the fragmentation effects of five point five six in Vietnam. Accused the U.S. of 'atrocities.' So Natick Lab demonstrated that their ammo fragmented worse. They shut up."

"Heh. I like it. How much do you have?"

"Two battle packs of two hundred rounds."

"How are you transporting it?"

"Since it's all going in our rucks and dropping with us, it's going in there. I'll mark off the issue stuff and load this instead. It's NATO, he may not even notice it's not U.S."

"And he can't do anything if he does."

"Right."

"This was a whole lot easier with Robash signing blank orders and handing us cash."

"We need to ask about cash," Kyle said, frowning. "I assume he'll want to carry it personally, but we better have some."

"That's your department. I don't even want to try to negotiate with him."

"Yeah, I know." The frown turned into a grimace.

All four rifles were laid out ready. All had threaded can type suppressors. It increased the length slightly, but reducing muzzle blast by 36 dB and all but eliminating the flash made shooting much more secure. There were four 100-round Beta C-mags for the M4s, which "could be loaded on Monday and shot all week." One of the SR25s had light olive green furniture.

"What did you do to the weapon?"

"Aftermarket furniture from Cavalry Arms. I've bought a bunch of AR components from them, they have a rough, sanitized idea of what I do, and they mentioned prototypes last time I spoke to them. So they agreed to send me some."

"Looks good, but why add the green plastic if all it will really do is piss off Wiesinger?"

"That by itself is enough."

"Gotcha."

"But it's also very stable and has better ergonomics." He showed the sculpted, adjustable ErgoGrip and the stock, which let the rear swivel be mounted sideways as well as underneath. The front free-float tube had rails on four sides for mounting accessories. Those rails were now green. "The color will help disrupt the outline of the weapon even before taping and camo. I'd endorse them if we could make endorsements."

"Yeah, I can see that. 'I'm Sergeant First Class Kyle Monroe, a U.S. Army Sniper. I shoot terrorist assholes. When I'm out dropping them like used rubbers, I always swear by Cavalry Arms for furniture for my rifles.' I'm sure that phrase would sell a thousand sets."

"Wade, you have to see it," Kyle said, "they do the desert tan everyone's getting in the Middle East, they do black, green, brown. Yellow and orange if you're trying to be found in the Arctic or at sea, and blue, purple, and frigging *pink* for style."

"I'll bet that would go well with your pumps." Wade was not going to let this go.

"Yeah, whatever. Anyway, if it helps me hide and pisses off Wiesinger, I'll do it." He really was enthusiastic about the plastic, though. Shooting was his life, and he tried to have the best of everything related to it, and he wasn't ashamed to extol the virtues of good hardware to others. "I've also got Bowflage tape to hide things."

"Fair enough. I've got a bit more on Indonesian culture."

"Good."

"Mostly secular. Prayers are announced every day, but most people don't bother. They do smoke. They do drink and it's accepted. The national philosophy of Pancacila stresses religious tolerance among other things. They really don't approve of religious curses of any kind, so keep the 'Goddamns' to a minimum."

"Useful, and good. I don't object to prayer, but watching it five times a day creeps me out. I guess I'm too Western." Kyle frowned. He didn't like being uncomfortable with other people's beliefs, but he also didn't care for those beliefs.

"So, we're dealing with a modern but different culture, not people stuck in the Stone Age."

"That's nice for a change."

"Don't get used to it," Wade said.

"No worries." Kyle wasn't a pessimist. But after fifteen years, he had a certain pragmatic realism.

Kyle got everything packed in rucks and harnesses and palletized for the flight to the Philippines. As he'd expected, Wiesinger didn't even look at his before it shipped, just asked Kyle if everything was accounted for and signed off. As everything he'd asked for was to the letter, it shouldn't be a problem. Wade's and his were different, but that fact would only come out if, or rather when, things went to hell. By then it would be too late, and hopefully he'd approve or at least ignore it. Kyle was going to do what he thought was right no matter what happened. The tricks he'd learned were the tricks that had kept him alive.

They briefed Wiesinger with everything they'd studied, except for the bits they'd gotten from Gober. Wiesinger had his own data, some of it woefully dated, some new to Kyle and Wade. But it would have worked better had he not been so remote throughout this. There were times when a unit needed to dispense with formality, sit around and bullshit and work the edges off. This was one of those. But Wiesinger had to do it the Army way, which worked fine for stand-up battles. This, however, was COIN—COunter INsurgency. It was almost always messy and in the dirt, and the rules were different. Kyle had a lot of reservations, but did his damnedest to impart what he could. He wasn't going to short the man on intel just because of personal issues.

"One important thing, sir," he said. "Terms of address."

"Meaning?"

"It's a bad idea in these circumstances, where we might be overheard, to be formal. 'Sergeant' or 'sir' or 'colonel' can twig a listener that we're military. We want to come across as journalists or common thugs or even mercs. If they think we're actually soldiers, it could escalate badly. So we need to use first names."

"I guess that makes sense. I go by Mel."

"Got it, Mel. We may use a 'sir' now and then, but generally, we need to start practicing now."

"Roger that . . . Kyle. I can't say I'm happy with the concept of missions that require that kind of skulking. In the future, we may need to address that."

Kyle didn't think there was any way to address that. "We can see, sir," he said. He was eager to end this processing and get on with the mission.

The next day, they boarded an Air Mobility Command C-141 toward California and Hawaii, there to transfer to Guam and the Philippines. After more than twenty hours in transit, the best Kyle could say was that Wiesinger had been mostly silent. The plane hadn't been silent, and his ears ached from hearing protection and pressure changes.

Then it was into another C-141 for the final leg, with their gear pallet with them, and the inevitable nerves.

4

KYLE TOOK ANOTHER TUG AT HIS LEG STRAPS. He'd once made a jump with straps insufficiently snug, and the shock of the opening canopy had almost crushed his testicles. It wasn't a lesson he would forget. He always double-checked his straps and triple-checked the legs and laterals, which held the bottom of the container firm against his back. They'd just donned the rigs now, and it hurt where the straps dug in. Wade had his adjusted and didn't move. He looked very relaxed. *Good act*, Kyle thought. Kyle was tense, sweating in the jumpsuit, even with it zipped open at the throat and the temperature in the plane down below fifty.

Wiesinger was fumbling back out of his container harness. Right. He needed to drain excess coffee in a hurry. Idiot. That was another reason not to drink coffee on the way in; it was a diuretic. There was no way to go around the gear, with the ruck hung in front. Kyle laughed silently.

It was a quiet half hour later before anything else happened. Kyle was reading a novel, his usual pulp SF with an exploding spaceship on the cover. He figured to leave the book for someone on the crew, assuming he didn't have to file it to prevent problems. He asked and was told someone would be happy to take it. He nodded and sat back down, leaning against the cargo webbing behind him.

They got the signal from the jumpmaster to go on oxygen. The signals were Army standard, even though the jumpmaster was Air Force. He was a Special Operations Weather Parachutist, who jumped before assaults and put out the data the pilots needed. He jumped along with a Combat Control team who provided landing, flight control, and terminal guidance for munitions. It made sense, but Kyle had never even known that job existed. There weren't many of them. Up here, in lieu of his gray beret, the man wore an insulated flight suit, parka, and oxygen mask, as well as a harness on a line to keep him inside the aircraft. Kyle secured his mask and plugged into the plane's bottle, then had to pop his ears as the pressure dropped. It got much cooler, too. For that, he was welcome. He'd been sweating his ass off inside his suit. The ramp cracked open, and a sliver of light appeared. It was a dark sky, light only in comparison. The air currents changed and roared and the temperature became decidedly chill. The sliver became a band became a hole into space, with a faint rumbling Kyle could feel. He'd done this only a few days before in training. It was different now. No recovery crew, and an international nightmare if they were found on landing—though from this altitude, any errors were likely to be in the first few seconds and fatal. He took a deep draft of oxygen to reassure himself, and stepped up.

The jumpmaster crawled to the corner of the ramp and the fuselage and stuck his head out enough to view conditions. It wasn't as if he could actually see the landing zone from here. That would require a lot of work on the soldiers' part to reach. He could check for storms, bad cloud cover, and confirm the approximate location just as a double check. That done, he stood carefully and held a thumb up. The jump light turned green, indicating they were over the drop point.

Kyle nodded. He shuffled forward, the ruck between his legs causing him to waddle. He checked behind and got a response from Wade, who was just behind him. Wiesinger was following, and gave him a nod that seemed to imply he should hurry the hell up.

Hampered by the ruck, Kyle took long, loping steps down the ramp and leaped into blackness.

The wind snatched at him, slapping him across

the front as he fell head down, then tumbled. He stiffened his body in a hard arch—arms and legs spread-eagled and drawn back behind the plane of his torso. It worked as it was supposed to; he became stable and face to Earth.

For just a moment, all was still, silent, and weightless. Add the blackness before the few dim light sources beneath penetrated his vision, and it was as close to perfect solitude as one could get. For that moment, Kyle was alone with nothing but his thoughts.

Then gravity started to return as friction with the air braked his acceleration. His weight built back up as the sibilant breeze increased to a buffeting roar. Icy daggers of wind stabbed through the edges of his goggles, chilling his eyes. It was like a motorcycle ride in deep winter, the rarefied air at 35,000 feet well below 0°F.

The jump was a cross between HALO—High Altitude, Low Opening, which was designed to keep troops invisible from observers until the last moment, and HAHO—High Altitude, High Opening, which allowed lots of time under the canopy to literally glide to a target some distance away. They'd left the plane during its normal flight path, and would fall to 25,000 feet, where they'd deploy their canopies and fly several miles to their designated landing zone.

The altimeter strapped to his wrist had a luminescent tritium dial. He glanced at it and read 32,000 and some feet. He didn't worry about the dividing ticks between numbers. All he was waiting for was the needle to hit the 25. Total free fall time should be about thirty seconds, as thin as the air was. Lower down it was seven seconds per thousand feet, roughly, but at this altitude the friction was lower and terminal velocity higher.

Below, the ground was dark, with bare, shadowy shapes of mountains. Off to the sides were lighted areas. Those were small towns, oil and gas operations, and far to the north, Lhokseumawe. First things first: Determine direction. That was north and down.

Kyle fell through wisps of clouds, the denser, wet air changing the sound of the wind to a rumble. Clouds could be very dangerous. At 120 mph, even raindrops could cause injury. Hail could be lethal. But these were just tendrils of high cumulus in an otherwise clear night. A dark shape falling to his right was Wiesinger. Everything was equally affected by gravity, but Wiesinger had more mass in the same area, so he had less wind drag. Kyle and Wade were close enough to barely matter. He bent and spun, seeing Wade behind and slightly above. Using the lights to orient himself, he turned back around. So far, so good.

The altimeter swept past 25 as his goggles started to fog. He brought in his arms, the left on his helmet, the right reaching and snatching for the release.

The pilot chute snapped into the air, trailing

the bagged canopy and its banded shroud lines. It stretched the lines taut, popped the fasteners on the nylon bag and began to unfurl into an inflated wing. All Kyle felt was a firm tug at his crotch and chest straps. The sound was that of a flag flapping in a strong breeze. Then he was half sitting, half hanging in the harness and facing the horizon instead of the ground. A quick glance let him reach for the brakes and tug them loose from their Velcro, and he was able to steer.

Working quickly, he drew his Night Vision Goggles from a pouch on his front and slipped them over his helmet. In a few seconds, he could see things much more clearly. He immediately looked up to see if his officially overloaded canopy had any tears. It seemed fine for now. He let out a breath in relief and looked below.

In the clear monochrome of the enhanced image, his trained eyes resolved dark areas as woods, lighter areas as fields, and found roads and industrial areas off to the horizon. Below was a hillside field, likely around 2000 feet, with a beacon flashing straight up. It should be exactly 2112 feet. That was their LZ. The "beacon" was a tiny pocket flashlight set to strobe, mounted in a can. It would be hard to see from the sides, but was plenty visible from above with image intensifiers.

Now it was time for a long, hopefully boring, ride. Another check didn't show any problems with the canopy, but he *was* coming down fast. That was to be expected with an additional forty pounds of weight on the harness.

He drew the left brake in tight and made a tight circle, moving his head rapidly to scan the sky with the narrow aperture of the goggles. There was Wade, above and behind, and Wiesinger below and behind. He'd fallen faster, being denser. He chuckled at the alternate meaning of that term as he completed the turn and resumed "flight."

The wind shifted as he fell through different levels of atmospheric movement. It required adjustment every few seconds to keep oriented. That was also due to the fact that no canopy was ever perfect once deployed. A single line tauter than the others would affect the steering.

He had been told the wind should be from the west, so he angled that way, wanting to stay upwind so he could be blown onto the LZ if there were problems. The ride took a long time, sitting in a harness much like a ski lift, only going down instead of up. He paid attention to his oxygen bottle. It should have plenty for the time involved, but if it ran out, his only option was to take a deep breath of whatever dregs he could and pull one brake in to spiral down as fast as possible below 14K feet.

The altimeter swept slowly, steadily down into the 14,000s, then past. He should be fine with ambient air now, but he'd stay on oxygen anyway. There wasn't any need to ditch it yet. He'd wait until 12K to be sure.

It was actually a nice night, though still cold. The stars were brilliantly bright. Below, they were matched by the glow of lights, warm and mellow from sodium in residential villages and the edges of towns, stark bluish where mercury vapor lights were in use.

They'd been dropped very close to the mark, and Kyle found he had plenty of altitude to spare. He was west of the LZ and still at 9000 feet and some. That wasn't a bad thing. He yanked down on the left brake and the end cells fluttered, lift lost. The right continued on at speed, throwing him into a counterclockwise turn that got tighter until he was almost facing down as he spun. After a few seconds, he eased off, steadied out and spiraled the other way to avoid dizziness. He checked the altimeter. Six thousand. Altitude for the beacon was supposed to be 2112 feet, which he couldn't rely on, and his altimeter was accurate to perhaps 50 feet anyway. Still, it was time to get into a landing pattern.

He zigzagged back and forth, losing altitude while remaining over essentially the same spot, as he turned upwind each time. Over the trees were rising thermals that held him aloft, so he steered over the meadow and the lower growth higher up. He dropped smoothly and steadily. In the last thousand feet, he turned downwind, past the beacon.

Then he turned upwind to reduce his forward velocity before landing, and removed his goggles. They offered no peripheral vision at all. He had done it right so far and was just where he needed to be. It was, in theory, a straightforward task, but in the dark, over unfamiliar terrain and with no immediate weather conditions, it was still a job to be proud of. He sailed into the clearing and watched nervously for terrain features, all of which were hidden by scrub that might be eight inches or eight feet high. The ground below was rough, bumpy and uneven. Tendrils of mist wove lazily among the growth tops. But it was either land there, or land lower down in jungle. Landing in jungle was not an appetizing option.

He'd seen Wade as he turned; he was just behind Kyle and turning himself now. Wiesinger was nowhere to be seen. He'd been below, and should be down already. But either he wasn't in the area, or he was very adept at hiding.

Kyle didn't think he was that good at concealment. Still, the only thing to do at this time was get down and hidden, then deal with other issues. He slipped the ruck and let it drop on its cord, which would give him much more maneuverability for landing, as well as lightening the mass to be supported by the canopy once it hit.

The ruck touched down with a thump and suddenly his descent was much more gentle. He'd made it, overloaded and without ripping the canopy and plunging to his death. Sighing in relief, he checked the steering brakes he'd use to land now. He was near ground, five meters, and preparing to flare, when gunfire erupted lower down, at the edge of a patch of stunted trees.

5

IT WAS ONLY A FEW SHOTS, BUT HE WAS ABOUT
as exposed as one could be without being
naked. He didn't like it.

Kyle kept his stance and didn't panic. When it
seemed he'd hit at any moment, he pulled both
brakes smoothly in until his hands reached his
crotch. The back of the canopy's cells closed,
slowing it and causing air to billow up. After a
few seconds, it would stall, drop and reinflate.
But he should be on the ground before then.

As soon as his boots touched, he rolled out in a
parachute landing fall. It wasn't always necessary, especially with the square canopies, but it
never hurt, and when taking fire, it was the fastest
way to get on the ground. He yanked at the left
brake, gathering the line in his fist until the
canopy came horizontal and folded to the ground
like a fan.

He wasn't watching that event. He was unbuckling the thigh and chest straps and grabbing the only weapon he could reach in a hurry: his Ed Brown .45. It cleared the holster inside his jumpsuit, and then he scurried backward into some growth, dragging his ruck with him. Once concealed, he pulled the night vision back on. Waiting for muzzle flashes as a means of identifying potential threats wasn't the best way of operating. He wanted to see.

A fluttering shadow would be Wade landing. Beyond that were occasional, deliberate shots. Deliberate was bad. Afghans would have been spraying the landscape with no hope of hitting anything. Slow, careful shooting was the mark of a professional. Several professionals. He marked several faint muzzle flashes for later reference.

Wade had seen where he landed, and rolled and crawled toward where he was now hidden. Once under cover himself, Kyle slithered over to meet up. He came face to muzzle with Wade's Beretta, which bothered him for only a moment. He knew his partner's skill and nerves, and trusted him to identify a target. It looked eerie in the monochromatic green of the night vision.

"We're here. Where's Mel?" Wade asked, lowering the pistol, sinking back down and all but disappearing into the ground. There was a ring of apparently clear air around them, a trick of the eye, but beyond that was a tarp of mist over everything, stirring lazily. Kyle made note to use that movement to watch for threats, who'd disturb the air as they approached.

"Dunno," he replied. "We need to figure out who we're making contact with, too." Great. A twerp of an officer, and he was missing, too. But it was reassuring in a way. A certain amount of trouble was inevitable. If it was going wrong already, they could hope for steady, minor screwups rather than a precarious balance until it crashed totally. And goddamn, it was hot down here. Insulated suit over BDUs, helmet, and warm, humid, tropical air.

"Well, the fire is coming from out there in at least two directions, and outgoing fire from the beacon area suggests our friends." He pointed downhill to the eastern edge of the clearing. "If the beacon was captured, I'd hope our allies would attack in a more vigorous fashion, especially as we're on the ground. Either that, or yell for us."

"Logical, assuming professionals. These are the rebels, however." Professionals were predictable. Amateurs were fuzed explosives, just waiting for the hammer to fall. "But it's either that, or wait until it's over and hope the good guys win."

"So what do we do? Seeing as our fearless leader isn't here?"

"That way," Kyle pointed, "and we'll try to get attention. Any reason not to use flares to backlight the trouble?"

Wade considered this as he drew his M4 from his harness and snapped the stock open. He had loaded it aboard the plane in violation of Air Force regs, and the crew hadn't even suggested he stop. They knew what troops on the ground faced, and they supported them. He clicked a shell into the M203 grenade launcher mounted under the little carbine and slid the breech closed.

"Can't think of any," he said. "Anyone with ears knows there's a fight here. If it's big, they'll be here before it's over. If it's small, we'll be gone before they get here. I count three to five enemies over there, about fifty meters by ear," he pointed.

"I agree," Kyle said. He was pulling the upper and lower halves of the SR25 from his ruck, and slapping the pins tight to assemble the receivers. He grabbed a twenty-round magazine and slid it in. At times like this, it didn't hurt to "ride the bolt" forward until it was almost locked, then tap the forward assist to finish closing it quietly. But the SR25 didn't have a forward assist. He let the bolt fly to close with the reassuring ratcheting clack of the locking breech. Then he removed his night vision again. It was bulky, eyes had advantages, and he had the scope if he needed it. He hesitated for just a second before unzipping his jumpsuit and squirming out.

"Sorry," he said, "but I'm about to cook."

"No problem," Wade said. He had shed his already. He leaned back with the stock low on his shoulder, sighted for distance, and then "aimed by ear" at the apex of the firing. He squeezed the trigger on the grenade launcher.

Whoomp!

"Let's move," he said, and shimmied out of the tangled brush into the open space between trees. They hid again before the illumination shell burst under its parachute. Both kept their eyes averted out of habit, to avoid affecting the night vision goggles, though the gear they had could compensate for the glare. The firefight paused for a moment, then rose to a brief, furious level. Most of the fire was generally outgoing from the snipers' area, which was a good sign, assuming those were the allies they were to meet. Then it got dark again as the illumination burned out.

They crawled forward, Kyle holding his weapon in his left handed. That meant they each had an arc of fire. If they'd had Wiesinger, he'd cover the rear and they'd be protected all around.

Wade would shift a few feet, knees splayed and spine flexing like a lizard. He'd take cover and pause. Kyle would choose his next position from wherever he was and move to it. The growth was thick enough to provide good concealment and cover, and the air was humid and dense even though it wasn't too warm. That meant noise would damp out faster.

They'd covered perhaps thirty meters when Wade signaled Kyle forward.

Kyle slithered up alongside. He said nothing, simply waited for Wade, who pointed. Ahead of them was an Indonesian with a Pindad Senapan Serbu 1, the Indonesian-licensed version of the Belgian FNC carbine. He was slowly approaching the parachutes they'd just left.

The trick now was to get his attention, without getting shot by him or letting anyone else locate them.

Wade reached a long arm out and shook a branch on a bush. It wiggled, and the Indonesian froze, weapon held ready. Wade shook it again, twice. Then three times.

"*Keluar*," the man said softly. Come out.

"Americans," Wade replied. "Coming out." He led the way, after a moment's glance to see if Kyle approved. The man simply faced him in a squat, ignoring another shot that was some meters away. Who or what the target was was impossible to tell in the dark, dank growth. Kyle slipped out and joined Wade.

"You are?" the man asked in English, looking cautious rather than suspicious.

"Kyle and Wade," Kyle said. They were just "Kyle and Wade"; no last names, nothing to indicate military rank or an employer.

"I'm Bakri. Pleased to meet you." He was very slim, about five foot seven, and had a scraggly beard. It didn't really suit him. Nor did the smile that revealed crooked teeth. But the name was right for their contact and he wasn't shooting at them. Incoming fire seemed to indicate his loyalties were with them. Good news, after a fashion.

"And you," Kyle said.

"We're under fire?" Wade asked, prodding for intel. The chat seemed out of place, under the circumstances.

"Just a skirmish, you say? We have met a different rebel patrol, I think."

"You think?"

"It's hard to say in the dark," he admitted. "Where is your other man?"

"That's what we're trying to figure out."

Just then, a round crack-snapped through the leaves above them. They all ducked.

"Wonderful," Kyle said. "Do you mind if we return some fire?"

Bakri grinned a mouthful of teeth. "Feel free."

Kyle and Wade had the best weapons in the area and were undoubtedly the best shooters. A quick glimpse through the AN/PVS-10 scope showed Kyle the shine of clothes that had been excessively pressed or starched. Someone was trying to look "professional" in their uniform, and was instead standing out like aluminum foil. He sunk lower for stability, aimed, and fired.

There was a thrashing motion and then nothing. One down. Wade had pegged someone else, and the locals had hit another. It was eerie to be in a battle, yet to have everything be so clean. After another handful of shots, the enemy faded away. It had barely been rougher than a field exercise, other than the fact that a dozen bullets had passed overhead.

"What now?" Kyle asked, as they finally shook hands.

Bakri whistled and his troop scurried in. There were four of them. They were introduced as Rizal, Fahmi, Hassan, and Syarief. Kyle nodded, but in the dark they all looked the same; skinny, grinning Malays in camouflage with rifles.

"What is your status?" Bakri asked.

"We're down, someone knows that men with parachutes are down, and we're missing a man," Kyle said.

"And this surprises you?" Wade asked.

"No, not really," Kyle admitted. He was lying. He was endlessly amazed by all the myriad ways things could drop into the toilet. "Bakri," he said, "We need to look for our other man. Any ideas?"

"Where was he when you last saw him?"

"About two hundred meters below us and two hundred downwind." The fat bastard had dropped like a stone, squeezed into his jumpsuit.

Bakri looked around, considering things. "That way," he indicated, pointing uphill and into the scrub. Then he turned and rattled off something in Achinese. Two of the others went off to check on the enemy and gather loot.

"You lead, please?" Kyle asked. "I'll navigate and Wade covers rear."

"Got it," Wade agreed. Bakri nodded and slipped forward, twisting so as to minimize disturbance of the growth. It was a casual move-

ment for him. The snipers were trained professionals with lots of experience in many terrains,
but Bakri had grown up here. The leaves and
stalks made barely a whisper as he passed by. His
men spread out to patrol for threats. Kyle was reassured. They were quite professional, unlike the
eager and brave but unschooled allies they'd had
in Pakistan.

It was a bit nervy, with the growth at the edge
of the treeline thinning quickly in just a few
steps. They all slunk down to the ground. Bakri
had an old, crude night vision monocular Kyle
didn't recognize. He and Wade had state of the
art American ones that were far more effective,
but they were unfamiliar with the terrain. It was
a toss-up who'd see Wiesinger first, if he was
alive and in the area.

Shortly, Wade spoke. "I see a figure up ahead.
Large, armed with an M four. Likely him."

"I hope so. If there's anyone else here meeting
that description . . ."

"Yeah, one of him is enough," Wade agreed
jovially.

Wiesinger had actually done the smart thing.
Once down, he'd buried his canopy and container. He was sitting, back to a tree, scanning
with his night vision. Kyle swallowed hard and
stood slowly, arms out and weapon slung. He
wanted Wiesinger to see him. He also didn't
want the man, whose capabilities were in question, to panic and take a shot. At the least, it

would attract attention. At the best, or rather worst . . .

"Halt, who goes there?" Wiesinger asked in a whisper.

"Kyle, Wade, and local allies. Good to see you, Mel," he said. Although it was only good in the sense of not having to fill out the paperwork for a lost colonel.

"Ser . . . Kyle. What's our status?" Wiesinger had almost forgotten to use names instead of ranks. Easy-enough mistake, but they'd practiced to avoid that. Kyle wasn't sure if he was just that military minded, or that in love with his rank. But he'd need to avoid it.

Kyle decided to keep patient. The man had been out of the loop. "We're down, uninjured, ready to travel, with our local contact and have repulsed a minor skirmish. We count two kills."

"Good start to the mission, then?" The colonel nodded as he rose and gathered his gear.

"Sort of. We're ahead." The fact that a couple of easy kills made the man think things were "good" spoke volumes. "Good" came from not engaging until necessary, and not being seen.

In two minutes they were all together. Kyle had an unvoiced theory that Wiesinger's stealth had been predicated by fear, not strategy. Still, they were all down, had their allies and guides, and were ready to commence their operation. Kyle wasn't enthusiastic.

If fourteen years of service had taught him

anything, it was that that meant things were about to drop deeper into the toilet.

"Okay," Bakri said. "We walk. About six kilometers. Downhill."

"I like that last part."

Bakri grinned, and chattered softly in Achinese. His troops spread out two ahead and two behind, with the Americans and him in the middle.

It wasn't a rough march, but it was no walk in the park, either. Each of them was carrying close to 200 pounds of gear, between ruck, harness, and weapons. Kyle and Wade tired but carried on quietly. Wiesinger was puffing in short order. Obviously, his PT had been pencil-whipped, too. But he did keep up.

"Permission to sling helmets, sir?" Wade asked.

"Yeah, it's rough enough as is."

Kyle didn't like that. Certainly, he liked removing his helmet in these conditions, and would have made that call. But officially, they should wear them anywhere it was potentially hostile. That Wiesinger, who loved the rules, would change them when the whim suited him was a bad sign. On the other hand, it did mean he could see reason, as long as it was poking him in the chest. Perhaps some field time would be good for him.

It took three hours for six kilometers. The terrain was rutted and steep in spots, heavily grown and with tangled roots. Downhill was both blessing and hindrance as it meant watching one's balance carefully. Despite the cool dampness, they were all sweating in short order. The Indonesians drank from canteens. The Americans sucked it from their Camelbaks. Kyle worshipped the man who'd invented the backpack-style water bladder with its drinking tube. He'd tried several times to build one when younger, based on mention of the idea in a Robert Heinlein novel from the 1950s. Some things just took a while to germinate, it seemed.

Eventually, near dawn, they arrived at a well-maintained and well worn Toyota Land Cruiser being guarded by a sole female soldier, who appeared out of the scenery when Bakri whistled.

"Haswananda," Bakri said. "She is very good at stalking."

"Hello," Kyle said.

"Hello," she answered with a nod. She was probably pretty under the sweat and grime, and had muscles like a runner showing on her arms. She was long in the limb and about as tall as Bakri. "I am called Anda."

"Anda it is," Wade agreed. Wiesinger said nothing, but shook hands briefly.

Rucks in back, weapons on laps, Anda and another troop sprawled over the gear, and two more soldiers on the roof rack, they started jouncing down a track that came to a road a few meters along. But the growth was thick enough it wouldn't have been found without major effort.

"Any updates?" Kyle asked Bakri, as Wiesinger dialed his cell phone to report them down.

"We have another group involved, I think," Bakri said as he drove. "Whoever was shooting at us. They seem to know where we were to be, and that makes me unhappy."

"Yeah, a leak somewhere," Kyle agreed.

Wiesinger asked, "Is there any way to split your group further? To avoid leaks?"

"I have done so, Mel," Bakri said. "That is why we are only six. But if I have men in their groups, they have men in mine. Some are hostile, some are seeking wealth or politic advantage, and some just talk much."

There was silence for a few minutes. The question and answer had both been obvious, and Kyle was embarrassed. Certainly, one should ask the obvious, but there were more diplomatic ways than suggesting one's hosts had missed something so simple.

"How far?" Wade asked, breaking the awkwardness.

"About an hour. It's only fifty kilometers."

Kyle nodded invisibly. He was glad for a helmet, and donned it again. The rutted road caused them to bump heads from time to time. Bakri was shorter and safe, but Wiesinger was even taller, and could be heard cursing quietly. At least it was quiet. The guys on the roof had to be taking a beating, especially when one considered the trees overhead. Then there were roots they banged over . . .

The good news was there was a camp at the end of it. Rather more than a camp. It was a village with buildings. They were concrete and block, Spartan but weatherproof, and the three of them were bedded down on mattresses in short order. They weren't much as mattresses went, but were better than torn car seats, truck beds of trash, airplane seats or cargo racks, muddy pits, dank caves, or any of a number of other things Kyle had slept on. And there was cold rice and fruit for snacking. They used flashlights sparingly in the growing half light.

"We rise at nine and get back to it," Bakri said. "Normal we travel by night. But we need to get start soon."

"Understood," Wiesinger said. "Post watch, gentlemen. I'll take third rotation."

"Yes, sir," Kyle said. It was a perfectly reasonable order and a fair privilege of rank to be last so as to get uninterrupted sleep. But it bugged Kyle anyway. He realized it was an overreaction on his part that he'd have to get over.

Wade said, "You first, I'll take middle. Works out to fifty minutes each."

"Thanks, buddy," Kyle said.

"No problem. You owe me."

"I always owe you."

Wiesinger snapped, "Keep it down!"

"Sorry, sir." Kyle sighed and sat back, weapon in hand and alert.

A few minutes later, he knew he'd have trouble sleeping. Wiesinger snored like a B52 on takeoff.

6

KYLE WOKE TO WIESINGER SLAPPING HIS boot. He rolled up silently, hand on weapon. It was a trained reflex.

"Get ready, we're moving," Wiesinger said in a taciturn voice.

"Roger that," he said.

Wade was already stretching and reaching into his ruck for a toothbrush. Health care is important, especially in the field. One can avoid soap so as to blend in with the brush, but hand washing, with at least water, and tooth care are vital. They tidied up in a few moments and were ready when Bakri stuck his head back in.

"Good!" he said. "We take trucks to a meeting point." He turned and left with just a wave of his hand. The Americans followed him out. Three trucks were in the village, two Land Cruisers and an ancient Land Rover. There were troops to fill them, including one with an RPK light machine gun and another with an RPG, a rocket loaded and a spare sticking out of his pack.

As they gathered around the vehicles, Wiesinger asked, "What is the plan, Bakri?"

"Meet up with rest of unit. Then travel to where we can observe the target. We have avoid it so far to keep cover, as requested."

Wiesinger faced Kyle and Wade. "The target at this point is the village of Khayalan. Our brief says explosives are going through there. This intel is secondhand from several sources. So we're going to confirm on the ground. If we confirm, we'll take appropriate action. If we do not confirm, we'll have to determine where the target is and reevaluate."

" 'Appropriate action' means shoot the guilty parties, or call in fire?" Kyle asked. He hated euphemisms. Sometimes, they were just politeness to avoid scaring the more delicate personalities. Sometimes, euphemisms meant the mission was officially disapproved and the operator would get hung out to dry.

"Probably the former," Wiesinger said, which was reassuring. "If we can take out the brains, it hinders the operation."

"Yes, Mel." Kyle knew the doctrine; he'd been doing this for a decade. Likely, Wiesinger was used to briefing non-snipers. This was one of those things you let slide, Kyle decided.

Wiesinger turned to Bakri. "Is there enough

room inside, or do we need to shuffle stuff around?"

"We'll fit," Bakri said. "We just need to put it all in."

"Sounds good. We're at your disposal to help load."

"We load now." Bakri grinned. "Climb in." They all boarded the first Toyota, Wiesinger in front, Kyle behind, and Wade behind the driver. Wade and Wiesinger had their M4s convenient to the windows. Kyle's longer SR25 would be a bit harder to get into play. The other one was still broken down and cased in Wade's ruck. The rucks were all in back.

For a first, their allies had hot food in paper cups. It was a chicken-and-rice mixture with what might be mangoes and spices. Sweet and hot, it was quite refreshing, and Kyle enjoyed it. So did the others.

"Native food adds so much to a mission," Wiesinger commented.

"When it's good, yes," Wade said. "I can't recommend Romanian style Mexican, or Pakistani dried goat and beans, though."

"Mnnph," the colonel replied around a mouthful of rice. "I'll take your word on it. But this stuff is good."

"Yeah, I'm partial to it. All in all, I'm not going to jinx things by asking what could go wrong."

"It'll happen soon enough," Kyle said, feeling pessimistically realistic.

With the other vehicles loaded with six troops each, the little platoon rolled off with cheerful waves. In this area, they could operate fairly openly, weapons ready in case of skirmish with government troops or another faction. But there were large sections of the country where weapons would get them shot on sight by overwhelming force. Kyle and Wade had both been under such circumstances before.

"How long is the trip?" Kyle asked Bakri, who was driving. Anda and another, even slighter, woman, Irta, were stuffed in back atop the gear. They were small enough not to be too inconvenienced, but they couldn't deploy until Kyle and Wade cleared the back, unless they shot out a window and risked cuts.

"About four hours," Bakri said. "One hundred kilometers."

Fifteen miles an hour. Yes, that wasn't a bad rate. American civilians were spoiled by superhighways and well-laid streets in good repair. Most of the world still had dirt tracks with the occasional two-lane road. Speed above 35 mph was very respectable. And under the circumstances, there was nothing to complain about. The vehicle was in decent repair, ran well, and didn't shake.

It was even possible to doze, until Wiesinger snapped, "Kyle, wake up and pay attention."

"Yes, Mel," he said. He grumbled slightly. It wasn't as if they could do anything as far as a fight. If fire came in, he'd wake at once. If not, he couldn't help navigate. But if that's how the commander wanted to do it, he could will himself awake.

The best way to do that was food and drink. He sipped a mouthful of water from his Camelbak and reached over his shoulder to dig a granola bar from an outer pocket of his ruck.

The key to staying awake was to nibble just a little every time one started to zone. He got an hour from the bar and a few sips of water and was thinking about a second one. It wasn't as if he couldn't use the calories anyway. Wade was reaching back to grab something from his own gear, likely the jerky.

A burst of machine-gun fire ripped across the convoy, stirring the thick air.

"Awas!" Bakri shouted. *Take cover.* The order wasn't needed. The troops were already diving for cover. Wade kicked the door on his side and rolled out, and Kyle was only an instant behind him. The drivers were backing up rapidly, but the rearmost vehicle took a hit and stopped. The driver convulsed and gurgled, then died.

As long as we don't land on a preset mine or a coordinated attack, Kyle thought as he rolled into the weeds. But staying in the vehicles would be suicide.

Another burst blew past, along with aimed shots from rifles. He heard the distinct snap of a bullet through the growth.

"Kopassus!" someone yelled.

"Oh, fucking shit goddamit no!" Kyle shouted. It didn't mean much, he was just pissed. Of all the things that could go wrong, a firefight with government troops from an elite unit was about as bad as things could get.

"We need to attack!" Wiesinger said.

"Negative, Mel. Cover and low." He scrunched lower into the ground. He was in a faint hollow between the roots of a tree.

"The proper response to an ambush is to attack, seizing initiative. Get them to attack!" the colonel shouted.

"Mel, you attack these badasses, you will *die*," Kyle said. "And they're friendly to the US. We stay low and attempt to disengage. Bakri, how many and where?"

The wiry little Indonesian was alongside in a crouch, and obviously scared but not panicking.

"Probably two squads," he said. "One with machine guns and grenade launcher. One rifles."

"Explosives?" Kyle asked.

"I assume yes."

"And that's why we don't charge, Mel," Kyle said. "Claymores, if this was a planned attack." He ducked as a round snapped past. "Dammit, they're along a long front. Suggestions?"

"Machine gun and grenade launchers," Wade said. "Puts us as close to par as we get. Then you and I pick targets." Kyle noticed he didn't mention Wiesinger.

•

"Roger. Bakri, you know how to use this?" Kyle offered the M4 with its underslung grenade launcher. He unfastened the pouch of grenades from his harness.

"I do." The man nodded, appearing deadly serious while grinning widely.

"Fine, get your men to drive them out, we'll shoot." He slid the weapon and grenades through the soft, damp dirt. He could clean them later.

"I understand."

"Wade, spot and backup?"

"Can do," he agreed. He slid the two halves of the SR25 over to Kyle, with one magazine. Kyle could bless him for remembering to grab an extra weapon.

"Mel, can you pick targets with the M four? Or should we swap?" He fitted the two halves together and pressed in the pins.

"I'll manage, *Kyle*," the colonel said. "I do know how to shoot."

"No such thing as a stupid question in battle, sir." He let the honorific in to try to defuse things slightly. "Stand by for targets."

Another burst was followed by a scream.

"Goddamit, they're good," Kyle said. "I don't want to fight them if we don't have to. For one thing, we're supposed to be allies."

"For another, they're pretty goddamned good," Wade admitted.

"Yeah. Bakri, flush them," Kyle said.

Bakri spoke a few words, and his troops and he

opened up with the RPK and the grenade launcher. With both support weapons and eight riflemen shooting at one area, it took only a moment for the troops there to pop smoke grenades.

"There they go," Kyle muttered to himself. Behind concealment of smoke, they'd hopefully not advance.

"Reference twisted tree, target, running, two five meters." Wade called it off in a rapid singsong.

"Sighted," Kyle said, seeing the movement. As Wade spoke, it resolved from shifting leaves to a camouflaged something into a running man. He led, squeezed, and the man dropped, clutching at a thigh. The German 7.62mm should have well nigh shattered the femur and mangled the muscle. He might not be dead, but he wasn't combat effective.

So, as Kyle realized he should have expected, Wiesinger wasted five seconds and a round putting the man out of his misery. No, it wasn't a bad thing to do. But at this juncture of a battle, the idea was to inflict as many casualties as possible. If the enemy thought the count too high, they'd retreat. And they were theoretically allies, dammit. The goal was to *not* kill them.

"Mel, we want them alive," he hissed.

"Right." The colonel nodded. He seemed overly excited. That was better than fear for the first real firefight he'd ever been in, but goddammit, Kyle didn't need to babysit anyone.

"Got 'im," Wade said laconically as he snap-shot another. There hadn't been time to call the shot, and there was no need to pass it along. "I also see movement at five zero meters, clumpy bush that looks like oversized grass."

"Roger. Pick anything that moves and nick it. Just nick it."

"Understood," Wade said. Wiesinger was silent.

"Bakri, can you see there?"

"I see," he said. "I should shoot?"

"Just in front of it. If that doesn't work, go into it."

"I understand." The little man squinted along the sights and fired. The shot was wide to the left. He cursed in Achinese in a way Kyle didn't understand, but sounded very earnest. He clicked the breech and started to reload.

A shot threw splinters off the tree right over his head, the shards stinging Kyle in the face. He flinched, but Bakri didn't, continuing with the motion to load and close the breech. Only then did he roll around the tree to a different position. That convinced Kyle that the man was *very* experienced.

The second grenade landed barely under the tendrils in front of the bush, blowing half of it away. The leaves were thick and stalky and absorbed much of the fragmentation, as did the soft dirt the grenade had landed in. Still, lots of growth was removed, and parts of what could be two figures started to bug out. Kyle slammed a round through someone's upper arm, causing a rough thrashing motion. Wade hit something else and screams became audible over the fire.

Then it got quiet.

"They have retreated," Bakri said. "They will move some hundred meters or so and regroup, then depart to treat wounded."

"What about the seriously wounded and bodies?"

"What of them?" he asked with a grin and pointed.

Kyle looked out to where the first target had been, the one he'd shot in the leg and Wiesinger had finished off. There was nothing but a rut in the grass where the corpse had been dragged off.

The hairs on his neck stood straight up.

"Holy shit, that's a good trick."

"Never a body. They, we, both the same game," Bakri said.

"You little bastards are the best skilled allies I've ever worked with," Kyle said reverently. The Bosnians were competent but not imaginative. The Afghans were eager but unskilled. The Iraqis were constantly fearful of turncoats. But the Indonesians were competent, cool, and devious.

"We were lucky," Bakri said. "They could have caught us from behind as well. Three more men made the difference."

"I'm glad it was a small patrol," Kyle said. "Back to traveling?"

"Yes, but we will be tracked. Kopassus always tracks."

"Wonderful. There goes our cover. What do we do now?"

"Leave the area," Bakri said. "They want stronger targets, is that how you say it?"

"Hard targets?" Wade asked.

"Yes. Operations. Not patrols they want. We were just a chance."

"Makes sense," Wiesinger said. "Where?"

"This way," Bakri said, gesturing.

Wiesinger stood up and started walking. Stifling a curse, Kyle tackled him.

"What the fuck are you *doing*?" Wiesinger snarled, his face hardening.

"Mel, there are still hostiles in the area."

He bit off the second part of his statement. *So stay concealed, you fucking idiot* wouldn't sit well. Weisinger's act was that of a man who was used to exercises that were called clear at the end, with no ongoing threat.

"Right," the colonel said, looking sheepish. He stayed down.

They advanced in three elements, covering all arcs with additional weapons forward, slipping along a few meters from the road. Wiesinger wasn't bad at concealment, Kyle thought. Nor was he good. He clearly had studied all the right books. But he had little practice.

It's like having an older, fatter second lieutenant along, he thought. He sighed. It was uncharitable, but the thought he had was that at least the man was large enough to stop a few bullets.

They finished an advance and wiggled into the dirt, to cover the next element. With eyes shifting around, Wiesinger spoke softly.

"Sergeant Monroe, U.S. weapons are supposed to stay in U.S. hands."

"Yes, sir, they are. And when the shit hits the fan, I want backup and I don't care who it is."

"We have no positive confirmation of their loyalties." Wiesinger really wasn't getting it, Kyle thought.

"Then it's a bad idea to have them behind us with rifles, yes?" he said reasonably.

Wiesinger jerked. It clearly hadn't occurred to him that there were armed men and women behind him with M16s, FNCs, AK47s, a Jagawana Forest Guard Gun that looked like a Sten and fired 9×21mm, and large knives.

"Mel," Kyle said, "things are never the way we'd like them to be on these types of ops. Our allies are usually poorly trained; we're lucky this time. The food can suck or be nonexistent. Plans change, people screw us over, others help us. It's all a guessing game. I'm guessing we can trust Bakri, because we have to. He could kill us in our sleep. Or turn us in."

Wiesinger said nothing, but nodded perhaps a half inch.

Two more advances brought them to the vehicles. One had a hole through the radiator tank, but one of the men was at work with a propane torch and solder. Another had the windows well shot out. There was one lethal casualty, a man they'd only nodded to, never been introduced, and two wounds and an injury—sprained wrist from a fall. With some grunting of pain, the three were bandaged as best could be and they all gathered around to discuss plans, their hosts speaking Bahasa for ease.

"So where do we go?" Wiesinger asked. The man had no patience. Bakri looked at him, then resumed talking.

Kyle and Wade sat silently, alert, while the Indonesians jabbered quietly around a map spread out on the lead Toyota's hood. It was Kyle's experience that after the locals had hashed things out, then they'd talk to the Americans and finalize things. But they needed time. Especially as no one liked to feel the foreigners were trying to run the show. There was a diplomacy issue here that Wiesinger's lack of self-confidence couldn't help.

"Here, Khayalan," Bakri said, just as it looked as if Wiesinger would butt in. "But to get there we must go this way." He indicated a circuitous route along the hills. "To avoid attention."

"How long a drive?" Wade asked.

"Eight to ten hours."

"Oh, that's not bad," Kyle said. Likely less than three hundred kilometers then. Narrow roads and convoy security would make a long trip even slower. "What's there?"

"Just people we can supply with," he said. "Then we go to Khayalan for the target."

"Got it."

It wasn't a pleasant trip, cooped up in a small, cramped vehicle, sweaty and worried about attack. But Kyle and Wade had been through worse. Well-trained troops were a confidence builder, and they were literate and experienced. There was food along, more fruit and some cold chicken and rice. Kyle wasn't a rice fan, but it was a staple for most of the world. The Indonesian spices varied from scorching to sweet, so at least it was interesting. This was a far richer area, resource wise, than the ass end of Central Asia.

Wiesinger was mostly reticent, which was a good thing. The man was just naturally abrasive. On the other hand, no matter how poorly one got along with teammates, knowing something about them was important for cohesion. But it just wasn't the thing Kyle wanted to mention, so they stayed each with their own thoughts.

They sank down low in the seats as they passed through towns that were five or six blocks long. One had a divided main road with a central canal. Whether it was for water runoff or transport, Kyle couldn't tell and didn't ask. He was busy being not noticed. That road was asphalted, but others were cobbled. There was a motorcycle with a rickshaw sidecar he found really amusing. People wore native garb, Western clothes and American or Chinese hats. The ramshackle houses had steep roofs of tile or tin against monsoon rains, and were different but not dissimilar from the colonial styles in Asia. Dutch rather than French, but with obvious cultural roots.

There were militia fighters on patrol, and Bakri waved to one group but detoured around rice paddies to avoid another.

"They would collect toll," he said. "Cost us time, money, and risk for you."

"Appreciated," Kyle said. "We're not in a hurry."

"Yes we are," Wiesinger muttered.

"Not to die, Mel," Kyle snapped back.

He did find the schoolgirls cute, on old-style bicycles in skirts and with traditional head coverings. They smiled and waved and were absolute dolls. He hoped they weren't targets for anyone.

Then they were back out into the wilds again, occasional single and multiple dwelling settlements carved out of the forest. It was a constant fight as the humans tried to go one way and the jungle resisted, even grew back.

Shortly, they pulled into an open field that was terraced down a slope like stacked plates. It was the brightest green Kyle had ever seen, thick with rice and palms of some kind. The buildings were low wood.

They stopped and obtained ammunition and food, and swapped troops around. It was done quickly, and the Americans stayed in the vehicles.

"People are needed for the crops, and they will

notice if we are gone for long. We can only patrol a few days at a time when the Army is here in force," Bakri said. Though obviously that "in force" was still a fairly token presence.

"What is important is that you not be associated with groups like ours, who want to negotiate," Bakri said. "Very risky. We must get you into area where rebels are common. Your target is there anyway."

"We appreciate the risk," Kyle said. "Good people all over the world are taking risks on this. We've been in other countries doing the same thing."

"What is it like?"

Wade said, "Rough, dangerous, but rewarding. There's no headlines over it. But you know you've done right."

"Yes, the same with us. I do this for my children," Bakri said. "They should not live poor, but they should not have to fight. If we can meet Jakarta partway, then ask for more, it is better. But if not, we'll have to fight more."

"Our government is trying," Wiesinger said. "But paperwork takes a long time. This is the first time I've been away from it in years."

Kyle felt a flash of empathy. He despised paperwork. Was Wiesinger pushed into it because of his father's legacy? The perfect staff officer, even if he hated it?

"Yes," Bakri said. "We were all happy when Timor-Leste became free. But the fighting was

fierce. We would like that, too. And we could negotiate on oil and gas better than Jakarta. We are
closer, so have less entangles."

"I agree," Kyle said. "But we can't make that
decision. Seems like every real soldier I've met,
even among Bosnians, Iraqis, and Russians, was
a decent guy I could drink a beer with and get
along with. We all hate terrorists."

"Yes, because they are cowards." Bakri nodded vigorously. "We and the Kopassus and Army
and Marines are all men, and fight like men. It's
frightening and dangerous, but that is the price."
He shrugged his shoulders. "Attacking journalists, drivers, women, children . . ." He spat force-
fully out the window. "I would like a hut in the
jungle and a week with each of them. Perhaps ten
days." His clenching jaw bespoke a far less cheerful and angrier side that Kyle hoped not to experience. "If you can, will you let one live for me?"

Kyle was silent a moment.

"We've discussed that before," Wade said into
the pause. "As enjoyable as that would be, there's
the risk of escape."

"Ah, yes. Better not to. But some deserve more
suffering than life offers. There is Allah offering
judgment."

"I pray for that, too," Kyle said politely. He
wasn't very religious. But he did hope for justice
as it was deserved.

"We turn onto a road now. Keep guns out of
sight."

"Okay," they agreed, and slid the weapons lower. They were all wearing camouflage of various kinds; still, people were more likely to twig on weapons than clothes. They came out into brighter light and onto a two-lane blacktop in good repair. Kyle removed his brimmed boonie hat and the others followed suit. That and keeping arms inside the windows should help reduce visibility. There were fields on either side, flat and a brighter green than any American growth. The forest stood back around them, tall and riotous.

Then they turned back off the road. They'd been on it only a kilometer or two and had passed one car going the other way at high speed. The three vehicles, spread widely and packed, could easily be mistaken for work trucks.

This trail was much rougher, but that was due to use. It was a dirt road and well worn. Sleeping was impossible, with heads bobbing around like toys as the suspension squeaked in protest. The light flickered occasionally as a fluke of nature left an opening in the thin rain forest. It wasn't as thick as South America or Southeast Asia, but it was thicker than all but the heaviest, tangled second growth Stateside, and much taller.

Bakri waved and pointed, and the second vehicle pulled off in a very narrow shoulder area to keep watch. The trailing vehicle squeezed through the gap and took second place. Kyle approved silently. Far better than others he'd worked with, for certain.

These were roads under here, Kyle decided. About like access roads on an Army training range. Some were graveled in sections, old and scattered and pressed into the mud. Some were grown with low grasses from little use, and some were plain mud.

It rained one day in three here. The daytime temperature was steady near 30°C, 86°F. At night it dropped to a balmy 72°. The humidity did the same, from 90 percent down to 70 percent, day after year after century. They were so close to the equator that weather, apart from monsoons, didn't really exist—only climate. It was hot and would stay that way, barring a few days here and there. The remaining escort pulled off onto a narrow path and disappeared.

Shortly, they were driving along a track so little used it was barely visible as a trace, the growth on either side brushing against the sides of the vehicle, scratching and scraping. The windows were still open, and everyone drew back to avoid getting jabbed.

Wade said, "I remember doing this once in Macedonia, along a trail."

"Yes?" Kyle prompted.

"Well, the next time someone tells you that something is better than a poke in the eye with a sharp stick, you believe them."

Everyone, including Bakri, chuckled. Everyone except Wiesinger, who seemed lost in his own thoughts. But he was examining the terrain and the woods, so Kyle figured it was just concentration on his part.

"We stop just ahead," Bakri said. "We are above and east of the target."

"Understood. What then?"

"Can you get closer on foot to observe?"

"We can do that," Kyle agreed. "Show me the map."

They were 1705 meters from the target, by Kyle's reckoning. He entered coordinates into his PDA, GPS, and on a paper notepad for backup. He planned to advance on foot the first kilometer, then on knees and at a crawl, and set up an OP—Observation Post—where they could see what was going on. Keep records of comings and goings, identify important persons and equipment, and then exfiltrate and determine proper action.

He explained what he intended, and consciously added an, "Is that okay, Mel? Or do you suggest something else?"

"No, Kyle, I concur," he said. Whether he actually did, or really had no idea and was letting an NCO lead, Kyle didn't know. But neither was really bad.

"Tell me about the area," Kyle asked.

"Khayalan is a small village. We avoided the road through it, which is unpaved. We are at right angles to it. The houses are block and sheet steel, and there is a small administration building. Occupants are one hundred twenty-three according to the last census, taken in two thousand.

They have a large number of young males, and I believe they have considerable small weapons. Vehicle traffic is approximately four cars per hour, including a patrol by the police every three to four days and vehicles transporting workers to the oil facilities at six and twenty hours daily. There is a small general shop, a bar, and a mosque. Two side roads lead into the woods for rubbish disposal." He pulled out a sheet of paper with blocks drawn on it. Each block contained a routine Bahasa phrase so as to look like a shopping list. But with a few strokes of a pen and some words added, it became a passable map of the target area. Good operational and communications security.

Kyle was agog. He'd never had a local ally provide such a thorough pre-mission briefing. "That's a very impressive report," he said.

"Thank you. We've gathered what information we can."

"But you don't know if our target is there?"

"No. I was not told who that is. They said it was a sensitive matter." He looked both amused and put upon.

Wiesinger must have felt everyone looking at him. "That was through CIA," he said. "Pursuant to new rules of intelligence release after September eleventh."

"Heck, sounds like we might have saved a trip," Wade said, a bare tinge of disgust in his voice.

"Well, shall we head in, Mel?" Kyle asked. "Get an OP set up and see what happens?"

"Yes. You lead, serg . . . Kyle. Wade can guard the rear. I can offer support if needed. I'll take this," he indicated the M4. "Will you be using the SR25s?"

"That's likely best," Kyle agreed. "Range and intel gathering. We'll talk through phones, make sure they're set on vibrate. Bakri, how will we meet up?"

"I will drive by, or you can call my telephone."

"Sounds good. Assume twenty-four hours. If you don't hear from us, be very cautious, and report it back. Do you have a number for that?"

"I do, to someone in Jakarta who speaks American English."

Probably CIA. That wasn't as desirable as the Army. CIA might take weeks or months to deal with it, based on their own assessment of how valuable the three men were. Army would go balls out to get them. But you worked with what you had.

"Shall we give them one of our numbers, Mel?" Kyle asked.

"I'd like to, but negative. Maintain security."

"Understood," Kyle agreed. He didn't like it, but it made sense. The phone number could be tracked. If it was to an intelligence service, that might be expected. But if it was traced to a foreign military, that was another thing entirely. "Bakri, you have it?"

"Tomorrow at the same time, carefully if I haven't heard from you and report it back. This is my telephone number." He showed it to them on the lit screen.

"Got it," Kyle said, as they all programmed it into their own phones. Goddam, this was almost like operating in the modern world, Kyle thought. He tried not to get too optimistic.

That done, Bakri got into the vehicle and quietly pulled away. Kyle led the way off the "road" and into brush. More concealment was desired.

"So, what is our probable target?" Kyle asked.

"Mosque," Wiesinger said. "The current assumption is that if the presence isn't obvious, it's in a mosque. They've been doing that a lot lately."

"Right. And we're looking for explosives?"

"Explosives, weapons, anything we can report as activity."

"Got it," Kyle agreed. Wade glanced over and thumbed up. He was busy digging the soft-cased rifle from its straps on his ruck. He took the one Kyle held, and handed over the modified one.

Kyle actually had it assembled before Wiesinger twigged on the green-colored stock and the rail covers over the hand guard. "That's not paint on that weapon, is it?"

"No, it's aftermarket furniture," he said, and braced for the storm.

"From where?" The colonel was clouding up.

"An outfit called Cavalry Arms." Kyle pretended not to understand.

"Acquired how?"

"Personal expense, Mel. Didn't want Uncle to have to pay for it."

"I wasn't aware Uncle authorized it, and I know I wasn't asked."

"Sorry, sir," Kyle said, slipping the honorific in again. "This was an experiment we'd already arranged, and I forgot to inform you."

"Are there any other surprises I'm not aware of?"

"I don't think so, Mel," he said. Heh heh. He'd pulled it off. It was only one little victory in an ongoing bureaucratic battle, but it improved his morale.

"Good. Let's get to it." He accepted the ghillie Wade handed over, and started pulling it on. "But don't try to cowboy this operation, Kyle. I will take you down."

There was nothing to say but, "Yes, sir." Goddam, the man got bent out of shape over piddly crap.

At least there was nothing the man could criticize about Kyle's ghillie. In addition to strips of shredded burlap, he'd used sections of camouflage netting to improve it. It was a coat made shapeless with tans and greens, more of the former, that being the predominant color in woods, and certainly on the ground. It was disruptive enough in shape to make him near invisible at a matter of feet.

Each of them grabbed food and technical gear, then stowed their rucks in a hollow. Everything inside that could be damaged by water was sealed in freezer bags. They didn't need the three hundred pounds of gear represented for recon. It would simply bulk up their profiles. Careful positioning under growth should hide it from any view. Kyle noted a tree and cut a blaze in the bark very low down, peeling it back with his Gerber. He noted the position on his GPS. That should be enough to let them recover it later. In a worst-case scenario, nothing inside had any names or official U.S. identifiers. It was just military gear.

The three were ready in a very few moments. Kyle stepped slowly forward, his weapon in a drag bag over his shoulder. With his face painted and dirtied, the ghillie tumbled over him and the growth around him, he looked like a shambling tree.

Behind, Wiesinger was a little noisier. It wasn't anything most civilians would notice, but Kyle did. If he did, another professional might. He gritted his teeth. Hopefully, the man would steady out in a few minutes. If not, Kyle was at least leading, so he could set the pace. After years of instructing, he was afraid Wiesinger would be a rabbit, hopping eagerly forward and drawing attention.

The first seven hundred meters were largely uneventful. They shifted through the branches, careful not to shake them, watching for clumps of brush that might get crushed, soft spots that would hold boot prints and roots that could trip them, not to mention boobytraps or sensors. They didn't anticipate any, but one doesn't until it's too late.

Once or twice they froze and sank into the growth because of noises. But none was threatening, and actual human noise was scarce at this distance. Trees and humidity damped a lot of vibrations. Still, the situation demanded caution. Hours of infiltration and weeks of intel were riding on this. A minor screwup could kill a lot of people and waste a lot of time and money.

The GPS Kyle held said they were a kilometer away. It was time to get romantic with the dirt. Slowly, he eased to his knees and down, gently laying the drag bag behind him. Gingerly, he put his hands down—he wore thin Nomex aviator gloves to avoid scratches, plant toxins, and insect bites. Behind him, he heard the very faint sounds of Wiesinger and Wade following suit.

It was hot. Under the ghillies, it was stifling. He sipped at his water, glad he had filled the Camelbak to overfull. He'd had 105 ounces forced into it, and had drank a good half quart before gearing up. He thought of water in quarts. This temp required a quart an hour when active. He sucked a couple of ounces when he paused again, and would bring the container to normal capacity in a few minutes. Bursting it would be bad.

At five hundred meters, he went from hands and knees to a belly crawl. It was essential to avoid a profile. From a secure position, he'd identify a new location, ensure the route was clear of debris or growth that would leave an obvious trail, free of wet or low spots, of which there were plenty, and not open to observation. That confirmed, he'd slink forward like a lizard after a fly, pulling with hands as much as pushing with feet and knees, to avoid leaving divots. Once he felt secure behind the mark, a tree with shrubbery at the base, he fished the phone out of his front pocket.

"Wade, Kyle. How do things look?" he asked when his partner answered.

"Clear, good. Did you know you rolled a limb as you crawled over it?"

Kyle felt a ripple of shock. That was an amateur's mistake. "I didn't even feel a limb," he admitted. Was he tired? Or was it just one of those mistakes that happen? Either way, he had to avoid that.

"Yeah. Eyes open, buddy."

"Will do. Please relay to Mel. Call me if you need me."

"Roger that." Here they were, on profile for a mission, halfway around the world. They were perhaps ten meters apart, and they were communicating through thousands of miles of space by Iridium phones. Were Iridium satellites, or the satellites they used, low orbit? Geosynchronous, high enough to orbit over one location? That was 23,000 miles and some, he recalled. But beyond that, he was hazy. Those details were out of his control, so he hadn't dwelled on them much, but he was curious now and would check.

He resumed a slow advance from concealment to concealment. That was something he had control over, and was expert at.

A half hour later, he had the edges of the village in view. He figured their distance as 330 meters. And Bakri was almost certainly competent enough to have done this. Instead, they'd come halfway around the world.

Oh, it made some sense, he thought, as he slithered under a vine that drooped between a bush and a tree. They could ascertain the target and make the call, and confirm the kill. A local could claim anyone as the target, as had happened in Pakistan. That had set off a tribal war that almost got out of hand. The CIA's after-action review had been very stern about confirming reliability of allies. And if the locals were paid money or favors for killing a target, it was hard to know if they actually had. It was hard to drag bodies in for confirmation, and claims of body counts were always inflated.

But that still made it annoying to see first-rate

troops kept in the dark and used as taxi drivers for a mission they were actually better qualified to handle.

At 275 meters, he decided the view was good. That distance was based on the road and the approximate center of town, and assuming Bakri's hand-written grid coordinates were correct. Somehow, he knew Bakri could handle a compass.

He dialed Wade. "We'll set up OP here. Spread out and we'll take shifts. Two on, one asleep, switching off every hour on watch, four hours to sleep."

"Roger that."

He relayed the same information to Wiesinger. "Does that work, Mel?"

"It does. Do you want to sleep first?"

"I could do that, yes, Mel," he agreed. He wasn't keen on trusting Wiesinger, but Wade would keep a good eye on him. One hour on, one off actually meant both were on, but one was responsible for notes and keeping an eye glued to a scope in case a shot presented itself. The "off" partner would still be observing while also watching for encroaching threats and other issues.

Issues such as weather. Kyle could hear rain beating on the leaves far above. He shrugged mentally, confirmed that Wade had the same info as the colonel, and hunkered down to sleep. It was hot and itchy under the ghillie, soon to be hot, damp, and itchy. That was the nature of the job. He placed his phone back in his chest pocket, where it was somewhat uncomfortable, but where he would certainly feel the buzz if he was called.

He folded his arms in front, laid his head down, and focused on a blade of grass. Things went fuzzy and he was asleep.

It was a restless sleep, as rain and sweat mingled and soaked his clothes, grass and dirt shifted and brushed him, and bugs ran over him. There were other animals in these woods—wild boars, orangutans, assorted rodents. None came near, but the small ones were annoying enough.

He felt the buzz of the phone, and woke at once. Years of practice kept him from jerking. He simply snapped awake and shifted a fraction of an inch. He reached gingerly for the phone with his right hand, keeping eyes and ears alert for a threat.

"Yes," he whispered softly. He had it close enough to his lips that he should be heard. A move that combined head and hand brought his ear to the other end, smoothly enough that it shouldn't show as movement, and quickly enough to catch anything that might be said. He also started flexing his muscles, to get circulation going and prepare for anything from a crawl to a charge.

"Wade here. Wakeup call."

"Roger that. You're next?"

"I am. You and Mel have it until twenty hundred."

"When is sunset and EMNT?" He realized it was getting dark. End Mean Nautical Twilight. Sun twelve degrees below horizon and eyes no longer adequate.

"One eight one six hours, another one seven minutes for sunset. Nominal four eight minutes for EMNT, but I'd guess three zero minutes with those hills."

"Roger that. Go sleep."

"Out," Wade agreed.

Kyle dialed Wiesinger.

"I'm on watch, sir, you're off, Wade asleep."

"Understood. We tracked a vehicle and personnel. Approximately two zero men arrived by bus at one seven four three hours."

"Understood, noted," Kyle said. Most of what they'd observe was routine or meaningless. Only if they saw one of the three targets or suspicious activity would they follow up. Whatever was here might not arrive for days, or might have moved on, or might never have been here. But with Bakri's initial recon, the odds were good there'd be trouble. Then they'd troubleshoot, to use a pun. Kyle smiled very slightly. Jokes like that and random thoughts kept him alert and sane hour after hour on missions like this.

He reached back into the drag and drew his rifle and scope. Assembling them, he now had a sturdy, bipod-mounted scope he could use in near total darkness, with a weapon to support it and to provide fire if need be.

Nothing had happened by 1900, other than dinner that he could smell from here, with fresh fruits, hot peppers, and rice. His slow sweeps of the scope had acquired nothing of military note, though he noted vehicles, and a mosque service. It was sparsely attended that he could tell, perhaps thirty or forty people, mostly male. Though others might be worshipping in their homes, within earshot of the imam's prayers.

He buzzed Wiesinger and ended the call before he answered. A buzz in response indicated acknowledgement. Gratefully, Kyle came off the scope, blinking his eye. It had been sweaty against the rubber guard. He allowed himself two minutes to zone while he dug for an MRE. He'd chew it slowly, component by component for the rest of the shift. The remains would be stuffed into the outer envelope, which he'd keep in his shirt so as not to leave any evidence. Shortly, he'd have to relocate slightly and dig a small hole to piss in. He'd been holding it since they left the vehicle and geared up.

It was incredible, Kyle thought, that with technology so crude and in an area so remote, a terrorist group could pull off the attacks it did. Not for the first time, he was disgusted that such effort wasn't put to productive ends. Or that brave and eager young men could meet real military recruiters rather than terrorists. He recalled the story of a Foreign Legion veteran who'd gone on to become a billionaire. And very many senior politicians and executives were veterans. Aggression was a very human trait. But it didn't have to be destructive.

Christ, it was hot, even in the "cool" evening at less than 80°F and 75 percent humidity. Sweat was not just running off him, it was running out of him as if he were a squeezed sponge. That would cause problems. While the book said to keep water in your body, in a case like this, one might as well pour it out. Instead, he decided to wait until he just barely felt heat effects, and his sweat thinned, before drinking. His water supply would last slightly longer, and that was important.

And perhaps it would rain again and he could suck absorbed water from a rag. But it was going to be a rough night. He blinked his eyes as liquid ran. At least the salt content was low, as much as he was leaking. His eyes didn't sting, but certainly were uncomfortable.

He kept ears alert for anything that might approach. Certainly Bakri had patrols in the area, but it made sense to be wary. Then there was the road. That had to be watched while Wiesinger watched the village.

At 1948, there was action. A group of men slipped out of the mosque, each with a backpack, and boarded motorcycles. Kyle made note of time and activity as they slipped away. He thought there were nine. He'd confirm with Wiesinger in twelve minutes.

Wiesinger didn't call at 2000. Kyle gave it five

minutes, then called himself. He had a creepy feeling he knew what had happened.

It took three rings, which made sense if Wiesinger was expecting a single only to alert him. Or unless it meant . . .

"Mel," was the answer, sounding very sleepy and confused.

"Oh, Jesus H. Fucking Christ on a crutch in a tutu!" Kyle swore in a whisper with his hand over the mic. Asleep, on watch. Something no soldier should *ever* do. Something inexcusable. And the man had in theory been to Ranger school, so he should know how to force consciousness when needed, even for days at a time.

"Did you get a count on that motorcycle activity, Mel?" he asked, knowing what the answer would be.

There was a long pause. "I didn't. Do you have it?"

"I have an estimate only, Mel. I was covering security." And it was taking every ounce of strength he had not to shout, scream, call the man an incompetent, reckless, derelict fucking idiot.

"Understood. I'll take next watch."

Kyle wanted to tell him not to bother. Instead, he decided to bull through the remaining two hours and cover both security and observation. Wade needed his sleep.

"Understood," he said, hating himself for lying. There was just no good going to come of this. He dug out a small camera that would take photos through the scope. Had he had any inkling Wiesinger would dope off, he would have had it all along.

It was a relief to wake Wade at 2200 and the two of them to go on together, even if Wiesinger should by rights take another hour. He'd worked with Wade and trusted him. They'd saved each other's lives several times, and Wade had pulled him out of deep depressions over dead friends. He synopsized the situation.

"Well," Wade said, "he's obviously lacking in field experience. So we need to cover him and us. Consider it a tradeoff with the better allies, who are really good, my friend."

"Yes they are, and I know we can't get a perfect mission," Kyle said, watching a caterpillar of some kind worm along a long leaf. "We'll manage. Wanted you to know. Here's the activity I've got—" He read off his log.

"Roger that," Wade agreed. "I'd say nine or ten men on motorcycles with backpacks leaving a mosque simultaneously is unusual. But I'm not sure what it means."

"Neither am I."

The forest was loud even at night, with bugs, birds, and larger forms all chittering, whooping, and cackling. It scared many people, but Kyle had spent so much time outdoors he only noticed when it stopped. Around here, he'd learned that such things presaged a vehicle arriving. So he was unconsciously leaning over his scope without realizing why when the truck arrived.

The truck pulled into the village using only parking lights and was ground guided by a man with a flashlight. It stopped quietly in front of the mosque. At once, a dozen men formed a line to unload it.

Boxes. The labels weren't English and weren't Bahasa, but were some Asian language. Kyle thought it might be Korean. It wasn't Japanese— it could be Chinese or something else. Kyle snapped a dozen pictures.

Boxes at night, lights out at a mosque, pre-arranged and being off-loaded in a hurry by a small group of young men might not mean anything to a peace-love-dope dove who wanted to believe in the good of mankind, but it did to Kyle. He wanted to believe in the good of mankind, too. But years of experience had taught him that those boxes were probably explosive.

Should they exfil now with the intel they had? He had sketched the markings as best he could, and would track down a translation somewhere. Meantime, more might happen.

There was activity at the mosque until dawn, after 0500. As the sun rose, things went back to normal village-in-the-boonies mode, with a few men catching a bus to the oil fields and a small patch of agriculture.

With a few thumb strokes he called Bakri.

"*Pagi*." That was *selemat pagi*, or "Good morning."

"Bakri, Kyle. We need to catch that ride now." His satellite cell was about as secure as one could get. But Bakri's went through an Indonesian telecom. It might be monitored.

"Okay, I'll send a boy over," Bakri said conversationally. "As soon as he gets off work."

"No hurry. We're outside waiting. Goodbye."

"Goodbye."

Then he dialed Wade. "That's enough. Wake the lump and let's start moving."

"Understood."

Wiesinger had other ideas, though. "The plan was to do twenty-four hours of surveillance," he said.

"Yes, Mel, but nothing is happening daytime. All the activity is now over."

"You don't know that." The voice was stubborn.

Kyle gritted his teeth for a moment. "Mel, I've already called to exfil. I apologize for not waking you, but it didn't seem the kind of detail a colonel needed to be bothered with. I believe we have what we need, and while we might get a little more, it's important to act on this quickly."

After a pause, Wiesinger said, "Very well. But remember who's in charge here, sergeant."

"Yes, sir," he agreed as he disconnected.

Kyle should be in charge. He'd worked at this,

studied it, done it. Wiesinger was a staff puke, and an egotistical one.

But he had a bird on his shoulder, even if it sat atop a chip. So it was necessary to follow orders a lot, humor him a little, and just pray the man wised up. The only other options were all capital crimes, and not the sort of thing Kyle Monroe would ever entertain. He was too professional, too dedicated to violate the Army regs.

But he might beat the hell out of them on this mission.

7

IN LHOKSEUMAWE, ANOTHER ELEMENT OF THE operation was quite pleased. Agung received the current shipment of incoming explosives and had it quietly stowed in the warehouse.

It was certainly an impressive sight, Agung thought. Part of him had a craving to take a photograph for the Movement's archives, and so he could remember this and smile. But that would be a risk. Evidence like that would get him shot in the spine by the Allah-cursed Kopassus, or executed publicly. It could get others killed or jailed, and there was the risk of rape and torture for the women. So he would settle for fond memories.

Instead, he would cause tears for others. He had 850 kilograms of explosives in five packages. One would kill the lackeys of Pertamina, who sold out to the Americans' Mobil Oil for money. One would attack an Army administrative office in Lhokseumawe. That one was pleasure, for what they'd done to his cousin, though it was business, too, as it would spread fear.

Two of the remaining were shipping overseas, through the Philippines and Pakistan. Whether or not those were the final destinations, he neither knew nor needed to. They'd go aboard ships, and as of then, his responsibility for them was ended.

That left one package of fifty kilograms of PETN-based breaching charge. That had a very special purpose. The thought of that one made him smile even wider. It would light a conflagration Allah himself would be able to see. The satellites in orbit should have a great view, and the images would certainly make worldwide news.

And a few thousand crisped corpses, plus the panic in the market, should drive the cost of doing business so high that the West would have to make the Javanese bastards come to terms.

Faisal was not smiling. He had never killed a man before.

Of course, he wasn't going to kill a man now, technically speaking. Decapitating a man would be like decapitating a goat. Or so he was told, never having done so. He was a city dweller from Medan. A decapitation death would cause blood to gush everywhere.

So instead, the man would be stripped and shot. Then, as the camera was turned on the dressed and set corpse, it would be knocked over.

Then Faisal would hack off the head with a large knife, in this case, a pedang—an Indonesian tribal knife.

The video would be sent out to the press to prove the act. Faisal's face wouldn't be visible, but his eyes would, beaming in triumph.

Except he wasn't sure they would be. There was little honor in killing a helpless, handcuffed man. There was little pride in butchering a corpse. It might be necessary, he believed action was called for, but was very distraught over it.

What Agung said was true: the West, particularly America, needed to know that its imperial ventures weren't popular with the typical Muslim, only with the elitists in power, who had sold out faith for money. It was true that the hostages they were taking were part of the military or industrial operations against Islam and could be considered combatants. It was true that they were infidels and nonbelievers, and thus by their own beliefs not harmed by being decapitated or dismembered. It was true they were taking Achinese oil and leaving the people bereft, then abusing them.

But it was also true that the Quran taught not to violate bodies, to allow them to be buried quickly, and, even if oil industry workers were helping the military indirectly, they were merchants and exempt from attack.

The different interpretations of the same scripture troubled him. He prayed as he should, hoping for guidance. So far, none had come.

Back at Bakri's village, tactics were discussed. First was to identify the boxes Kyle and Wade had seen.

"I don't recognize the language," Bakri admitted.

"No problem, we know someone who does," Kyle said.

"If you're thinking of your civilian, forget it," Wiesinger put in. "He doesn't know we're here, and to tell him now would create all kinds of hassle."

"Mel," Kyle said, "he's an ethnologist. He's the best chance to recognize a bad photograph from a scope image, and be at least able to guess the language."

"And if that picture says 'TNT' or 'Pentolite' and he knows we're in Indonesia, it tells him a lot more than that. Compare to images online."

That would be totally fruitless, but, "Yes, Mel," Kyle agreed.

An hour later, even Wiesinger was convinced. Without knowing what language, one couldn't even guess the meaning.

So Wade file transferred and painted it up in an art program, a copy of a copy of a photo taken through the image intensifier of a scope looking through humid air late at night. They attached it to an email and politely asked Gober if he could identify it. Oh, and by the way, could he hurry, they were in Time Zone–7. Please forget any reference to Indonesia you may have heard implied. Kyle phoned Robash's office, where a polite sergeant took note to call Mr. Gober and let him know there was a message waiting.

Lunch was brought in as the conference continued. Bowls of rice with aromatic seasonings, chicken, and more mangoes. It was good, Kyle reflected, that he liked tropical fruits. There were a lot of them in these dishes. And one of the bowls could legally pass as an incendiary. He'd had Pakistani curries, Tex-Mex chili and genuine Thai cuisine. But this stuff was flaming gasoline by comparison. He nibbled at it in between bites of the sweet stuff, which was a combo he'd have to remember. It was quite interesting.

"We never saw a truck with crates before," Bakri admitted around a mouthful of the firebomb. "And it sounds as if it was sent away quickly. Also the men on motorbikes are curious."

"We'll need to follow up on that," Wiesinger said. From his tone, Kyle guessed he wasn't sure how.

"I was surprised at the low attendance at the mosque," Kyle said.

"Oh?" Bakri asked.

"It couldn't have been more than a third."

There was silence for a few moments. Then

Bakri spoke. "One third is quite high. High enough to be of note. I would expect that for a holy day, not for a normal workday."

"Oh," Kyle said. He'd assumed near 100 percent attendance, as in Pakistan and Iraq. "They were mostly young males."

"Then that is certainly a sign of one of the more militant factions," Bakri said.

"Damn." He hadn't realized how secular people were here. Actually, he'd only heard Allah mentioned once in a day and a half, now that he thought about it.

"We need a better look, then," Wiesinger said, "to figure out what's there."

"You stand out," Bakri said. "Better if one of my men goes in."

"How do we do that?" Wade asked.

"Watch." The grin on his face was inscrutable.

Wade was as antsy as Kyle, and had been checking mail constantly. "Response from Gober," he said.

"What do we have?" Kyle shifted attention at once.

"'Gentlemen: As near as I can tell, that pictogram is a logo that closely resembles the Thai word for "explosive." Hope this helps. Signed: E.'"

"Well, we had guessed that," Kyle said.

"Is there any legitimate reason they might have explosives there?" Wiesinger asked.

"Not without government people bonding and delivering it. Foreign marks are a sign of smuggling," Bakri said.

"Definitely the right track then." Wiesinger smiled in satisfaction.

Kyle wondered why. It wasn't a difficult conclusion. It didn't bring them a target or any way to stop whatever events were happening. It was only a report.

But, he realized, the colonel lived for reports. To him, this was a major event. He sighed. There were two types of soldiers in the Army. Wiesinger would never understand Kyle's type, and he would never understand Wiesinger's.

After a nap, they were back out on the road, on a slightly different route. There was still a Kopassus unit south and east that might come looking for them, and anyone tromping around in the woods from the village might see traces. They circled wide and came down from the hills south of the town, moving through thicker brush as they did so.

Kyle was again impressed. Snuggled under weeds and a ghillie, sweating a little less than the day before now that he'd had some time to acclimate, he watched two of Bakri's men, Rizal and Fahmi, slip to the edge of the village. They were young, and eager, and grinned a lot, but had shrewd looks when faced with problems. Both were very mature and wise for their ages.

He wasn't sure, but he thought both were about fifteen.

The buildings on this side were older. Trash didn't seem to get dragged into the woods as often, but rather was left carelessly against the back walls or just tossed a few feet. Disgusting. Even animals knew to shove waste out of the nest. The professional in Kyle, who had studied camp security from day one, was appalled.

There was another truck tonight. It was smaller, a decrepit old stake-bed with canvas covering something in the back. In front of the mosque, two figures peeled the cover back. With a faint whistle, the line of men materialized to unload it.

And Rizal and Fahmi stood up and walked into town.

It took serious balls to do that. But it would probably work, Kyle figured. If you acted as if you belonged, people generally didn't question you—though there was the risk that everyone in the group knew everyone else. Still, it was dark.

They joined the line and passed crates for about three minutes. As the last few were being dragged along the splintered wooden bed, Fahmi took the box in his hands and walked straight into the mosque. Less than a minute later, as the last crate came down, he appeared outside the back door. He gingerly picked his steps through rotten timber and packing boxes for mundane stuff, and headed into the woods at an oblique angle, quickly but with caution. Rizal appeared around the side, dropping into the undergrowth and starting to crawl. In seconds, he was lost to Kyle, who was a trained professional with a night vision scope. No amateur should find him, certainly not ones who had no reason to suspect him.

Two hours of crawling and sweating later, they were back in the vehicles and heading for safety, the crate in the back unopened as of yet.

8

CAPTAIN HARI SUTRISNO DIDN'T LIKE FILING reports that would lead to greater interference from Jakarta. Still, certain events required a report, and this was one of them. Nor was it the first such, and that angered him. Indonesia was quite modern, a producer of electronics and raw materials, but the damned Europeans and their lackeys seemed to think it was a backwater like Iraq or Yemen.

He started the page with date, rank, name, and unit, then noted the incident by date and time from his records.

> "While on patrol for operations or training missions by GAM elements, encountered three technical vehicles with suspected insurgents.
>
> "Upon sighting weapons, improvised ambush and attacked. One vehicle was disabled.

"Unit consisted of rifles and RPGs with one known machine gun and a 40mm grenade launcher. Estimated force of 15–20.

"During the engagement, private Edi Sudradjat was killed, two wounded. Estimated enemy casualties four wounded.

"Faced with strong opposition, I withdrew my forces and planned for pursuit and observation. Enemy disengaged in a fast, professional fashion and took casualties and all equipment.

"For note: estimate two Caucasian males in unit. Possible Australian or European. Concern is potential mercenary forces assisting rebels. Recommend all units be alert for other incidents of this type.

"For note: force was quite highly trained, far better than typical for GAM. Consider possibility that Caucasians are military advisors. No purpose comes to mind other than to foment insurrection and separate Aceh, thus leading to negotiations for resources."

He listed routine operations, requests for supplies, and wrote, by hand—for he was formal about such things—a letter to Private Sudradjat's family, praising his service.

The email report went out at once, and should be looked at by 0900. The handwritten letter would take days, but it was best, he thought, to have a personal memento to go with the harsh truth.

While a competent enemy was a challenge, it also was a threat. And who were these foreign troops? Could someone be trying to split Aceh? Cash in on arms sales? Create trouble with Mobil and put pressure on Jakarta?

He didn't have enough intel to guess. Nor was that his problem. But he would find and if possible capture these strangers.

The crate contained blocks of TNT. Forty-eight of them, half a kilogram each. That was a standard size for most of the world.

"How many crates were on those trucks?" Kyle asked.

"More than twenty last night, ten more tonight," Wade said.

"At least twelve hundred and twenty-four pounds of HE. Someone is planning a party." Kyle had seen lots of HE—high explosive—military and civilian. He was fine with it as a military materiel. The thought of sociopathic freaks with it gave him the creeps.

"Could be more than that," Wade reminded them.

"I am most unhappy," Bakri said.

"Why, specifically?" Kyle asked.

"Because if this is used against Mobil or the government, it will make our struggle that much harder. If someone has this kind of resource, they should be sharing their skills and helping us. This can't help. And if it's being sent elsewhere, it will make my people look like terrorists." He was quivering in anger.

"We'll report back what we can," Kyle said. "We are usually listened to as a source of intel." But inside, he knew if State wanted a scapegoat and couldn't ID the real culprit, they'd use Bakri's men to take the fall, to improve relations with the Indonesian government.

Wade offered a more useful comment. "And if we ID these bastards positively, we'll dispose of them."

"Good," Bakri said, nodding vigorously. "But we must find where this is going, or at least where some of it is going."

"Do you have any ideas?" Wiesinger asked.

"I am guessing some of it will head for other groups. I can inquire carefully. But I don't know where else they might be using it." Bakri looked rueful.

"Well, what do we know, Mel?" Kyle asked. "Any specifics as to groups?"

"We really aren't supposed to discuss that outside of our own channels," the colonel said. He looked at the glares he was getting from those around him. Disgust from Kyle and Wade, offense from the Indonesians. "But I think we should," he added, almost too quickly.

"The group in question, the Fist of God, is a fringe group of Jemaah Islamiyah." His pronunciation wasn't the best. Obviously, he'd read but not talked about it much. "They've been con-

ducting attacks on U.S. personnel near Lhokseumawe. So far, there are two hostages unac-
counted for, just disappeared and presumed
dead, and a third was decapitated two months
ago. We have another hostage at present. They—
Fist of God—are believed to be one of the
sources for the explosive that you . . . tracked on
your last operation," he said, referring to Kyle
and Wade's mission in Romania, intercepting explosives as they came across the Black Sea into
Europe.

"And we now have that explosive to compare," Kyle said. "And it looks much like the
TNT we intercepted, only in different crates."

"It also looks like the stuff they're finding in
Iraq and Pakistan," Wiesinger confirmed.

"I know of that group," Bakri said, and they
faced him. "Very dangerous. They are threatening to attack the oil."

"Why?" Wade asked. "Isn't the oil necessary
to Achinese independence?"

"Yes," Bakri agreed. "But they have come beyond independence to jihad. They want an imag-
inary paradise according to the oldest form of the
Quran. They want to kill all Hindus and Chris-
tians, split away from the modern government in
Jakarta, and live as wanderers, nomads. It won't
work."

"So they'll attack a refinery? A well? A terminal?"

"Perhaps all of them," Bakri said. "But we'll

need to find out. I may actually have to talk to the government and tell them of this." The expression on his face was at once amused, perturbed, and amazed.

"No," Wiesinger said, shaking his head. "They don't know we're here, and the repercussions would affect U.S. interests."

"What about my interests? And those of my family?" Bakri asked.

Wiesinger froze. Obviously, this had gone from an office plan to a real world fight in his mind. He now had no idea what to do.

"First we find who and where," Kyle said firmly. "Then we sit down and discuss who's affected how. Then we decide what to do. We may need silence, backup from your government or ours, or a quick raid and vanish. It's too early to make calls. But Khayalan isn't the root source, merely a way stop, right, Mel?"

"Yes, so it seems."

"I would have said so, if I had been asked," Bakri said. He was smiling, but obviously exasperated underneath.

"Sometimes State and the CIA really piss me off," Kyle said. "I'm sure they meant well, but they didn't cross-check well enough, and now we have a dead end."

Wiesinger said nothing. He had his phone out, and wandered away for privacy. Kyle let him. Hopefully, he'd get some guidance from somewhere. As it stood at present, the mission was a wash. Oh, they could still shoot a player in this and hinder the operation, and that was better than nothing. The brains behind the program were still at large, however. Depending on where, he or they were probably unreachable.

If it came to an urban engagement, Kyle intended to refuse. That had worked in Romania with lots of CIA backup on scene and favors from the host nation, and it had still resulted in several international incidents. Then it had taken a crack anti-terror squad as well. There was just no way to set all that up here, he figured.

The colonel came back. "Okay," he said, "that took a three-way with our people, State and Intelligence. They want us to acquire more intel at Khayalan and determine the source if we can, or follow further up the chain. Then they'll tell us whether we shoot or pull out." He looked quite unhappy.

Kyle knew the look. Wiesinger felt the mission was a wash, and he'd just become a cog for a possible future one, rather than a commander. Kyle had felt that way several times early in his career. It was the nature of the business. And no mission was ever a waste: Just ruling out bad intel was useful, though it could be hard to be so objective halfway around the world.

"We know which way they traveled," Bakri said. "We can travel that route and observe. Also, we can set up posts to see what else comes along there."

"How many men do you have for that?" Wiesinger asked.

"Enough," Bakri said. "But I'm not sure I should discuss such matters." His grin was cruel.

Thankfully, Wiesinger didn't take the bait. He didn't manage to hide his anger and distress, though. The man wanted control, and wasn't getting it.

Bakri had two cell phones for his group. The Americans had three. That suggested five groups with a total of nineteen people. Fahmi would lead one group, Bakri another, and each American one. Each group would take a different part of the route and watch for traffic in and out of Khayalan.

Kyle wasn't keen on letting Wiesinger operate without Wade or himself along. But it was just observation, and the man was steady enough under fire and could move adequately. Sighing, he realized he was running the show while maintaining the pretense of a subordinate. And everyone knew it. If Wiesinger could just come out and say he was an observer and advisor and let Kyle run things with the locals, it would be easy. But the ego the colonel carried would never let that happen.

And maybe he'd fall asleep again, leaving the work to soldiers. No, it wasn't a kind thought.

By nightfall, they were distributed in five groups along two roads that diverged from the track through Khayalan. A third route was, as Bakri put it, "An easy way to meet the Kopassus." It was unlikely the explosives had gone that way.

Kyle was sure enough of his element, four of Bakri's men including Rizal, who spoke some basic English. Combined with Kyle's very rudimentary Bahasa and the commonality of many technical words, they were able to communicate adequately.

His phone buzzed and he grabbed it. "Kyle."

"This is Mel. First item, truck, one one three zero hours. Same vehicle as last night. Eight items same as last night. Over."

"Roger."

"Item Two. Six motorcycles departed zero zero one five hours. Backpacks medium. Likely capacity three zero pounds each. Over."

"Roger." So they might see stuff their way soon.

"Item Three. American Mobil employee Frank Keller reported killed, decapitated according to video released by Fist of God. State Department and Indonesian ministries following up. Over."

"Roger. Shit." Someone else dead, just as a childish gesture. Kyle gritted his teeth.

"Any chance of recovering one biker and contents of ruck interrogative. Over."

"Yes, Mel. If I see any, we'll get one silently. Shall I relay to Wade interrogative. Over."

"Have done so. Plan to intercept one rider. Over."

"Roger. Out."

"Out." The exchange wasn't entirely by the book. He suspected Wiesinger was shaky on radio operations. Besides, these were cell phones. One could be conversational.

Kyle looked carefully around, then relocated by several feet. He wanted to be well away from the road in case of observation or attack, or some geek hopping out to take a leak on the side of the road. He also wanted to be where he had a good field of fire. If the opportunity presented itself, he intended to take out the last rider in line. The goal was to make it appear an accident or have it be beyond sight of the leaders. That would give them time to get the road swept clear and neatened.

He found a nice spot, a slight depression still damp from the rain the night before. There was a ridge next to it, likely caused by some near-surface root. It was shielded from the road by some thick, leafy scrub that would make him effectively invisible. The mound would provide cover, and he had a great long oblique view along and across the road. Two trees marked the right and left limits of his weapon. So it would be like skeet shooting through a window.

A couple of soft whistles brought Rizal and the other three over. He explained what he was going to do. He used a lot of gestures and simple words.

"I understand," Rizal said. "You will shoot, we will catch."

Then it was back to waiting. It could be twenty

minutes or more, assuming the bikes were even coming this way. Two lonely trucks had passed all evening. This was about as far into the boonies as one could get.

Far in the distance, Kyle heard the sound of engines whining. He quivered alert. The sound faded out, then came closer. So they were probably heading this way, but that could mean business for Wade, too. Or both of them if the group split up.

Then the whine rose and came up the slope of the road.

How many? At least three were present, but were all six? It was critical to hit the last bike and not one in the middle. No matter how good a shot Kyle was, and he was perhaps the best anywhere, a target that fast was hard to hit. If the bikers thought it was an attack, it was probable the rest would just ride on. He snuggled into the rifle and checked his scope.

Then they came into view.

The riders were in a perfect bell curve distribution. One machine was out ahead, then another, two side by side right behind that with the fifth close in and the sixth a good twenty meters back. Kyle could take a shot, but there was no margin for error.

The first cycles flashed through the field of view, and Kyle assessed the lead at an unconscious level. He stretched his left hand far forward on the handguard. This would be like shotgunning a clay pigeon on a sharp left launch. He grumbled to himself for not taking the other side of the road.

But then the last one was in front and he swung, using a technique he'd learned from Peter Capstick, an outdoor writer long dead but whose books had fascinated Kyle. With his left hand out and the rifle pulled tight into his shoulder, he waited as the image of the speeding rider in the blur of trees passed through the swinging scope. The reticle aligned with the rear wheel's upper arc and he snapped the trigger, letting the rifle finish its swing.

The suppressor caught most of the gases and muzzle blast, but still left the supersonic crack of a boattail match bullet. But that wasn't obvious as a weapon sound to people not trained to recognize it. Indeed, the other riders didn't seem to have heard it above the banshee howls of their engines. They disappeared in a whirlwind of leaves.

Meanwhile, the last rider skidded on the edge of control. The bike slewed and went down. He'd held it just long enough for the others to be over a slight rise. So unless the rider ahead was very nervous or well trained, it could be minutes before he noticed his buddy missing.

"Go!" Kyle whispered hoarsely, and Rizal nodded.

The driver had laid the bike down well, and was just standing to dust himself off as he was swept off his feet by a torrent of small figures. He was beaten senseless and carried off. Rizal righted the bike and began rolling it as the other two scuffed over the tire marks with branches. Unless the other riders dismounted and made a good search, they should have trouble seeing any signs.

Kyle was already on the phone. "One target recovered. Stand by." He left it at that as his small squad sought deeper cover. Sooner or later, the riders would notice. They might return, press on or call for someone else to investigate. It wouldn't do to be around.

A kilometer later he was badly out of breath. It wasn't the distance, it was the encumbrance of the ghillie, the mass of his ruck, the weapon and the very uneven terrain that required a loose-jointed, shifting run. The distance should give them plenty of time to respond to happenings on the road.

Twenty minutes later, the other bikers hadn't returned. That meant either they were calling for other forces, or more likely, had no idea where the incident had actually happened. They might have no idea it had happened at all, depending on how observant they were.

The bike had been pushed a good two hundred meters back the other way and dumped on the other side as misdirection, in a small rivulet. Kyle's shot had taken it through frame, rim, and tire. He figured the odds of a perfectly aimed shot at the wheel having about a one in three chance. Sometimes, luck did matter.

Rizal had the captive trussed with parachute cord and duct tape. He hadn't taken any liberties, but he hadn't been gentle about it, either.

Back on the phone, Kyle called Wade. He gave his coordinates. "Relay and we'll meet here. I'd like extra firepower just in case, and I don't want to try to drag a prisoner too far."

"Understood."

While they waited, Rizal left the man gagged but started softening him up. His methods were direct and brutal. By the time Wade showed up, the victim was wincing and crying, snorting for air through his nose because of the gag. Rizal handled that by gripping the man's nose shut with pliers.

The snorts turned to whimpers and moans. Wade arrived, then Bakri and his other man, Syarief, with Anda covering the rear. Wiesinger was last and following GPS. He still held a compass but wasn't using it. Kyle said nothing, but he and Wade exchanged glances. GPS could be spoofed, batteries could die. If you couldn't find your way with a compass, you didn't belong in a task like this.

Wiesinger was smart enough or scared enough not to mention the battered and bleeding body in the middle of the group. He simply remained nearby in a squat, as most of the troops spread out for a perimeter. Kyle decided to tweak him. He pulled out an MRE and started slurping cold spaghetti and meatballs. The colonel faced away.

There was trouble when Bakri stepped over and peeled off the gag. The man started to scream, either curses or cries for help. A boot to the teeth shut him back up, but it was clear answers wouldn't be forthcoming.

That was, until Anda snapped off the man's belt and tugged at his trousers. Rizal clacked the pliers suggestively and the response was nodding so hard it might cause a sprain.

Kyle didn't approve of torture, and officially should have stopped it. But this wasn't his country, or his troops. They weren't even legally troops. And this scumbag was helping kill people anyway. Innocent people. Kyle didn't approve. But he wasn't about to stop it.

"Ruck contains fifteen half-kilo blocks," Wade reported. "He claims a destination of . . . where was that?"

"The oil terminal," Bakri said. "They are planning to attack that, as well as civilians."

Kyle frowned. There were literally billions of gallons of petroleum at the terminal. A properly staged attack would destroy it beyond any hope of salvage, and kill hundreds, perhaps thousands of people.

Those were headlines that would cause corporations to pull out. Add the death toll to that, and it could be considered a victory for the terrorists.

Or would they pull out? There were trillions of dollars at stake here. Perhaps Indonesia would respond with more military force. If so, that escalation could be as bad. Thirteen hundred islands, 200 million people held together by a government bureaucracy, not any common heritage. What was the term he'd heard? *Disintegrasi.* Not something that was considered funny here. Indonesians were either very protective of their nation or wanted out. There was none of the humor that accompanied the comments of say, Massachusetts or California seceding from the United States. National disintegration was something most feared.

Some more cuffing and kicking yielded very little more information. The "man" was about fourteen and scared. He knew little more than hearsay. But he had the explosives and an address to deliver them to. When it was clear he wouldn't be of more use, Rizal drew a large, leaf-bladed knife, bent over and made two brutal chops. The first split the skull like a bloody melon. The second severed the head.

Wiesinger looked rather green. Obviously, he hadn't seen many, if any, deaths before. Kyle couldn't say he was enthused by the activity. But there wasn't much he could do, and they did need the information. He had to deal with his conscience on the grounds that he had neither suggested, encouraged, nor endorsed the activity. But a lot of things in this job were disgusting.

"What shall we do?" Bakri asked. "I am reluctant to start a local war against other Achinese. It could only spread."

"Yeah, I see that," Wade said. "Their friends, your friends, and the government all on you."

"Is there any way to share that intel with the government?" Kyle asked. "Without admitting we're here?" he added for Wiesinger's benefit.

"There are sympathizers in the Army," Bakri said. "But the Army would claim in propaganda that we were all involved. They'd send more forces after us to thank us."

To which Kyle said, "Oh." Of course. He knew that and had been briefed on that. Were it mentioned to the government, the operation would disappear overnight and crop up somewhere else. The Army would attack what rebels it could find to show it was doing something. That would make things worse for their friends and do little about the real threats—a hostage and an imminent attack on the oil terminal.

"We need a more informed captive," Wiesinger said. "Can we arrange that?"

Bakri considered. "I'm sure we can, given time. But who would know? The lorry driver is not likely to know. These message boys," he pointed at the corpse, "don't know."

"What about the imam at the mosque?"

"He would make a good target," Bakri agreed, "if we could get him to come out."

"He always greets the truck, right?" Wiesinger offered.

"He did twice," Wade agreed. "It's a pattern."

"Hijack the truck?" Kyle asked.

"If there's a way." Wiesinger wasn't stupid, Kyle realized. Just bad-tempered, inexperienced, insecure, and conceited.

"But will he talk?" Bakri asked. "The imams are quite agitating in the news. Very stubborn."

"Bakri, it's my experience that such men talk a lot, and are happy to send young men to die, but have no balls for a real fight." Kyle had seen such press releases. Men who vowed to "fight to the last drop of blood" when the blood wasn't theirs.

"You may be correct. Certainly I've not heard of their exploits."

"Camp out here today?"

"I think we must. And at nightfall we must move quickly." Bakri looked around at the growing dawn. "And we should travel some more distance now for safety."

"Let's move, then," Wiesinger said, sounding as if he was in charge. Kyle wouldn't mind that if the man actually did take charge and do it well. He seemed to want the glamour but not the work.

They compromised on moving south, toward the hills. The ground rose only a few meters overall in the five kilometers they traveled. Rain started to fall, large drops splatting through the trees, and they were well soaked in short order.

They traveled a narrow path that might be for game or people. Such paths were often dangerous, but it was fast and they carried substantial firepower. Several wild boars trotted by, but upon seeing a large armed party, snorted and gave them a wide berth.

They passed a troop of orangutans who squeaked, which made Kyle nervous. Certainly there were other reasons for them to sound off, but he was still worried about the attention. And the squeaking was almost creepy. He'd expected bellows or shouts from orangutans, not the high-pitched sound.

It could be worse, he thought. Various parts of this archipelago had saltwater crocodiles, kraits, and komodo dragons. There were tigers around here, too. Life seemed so much more interesting away from home. But it didn't interest Kyle that much. Each was a challenge and a curiosity, but he preferred to go home afterward.

The sun began pattering through the trees after the rain lifted, and they sought shelter. Various downed giant timber, broad, leafy bushes, and hollows served as such. They posted watches and tried to sleep in the oppressive heat and humidity. Kyle was down to just a T-shirt, over Wiesinger's complaints about camouflage and insects. But if he couldn't sleep, he'd be no use, and the bugs weren't deterred by thin fabric. Wade followed suit. Wiesinger didn't, no doubt to lead by example. Kyle saw him sleeping while on watch. He tossed and twitched, sweat running off him in rivulets rather than beads. Kyle was merely beaded and his shirt stuck. That was enough for him. He shook his head at the mentality of his officer and turned his attention back to potential threats.

9

FAISAL RIPPLED WITH EXCITEMENT AS HE stood before the camera. An hour earlier, the man beside him had been tied down and shot through the heart. After a few seconds of thrashing and screaming that echoed over the gunfire still ringing in Faisal's ears, he'd stared and stiffened and died. A couple of large bandages and a change of clothes, and the stiffening corpse "sat" on a chair, propped from behind by well-directed hands.

"Everyone look at the camera," Erwin said. "Good. We'll add the audio in a moment, so get ready . . . and . . . now!"

Screaming "God is great!" Bambang and Wismo wrestled the chair and body over, fighting each other as much as it. Wismo was a monster of a man, almost six feet and near two hundred pounds. The head struck the floor with a thunk, and that was a good pretense for unconsciousness. Faisal took his cue and jumped astride the dead man's chest.

He was dizzy and remote as he worked. It almost felt as if another were using his hands. The long, slim pedang grated off bone and gristle, slicing and sawing and hacking. The lime and arsenic etched blade left streaks of black oxide in the flesh as blood smeared the knife. Erwin moved in close with the camera, to get a nice shot of the opening gap. Bambang got close to the body and the microphone and gurgled a scream that sounded horrible. This really would come across as a killing.

Then it was done. Faisal took the head by the hair and held it up so Erwin could get a close shot. Then, in carefully rehearsed Arabic, he said, "Thus to all infidels who oppose the will of Allah."

Then the camera was off and they were all singing, shouting, and dancing. "God is great! God is great! Now you are a man!" and clapping him on the shoulders.

He smiled, but wasn't sure he felt it. How much of a man did it take to butcher a corpse? How honorable? It wasn't something he felt like boasting of. His brother had shot men, soldiers in battle. This couldn't possibly compare.

But he did smile, and took the accolades. This could be a start to greater triumphs.

* * *

The video would receive attention in the press, though it wouldn't have the effect the Fist of God desired. In America and to a lesser extent in Europe, the TV-watching public had seen enough beheaded corpses to not be shocked. Every week or so, another headless corpse. Every day, another twenty Iraqis, Palestinians, Afghans, or some other people dead. Every month, a few Israelis. It was a status quo that they didn't really have any hope of changing.

Beneath that, however, was a growing undertone of disgust. Some knew that the killings were a violation of the Quran's teachings. Many others didn't care, and simply wanted revenge. The military and intelligence services were frustrated and angered at the inability to respond because of the political and diplomatic hogties they wore. In short, the problem was growing, neither side willing to back down, and one far more powerful than the other, even if it was showing restraint so far. But sooner or later, something would snap.

Then the terrorists would get the rivers of blood they prayed for. But much of that blood would be theirs, and those of the people they spoke for, whether those people supported them or not.

Kyle heard the shot through his sleep. He wasn't sure if it was incoming or outgoing as he rolled over. Trained reflexes kept him on the ground as he snicked the safety off his rifle and got ready to rock. Someone had discovered them and was deemed hostile. But Kyle needed to know who and why before shooting. Fratricide was bad. He twisted to his belly but stayed under the leaves.

Wiesinger woke, too. "Report!" he snapped, loudly enough to be heard but not give away position.

"Unknown, Mel, I'm standing by."

Wade dove in nearby and said, "Hostiles, small arms. South and closing." He was close enough to talk and spot, not close enough to be caught by the same area effect weapon.

"Roger that," Kyle said. "Outgoing!" and hunched down for a target.

Except it was very tough to see in this terrain. Nor did he want to stick his head up. Bakri was shouting something, and the machine gun opened up with a two second burst. Another fired back, shredding leaves a dozen meters away.

In the pause before more rifle fire, other voices were yelling.

"Was that English?" Wade asked.

Kyle had heard it, too. "I think so."

"Hold fire," Wiesinger said quietly. "What's the phrase?"

"*Jangan tembak*," Wade supplied. There was no need for it; Bakri spoke English.

Bakri looked at them quizzically from his position, but relayed the order. The outgoing din died down, and everyone hunkered behind cover. A few seconds later, their opponents also slacked off. Into a momentary lull, Kyle yelled, "Do you speak English?"

"Bloody right. Who wants to know?" The English was clear, but there was an accent. Whoever spoke it was well educated.

Wiesinger shouted, "U.S. Army. Who are you?"

"Australia." Nothing happened for several more seconds, until the other party said, "Want to call truce and parley?"

"That's probably a good idea," Kyle said. "Weapons down, everyone." He turned to Wiesinger and quietly said, "Is that okay, Mel?"

"Do it," the colonel said.

Cautiously, Kyle stood, his right side behind a tree and ready to dive for cover. Ahead, a man dressed in Indonesian camouflage, but clearly Caucasian, also stood. He was carrying an M4A1 with an M203 grenade launcher and an Advanced Combat Optical Gunsight, pointed at the ground.

Kyle cautiously hefted the SR25 into a low port and stepped forward. The other did likewise. In the thick growth, they were only about twenty meters apart, but had been well hidden from each other until they stood. It was a wonder they'd met up at all. They could have skulked within meters and not known.

Wiesinger had been way too incautious by adding the "Army" to "U.S.," in Kyle's opinion. "We're Americans" would have been enough to start the negotiations. There'd been no reason to announce their identity to an unidentified force, which still could contain hostile elements.

They stopped about ten feet apart. The other man was skinny, about five foot eight, and had a rugged moustache. They looked each other over, then looked around surreptitiously for any observers or other presence. They'd been doing that as they walked, of course. The obvious act was just part of a meeting between two soldiers unsure of each other.

"Kyle Monroe," he identified himself softly.

"Jack Stephens," the other said. "U.S. Army?"

"Ranger, Sniper, sergeant first class." He nodded.

"Staff sergeant, Special Air Service. This is Akbar." He gestured at his local guide, who was shorter but stockier than Bakri. "What the bloody hell are you doing here?" His trained speaking voice slipped for a moment, to a Western Australian accent.

"I could ask the same thing," Kyle said reasonably. He eyed Akbar. Presumably he was loyal, but he was still only vouched for by a probable ally. Akbar nodded back with a surly but not unfriendly expression.

"Right," Stephens agreed. "Should we both guess, or admit we're hunting Jemmies?"

"Jemmies. I like that." Kyle grinned. It was hard to find an obvious but rude term for Jemaah Islamiyah.

"Yeah, what do you call 'em, mate?" Stephens asked.

"Dead, whenever possible. Scum when not."

"Good man." He returned the grin.

"Do we need to get together and talk?" Kyle asked. "All of us?"

"I reckon that's an idea," Stephens agreed with a curt nod. He turned and whistled a sibilant note.

Slowly, his unit stood. There were two other Aussies and six Indonesians.

Kyle nodded to Wade, who turned to both Wiesinger and Bakri, and their force rose and moved forward. Shortly, all twenty-five of them were in a loose huddle, a circle of squatting and lounging men and women in the trees, with three of each team, including one Aussie and Wade, facing out on watch. It was quiet now, except for dripping condensation. As his hearing recovered, Kyle could hear the fainter sounds of animals and shifting growth.

"Wiesinger, colonel, U.S. Army. I'm in charge of our op." Kyle could see he'd started already, insecure and making sure everyone knew it, while imagining he was coming across as confident.

"H'lo, sir," Stephens nodded, then turned his attention back to Kyle. Kyle forced himself not to grin. That the colonel was a REMF was obvious to an operator like the Aussie. "So what shall we talk about?"

The negotiation would be as delicate as seducing a virgin, Kyle realized. They both knew what the other was doing, but neither wanted to be the first to say so. They likely had a lot of intel in common, and some peculiar to their respective services that could prove useful, or horribly wrong or worthless. The trick was to not give away bad intel, or swap good intel too cheap, or wind up offending erstwhile allies, or letting anything slip to locals of untested loyalties, or . . .

Kyle grimaced to himself. He wasn't a diplomat. He was a shooter. He *should* pass this off to Wiesinger, except the man clearly had no clue.

"Yes, we're hunting Jemmies," Kyle admitted quietly, but in a rush. "Specifically, ones interfering with our personnel and interests, though we're open to others if they're in the way."

Stephens was partially hidden under a broad leaf, shadow disrupting his silhouette. It was an unconscious move that marked him as a true professional.

"Makes sense," he said. "We've been handling PNG, and there's ties to Timor-Leste, Sulawesi, Borneo, and here." He pronounced them correctly, rather than in Aussie Strine.

"You probably have far better intel than we do," Kyle admitted ruefully. The Aussies had been in and out of Papua New Guinea for decades. He knew of it vaguely, had read a brief on

East Timor, and knew of attacks on the others. That was it, done for intel.

"Well, if you're not adverse to lending a hand, I don't mind swapping some for what you need. Tea?" Stephens asked, his smile broken by camouflage paint as he held up a small cooking pot, a "billy."

"Sure, why not?" Kyle agreed.

Wiesenger proved again to not be as bad as he came across. He'd been quiet so far. When he spoke again, he said, "I assume the ties you're referring to are Laskar Jihad from Sulawesi, and Organisasi Papua Merdek from Papua?"

"Indeed," Stephens agreed as he unfolded a small trioxane stove, pulled open a previously used and tightly folded fuel package with his teeth and broke another third of a bar of fuel off. He slipped it in place, flicked a butane lighter, and pointed at his back. One of the reticent locals pressed on his Camelbak, squeezing water up through the plastic straw and into the pot.

"But they're all linked, about like we are," he continued. "They scratch each other's backs and share intel on targets and techniques. Better than we do, a lot of the time. They really care less about the credit than they do about killing Americans and 'your lapdogs.' "

"You, the Brits, the Saudi government, the Poles, the Filipinos, the Japanese . . ." Wiesinger offered.

"And Bali and India for daring to be Hindu. Then there's Singapore across the water."

"Singapore is involved?" Wiesinger asked, surprised now. So was Kyle.

"Yeah, they have a team around here somewhere, too, because of Kumpulan Mujahedeen Malaysia. The Kiwis don't yet, but likely will if they ever catch some fire or think they will. The Filips do. The Brits have had teams in these parts since Malaysia in the sixties."

"Pity we can't all team up," Kyle said.

"Yeah, that'd be nice. Of course, Indonesia wouldn't like that, and the Kopassus is running a lot of ops, too. Some of which get out of hand."

"Yeah, we know," Kyle said. He didn't admit to having a shootout with them. "Christ, what a mess."

"Yeah, a big one. Even if we settle out the Middle East, we'll still be fighting this one in twenty fifty."

"So who are you after?" Wiesinger asked.

"Straight to the point, eh?" Stephens asked. "We're looking for Ibrahim Beureueh, who we think was the thug behind that second Bali bombing. But he's with the GAM and they're slippery—not all of them are bad, and we're not opposed to GAM in principle."

"Yeah," Kyle admitted. "I've got to say these are some of the most respectable indigenous forces I've ever worked with." He nodded to Bakri, who returned it.

"Indeed. We don't want to help the Indo government, but we don't want to step on their toes. It's ripe for being used as someone's bitch to settle a score."

"Heh. Been there, done that, somewhere else," Kyle said, recalling being used to fight a tribal war in Pakistan. He sat back on a damp log. It didn't matter. He was soaked with sweat and humidity anyway. He reached into his gear for a canteen cup.

"Sorry to hear that, mate," Stephens said. The water was boiling and he fished the pot off the stove with his hooked finger through the bail. He dumped in a handful of tea leaves and set it down to steep. Then he blew the stove fuel out before leaning back again.

"So we're creeping around until we find this bugger."

"We'll add him to our list, but we're mostly west of here," Wiesinger said.

"Right. So what about you?"

Kyle glanced at Wiesinger, who nodded at him.

"We're looking for incoming explosives, and whoever's been snagging hostages," he said.

"We heard about the hostages. Fucking animals. But what about explosives?" Stephens asked. He looked interested.

"Whole pallets full. Wade and I stopped some last year on—" he glanced again at Wiesinger— "the Black Sea. Coming out of Russia, most likely, through the 'stans, then into Europe and now down here. Literal tons. Mostly just commercial HE. But enough to blow craters."

"Kee—rist. That's something I should report," he hinted.

"Go ahead," Wiesinger agreed.

"Thank you," Stephens said, waving at one of his troops, who'd been professionally silent. The man handed him one of two phones. Stephens was going to report it anyway. Doing so now meant they all agreed to it, and the Australian military would have more lead time on what it was doing. Meanwhile, Wiesinger whipped out his cell phone.

Wiesinger said, "Wiesinger here. We've met an Aussie SAS patrol seeking Ibrahim Beureueh, I spell, Bravo Echo Uniform?" He looked at Stephens and relayed the rest of it, "Romeo Echo Uniform Echo Hotel. Have agreed to swap intel on my authority. Discussed deliveries being made to this location. Recommend our assets communicate with theirs. Mission on profile otherwise. No additional intel . . ." There was a long pause. "Yes, that is good to hear. Thanks. Relay our support. Wiesinger out." He closed the phone and said to Kyle, "Robash is out of the hospital, recovering at home on convalescent leave. His heart looks good, his cognitive function is back and he should be back on duty in a few weeks."

"Kick ass," Kyle said. That was cheering news.

Stephens finished his own call to some Royal Australian Naval vessel, and then poured tea into the Americans' cups, just a few mouthfuls each, then some for Bakri, his own men and his local liaison. The billy was refilled and put back to brew another batch. It wasn't that a hot drink was needed; it was more of a social issue. They were agreeing to sit, talk, and share a supply, no matter how small. Kyle recalled with bemusement the serious issues around such in Pakistan, where you weren't fed until they decided they weren't going to kill you.

"So where did you meet the Singaporean unit?" Kyle asked. He wouldn't have expected that one. The others he could deduce.

"Tiny island called Sulawan in the Karimata Strait. Friendly natives, lovely beaches, and a gorgeous crater lake. Oh, and kraits, saltwater crocodiles, roving pirates, and typhoons."

"Sounds like a charming place."

"Actually, I could retire there. I just might. One of the girls . . . anyway. They were staging from there to Borneo for some Irian Jaya mixup."

"We really should pass that to State to follow up with, don't you think, Mel?" Kyle asked Wiesinger.

"Yes, but let's hear more." Wiesinger was attentive as Kyle had never seen him. The man thrived on details and reports. He was probably great in the Pentagon. Better than he was out here.

Stephens nodded. "The Filipinos are operating in Sulawesi Utara, of course. Stuff comes from there up into Mindanao, which makes it their problem. The Brits and Malaysians and Singaporeans are worried about stuff flowing up the Malay Peninsula, and of course from Irian Jaya, and through India to Pakistan. That tells you how effective we're all getting at stopping their shipping."

"That's odd," Kyle said. "We just found explosives coming *in* from Thailand."

"Not really," Wiesinger said. "They sanitize it by doing that, and draw attention from it going the other way. Also, it wouldn't surprise me if it's being stolen or is pirated. These routes are never efficient. That's the one major advantage we have."

It was amusing to hear the government bureaucracy referred to as "efficient," but under the circumstances it was probably accurate in this context.

"So this is becoming a major point?" Kyle asked.

"Yes," Bakri said. "Some of my brothers will take any ally, no matter the reputation. And they have taken these. For transporting the explosives, they get a portion. They get training in it. They get to cause trouble for the government. But there is trouble the government will negotiate over, and that which they won't. The terrorism . . ." he tapered off.

"Right. And we can't tell said government," Wade said.

"Wish I could help you," Stephens said. "But we can't do anything that might wind up jeopardizing us. I'll give you support, but I can't get directly involved."

"Fair enough," Wiesinger said. "Likewise, I can share certain data, but I can't get into your op without clearing it through our government. That would take some time." That was an understatement, Kyle thought. That would take years.

"Right. So what more should we talk about, and should we head somewhere with better shelter? I think I feel a storm coming."

"We're heading south and east," Kyle said.

"We're south. If we hurry." He looked at the patches of cloud through the canopy.

They rucked up and started slogging. With a combined unit this size, there was little to worry about. They made good time.

"What's with pirates?" Kyle asked. He'd heard of that, but not in detail.

"Various," Stephens said. "Sometimes they grapple a pleasure boat or small tramp. Steal the valuables, kill the men, gang-rape the women to death, and abandon it."

"Oh, charming."

"Worse sometimes," one of the other SAS men said. "Rod Iverson, sorry. Good to meet you. Anyway, they've been known to fake lights or logos and pretend to be customs inspectors for some nation. Same story. And some of the customs inspectors are pirates, or as close as you find—milking the job for sex and cash bribes. Wouldn't surprise me if that's where some of the explosives are coming from."

"Always a way to make money," Wade said.

"Yeah, pretty much. Also some people buy scrap vessels and register them with valid names, then hunt down an appropriate matching ship in good shape and take it and all cargo, minus crew of course. They sell the cargo, and sometimes sell the fucking boat for a few million, then skip. By the time insurance for the real owners and a government catch up, they've got a small fortune."

"Devious," Kyle said. It pissed him off. With his skills, he could be rich if he didn't have a conscience. A highly trained soldier who could kill at two thousand yards? He could charge a hundred grand a hit anywhere in the world and get it.

Two hours of forced march and eight kilometers later, they were in a clearing with very crude huts—timber and woven boughs with leaves, some with tin roofs. The rain started beating the upper canopy as they slid into a large hut that belonged to a local headman.

Whatever language he spoke was quite different from Bahasa. Kyle could barely recognize one word in twenty as being close to something he'd heard. He settled for listening to Stephens and his guide-interpreter, Akbar, jabber away, while he studied their host.

The man was Malay, with a slight paunch. He looked sixty but might be forty. He was adequately fed and had all his teeth, save one up front. He wore Adidas shorts acquired from some Western source and was armed with a kris, a spear, and a revolver. It appeared to be an ancient Webley .455, and held only three cartridges. The canvas holster was worn in front, somewhat like a codpiece. The kris was buried in its wooden scabbard and looked to be rather old. Clearly, these were more ceremonial than functional. Several of his advisors, guards, hunters, whatever they were, were gathered around with light bows and spears and blowguns.

All smiles, the chief, whose name Kyle wouldn't even try to pronounce, came over and clapped him on both shoulders. Glancing at Stephens and getting a nod, he returned it. Then Wade and Wiesinger did, too, and Bakri. It appeared there were status issues. The other Indonesians were ignored.

The rain was reaching a torrent, though not as much as it would during monsoon season. Quickly, they were broken into groups and ushered into other huts. Kyle and Wade wound up alone in one, the occupants apparently hunting or gathering.

Outside, the rain poured down, splashing craters in the mud and the puddles already growing. It was dark, almost twilight, as the pools merged into a lake, then a sea, with stalks of greenery fighting to float above it and twist in the current. The tin roof shed water well, but the sound was a cross between being inside a snare drum and standing under a waterfall. Conversation was near impossible for several minutes.

Kyle stood, watching the water rise until it lapped at the lip of the floor, then slowly oozed in in a growing arc, then spread out to cover the worn, smooth gray planks. Through the frame of the door, the forest was a dark green-and-gray world, still in stark contrast to the flatter, artificial color of the walls.

With no one else nearby and Wiesinger gone, it was safe to actually talk about him. Still, Kyle looked surreptitiously around before speaking, and kept his voice low.

"You know, it's not that he's wrong so often, or shits a screaming worm about it . . ." he offered.

"It's that he never comes out and says, 'I was wrong' or 'I'm sorry,' " Wade supplied.

"Right."

"He can't be the first officer like that you've met."

"No, not at all. I just don't understand why they stick around so long."

"In his case, he's a daddy's boy."

"Yeah, I sorta noticed."

"Right. He wants a star so bad you can *see* the hard-on in his eyes. Just to prove he's as good as Daddy. And he's insecure enough to be a micromanaging ass."

"How did he wind up under Robash? They're nothing alike."

"Dunno," Wade said. "I'd guess he pulled strings but . . . how often do we have to deal with him?"

"Briefly on logistics last time," Kyle said, thinking, "and I had the general slap him down on some stupidity. We're dealing with him now. Other than that, maybe a dozen unpleasant phone calls."

"Right. He doesn't like the job. He doesn't like any job. He just wants to be a general like Daddy."

"Perfect problem for the Pentagon wienies; they can shuffle him off. Not so good for out here."

"You have a gift for understatement I envy, my friend," Wade said, smiling. It wasn't a happy smile.

"And he's not stupid. He's studied a great deal. But it's all book knowledge. Like that sleeping in full uniform in the middle of a jungle. It'll kill him from dehydration."

"Yeah. I've heard about officers like that in Vietnam. Damn near or did get their men killed."

"Well, time to kill. Euchre?" Kyle grabbed a barely used deck of cards from a pocket on his ruck. They were sealed in a plastic bag.

"If we must."

The hut had two chunks of carved log to sit on, a table of bamboo and split wood, and a window with a shutter. It was rustic but well built, and apart from the wet floor, quite tight and dry.

There were two pallets at one side, presumably for adults and children, and a hearthplace. With the oppressive humidity inside and the hissing rain outside, it was quite soothing. Kyle felt lulled.

He kept busy and awake by sorting through his ruck. No matter how careful one was, trash built up, and that was weight one didn't need to carry. He stuffed all the odds and ends into an empty MRE packet, and placed it in the top compartment where he could easily reach it for disposal at a convenient time—fire by preference, buried if not, civilian trash if need be. There was nothing that specifically linked him, but there was no need to advertise anything American.

Wade beat him three rounds in a row. "Damn, I'm tired," he said.

"That's what they all say. Want to take a nap? I'll cover."

"Yeah, if we can get fifteen minutes each or so, we should. Thanks."

He leaned against a timber and barely heard Wade's, "No problem."

10

THEY WERE REFRESHED BY LATE AFTERNOON, and invited for roast boar. Kyle ditched his trash in the fire, and the local children were delighted at the chemical colors of the flames. The Malay were an attractive people. He could see why Stephens had found a girlfriend on whatever island it was. Even the few overweight ones had nice skin tones and features. A couple of the women were absolute babes, and knew it—they batted eyelashes and the works. He thought of Janie and wondered how this mission would end up. He was only a little dinged so far—scratches, aches, bruises. It would be nice to avoid major wounds or stress that would hospitalize him. This time.

The families stayed mostly in their huts, though it was from politeness. The children played around the edges, in awe but not afraid of the strangers. The boar, roasted in thin strips rubbed with local herbs, was quite tasty. "Good grub," Stephens said. "We encountered the village by accident, and occasional gifts keep them quiet. Pocketknives, flashlights, lightsticks. They're too savvy for trinkets, but are in a rather remote location."

Actually, they weren't more than thirty miles from a huge industrial operation. But in this jungle, that was a considerable distance. There was little road other than the coastal highway and in the cities.

But they were nice people, and between game and fruit didn't seem to have to work much. One of the few tropical paradises left, and assholes were trying to tear it apart.

"Where do we go from here?" Kyle asked the group.

"South and East," Bakri said. "We should come up on the road and then set our ambush."

"Ambush?" Stephens asked. Wiesinger looked unhappy. There was just no way to keep track of the information here. It would be better if he just shared everything, Kyle thought. They were all on the same side and the enemy would know soon enough.

"We're going to capture what we hope is a leader and get more intel," Kyle said, watching Wiesinger to see if he objected to sharing the information.

"Right. Leave us out of that, then," Stephens

said. "Intel sharing, fine. An attack on anything concrete that will get headlines, even if we're not in them, fine. In between is a whole range of items that don't fall under 'winning the war' or 'staying discreet.'"

"Any way to get back together afterwards?"

"As long as there are no embarrassing bodies to talk about, certainly. Call my mobile. I'd kiss the arse of the man who invented those. Before that, it was pay phone, weeks with no reports, or lug a radio with all that entails and the risk of discovery."

Wiesinger accepted the number, and Kyle made note of it. That earned him a look of disgust from the colonel.

"Always good to have a duplicate, sir," he said. He wrote it as a simple series of digits with no breaks. It shouldn't be readily identifiable if found.

"Right," Wiesinger agreed. That was from the book. And it was something Kyle used because it made sense. An error or a casualty could leave them without contact information. "We'll call in a day or two. Good luck to you."

"And you." In seconds, Stephens's unit had disappeared into the brush.

"Our turn," Kyle said. "And we need to hump fast."

Bakri had a map out. "Here's where I recommend. It's where the trucks have been coming through."

"So we seize a truck and roll into the village?" Wiesinger asked.

"That is what I suggest. If they notice the driver is different, we can delay them a few seconds and apply force. Most of them don't carry weapons at hand."

"Could get nasty up close."

"Yes, but we should win. We have enough soldiers, and surprise."

Kyle was willing to risk it. Enough fire fast would make most people duck for cover. It wasn't sniping, but it should be over quickly. Wiesinger took a few moments to assess the risk, and agreed.

They headed out at a fast walk, two locals leading, two trailing, and the others switching off two on each flank. After an athletic hour of sweating and gasping for air, they reached a road.

"Not the safest way to travel," Wiesinger hinted.

"No," Kyle said, "but the traffic is light and we have a scout well ahead in case of trouble. As long as it doesn't get too mushy, we won't leave much sign."

"Very well," the colonel conceded. He did seem to be coming around, albeit slowly.

It was one of those marches where one quickly zoned and didn't notice the passage of time or distance. Kyle had done this for years, all over the world. He had good-fitting boots, a well-designed MOLLE ruck with contents suited to him personally, and a weapon he was comfortable with. There was nothing to do but pick up the feet, put them down, and pace off the distance. They were covering about three kilometers, two miles an hour, and would do so for a solid eight hours. That would put them where they needed to be for the ambush, hopefully with time to set it up. If not, they'd camp a day and try again. If that didn't work, they might need to actually assault the village and kill a few.

Kyle wasn't opposed to that on moral grounds. Most of them had to know what was going on. The darkness was merely a cover. But there were undoubtedly children, women, and a few men who really weren't in the loop. Besides, taking out towns was sloppy and attracted attention. That's why he'd opted for the surgical task of sniping. He'd changed entire battles with less than five bullets.

They were in darkness again before 1900. It was perhaps the darkest night Kyle had ever experienced. There was no light pollution from cities, the moon was invisible behind clouds and canopy, and no one was using any lights. Even Kyle's night vision goggles showed little detail. All was fuzzy and indistinct. But he could see ruts and worn ground well enough, and kept moving, occasionally feeling with his foot or shifting when he found a dark spot. "Dark" on NVG meant a hollow, but whether three inches or three feet deep was much harder to tell.

They took no breaks, eating and drinking on the march, no smoking, stopping with a buddy on guard to take a leak and then catching up quickly. Wiesinger seemed very bothered when the two women stepped off the track and squatted. But hell, they had to drain too. The act wasn't of any interest to Kyle other than as an intellectual observation that they were adequately hydrated if they needed to go. The process was familiar. That it was a little more awkward for women than men in these circumstances was a minor note, but if they didn't complain he saw no reason to. Wiesinger really needed to relax.

It was hard to tell how many of them there were, and Kyle was within the group. The noise discipline and movement skills of these people were excellent. That was of far more interest. On the whole, it had been a lot smoother so far than it could have been, and that was with sporadic firefights.

"Twenty-three hundred," Wade said as they stopped. He was panting. "Should give us an hour. We're about five kilometers east of Khayalan, I think." He pulled out his GPS to confirm.

"What's your suggestion?" Wiesinger asked.

"Well, Mel, they seem to have a driver, shotgun, and someone in the back. Two good shots will deal with the shotgun and cargo guy, but someone will have to tackle the driver of a moving vehicle. Ideas?"

Bakri said, "I think Syarief can do that.

Syarief?" he switched to rapid fire Achinese. The man smiled and nodded. "Sya is a master of pentjak silat. I think he can silence the driver and keep the vehicle on the road."

"Good. Both shots from the left?" Kyle asked. He knew silat was an Indonesian martial art. He wasn't aware of any details.

It was agreed that on a blank signal from Wade, spotting, Kyle and Wiesinger would shoot the passengers. Syarief would swarm up the side of the truck and subdue the driver, who would be kept alive if possible. Then they'd see about securing the imam.

There wasn't time to waste, as the truck could be along anytime. The forward scout was only two kilometers away, which would be only a few minutes of warning. Syarief darted across the road. Wade cuddled up to a tree and laid his scope over a low branch. Wiesinger stood by another bole, and Kyle ascended a few feet with the help of two men. He wanted to have his sight plane a good ten feet up to ensure plenty of window for the man riding shotgun.

He stood on two men's backs, scrabbled up over a branch, and wrapped himself around the trunk. It wasn't a largish tree, but it was thick enough to hide him. And, he discovered, thick enough to make shooting awkward.

Then it was time to wait. This was the approximate time the vehicle had been observed on previous nights, but there was a variation of nearly an hour. Nor did it come every night. But it did seem they were moving a lot of stuff at present.

His phone buzzed. It was Bakri announcing the truck. "Two kilometers, forty kilometers an hour. About three minutes."

"Understood."

Kyle found a position with his rifle steady, both feet twisted and placed for something approaching stability, and the truck came over a slight rise.

Wade fired the empty cartridge from his pistol, the primer explosion a loud snap like a firecracker, and the slaughter was on. A thrown coat spread across the windshield, surprising the driver and causing him to let off the accelerator. Kyle's bullet blew through the skull of the passenger and out in front of the driver. Wiesinger caught his target in the shoulder with the first round and finished him off with the second, though a solid scream escaped. The man's weapon tumbled over the side. Syarief clambered up the cab in a move Kyle would like to have seen, since the truck was still going at a respectable sprint, and grabbed the driver, who was busy staring in horror at his passenger. With a quick twist of Syarief's hands, the driver was thrashing and choking, panic evident on his face as his breath was cut off. Syarief wrestled his victim away from the pedals and the truck slowed.

In a matter of moments, the corpses had been carried far back from the road and left, guts slashed, for the scavengers. Both rifles held by the truck's security detail were in the hands of Bakri's men, who engaged in a quick shuffle down the pecking order. Lesser weapons were handed down to those in need, kept as trophies, or stripped for needed parts as called for. The remains wound up in someone's backpack. The corpses' possessions were looted, as were the driver's: cash, web gear, boots. The clothes were stripped and dumped elsewhere. Likely, there'd be nothing in a day or two.

That done, Wiesinger and Wade boarded the back and stashed themselves between crates. There were not only explosives here, but there also were three AK47s and a box of clothing and gear, as well as two other large cartons of produce and dry goods. Kyle now swapped for the M4. He left the SR25 behind with one of Bakri's men, whom he cautioned not to use it. Wiesinger still looked shocked at letting non-U.S. troops handle the equipment, but it wasn't possible to carry a ruck and a spare rifle for this. Kyle was worried, too; he didn't want the weapon jarred or the sight played with.

Bakri slipped in alongside the driver. From what Kyle had overheard, the driver had the muzzle of a pistol against his testicles and was being told that cooperation would save them, trouble would get them shot off.

Still, Kyle was nervous. Was there some sort of signal to be given as the truck arrived? Had they already been sighted? A firefight with him on a raised platform in the middle didn't appeal. Worse, he'd not donned even the light body armor he'd brought. He hadn't had time. It was still in his ruck, being watched by one of the Indonesians. He had grabbed his helmet and wished he hadn't. It had an obvious profile and made it harder to squeeze in.

But there was nothing to do but soldier on. In six minutes, more or less, they'd know. He checked the chambering on the carbine, hefted it again, and got ready. He and Wade would try to subdue the imam and load him into the track. If need be, Kyle wasn't opposed to a leg shot to make the bastard easier to carry.

One other thing bothered him. The passenger had been a woman. She'd held a rifle and was definitely a combatant, and a probable supporter of terrorism. Still, he'd never shot a woman before, and hadn't been expecting to. It bothered a chivalrous part of him. It didn't reassure him much to realize she would have done likewise. There were Anda with her Pindad SS1 carbine and Irta with her AK47 on this side, both of them fair targets for any opposition. People armed and ready to shoot were combatants.

Then he stopped worrying, because they were slowing and there were voices. Bakri had said he'd face the driver, so as not to be seen himself. But would the driver cause problems?

That was answered when Bakri fired. The driver screamed. Kyle cursed and came up.

Luckily, the men unloading the truck were not armed. He dropped off the bed and grabbed the imam by the shoulder.

The cleric was skinny, bearded, and wearing a black cap. He spun and started to shake Kyle off before realizing Kyle was considerably stronger. Then Wade caressed him with the stock of his M4, leaving a butt imprint in the fabric of his cap, and probably in his skull as well. The man staggered and fell.

Kyle heaved the limp form straight up and Wiesinger caught him. Then someone behind Kyle grabbed for the carbine.

He shoved, punched, and pulled away. He really didn't want to fire a burst. Their stealth was obviously blown, but bodies would make things worse.

Then the truck was rolling backward as Bakri reversed them out of the area, and Wiesinger was pulling at the back of Kyle's shirt. It cut into his throat momentarily, until he got an arm on the bed and heaved. His left leg caught on the wheel and was pushed up, causing him to swing.

Suddenly, he was up, Wade pulling on his arm. He wasn't sure how Wade had beat him to the bed, but he didn't care. They were moving.

As they picked up speed, there came a shot, and the sound of revving motorcycles.

"Well, at least they're all combatants," Wade said. Bakri was driving now, the old driver having been unceremoniously dumped out. The truck careened into one of the turnarounds, then spewed dirt as it accelerated. Kyle scrabbled around, unchoked himself and got a good grip on his weapon. The cycles came in pursuit, and he started firing.

It wasn't sniping. It did take calm nerves and precision, but it wasn't sniping. They were all moving, the terrain shifted and there was nothing to call a baseline. He rapped out bursts and kept them low. With a hundred rounds in the double drum C-mag, he could get thirty-three such bursts.

Overhead, Wiesinger *was* trying to snipe. The bullets snapped over Kyle's head. They didn't hit anything. Moving platform to moving target was a tough shot. It was something Kyle wouldn't attempt, and he had had a hell of a lot more practice than Wiesinger.

He and Wade had each fired a half dozen bursts before the first bike went down. Two others collided with it and the rest gave up in a slewing, swerving tangle.

"Well, that was royally screwed up from the word 'go,'" Wade said.

"That's because we're playing this like cowboys and not soldiers," Wiesinger said. "Dammit, from now on I will be the voice of reason."

"Oh, can it, Mel," Kyle said, anger welling over. "We're all unhurt and we have the objective. We've got good intel from allies and locals. We're in a better position to follow up on our primary objective. All that despite you falling asleep on watch."

Silence reigned. He wasn't going to look at the glare on Wiesinger's face; he could feel it. Wiesinger wasn't going to discuss his mistimed nap. Wade wasn't going to get in the middle. Absolute silence and stillness reigned for several minutes. Wade took the time to check the imam for injuries and lash him into a pretzel. Kyle watched the rear. He didn't give a rat's ass what Wiesinger did.

They were well ahead of pursuit for now, but there were no turns on this road. Additionally, radios or phones could have a roadblock waiting for them. It would only take a log or a few seconds of rifle fire to stop the vehicle. They had to ditch the truck soon.

"Here!" Bakri announced. The road angled downhill. Everyone dismounted, two of them carrying the bound and gagged imam. Bakri slipped the vehicle into neutral and bailed out.

The truck spent most of a kilometer oscillating in greater sways until it caught enough brush to stop. That should help confuse the issue. There was a solid 1500 meters on both sides they might have taken. So the crucial thing was to take the opportunity now and maximize that cover. There would definitely be more forces coming.

Meantime, an entire shipment of the explosives was in Bakri's hands. His troops each carried a few pounds stuffed into their bulky, shapeless packs. They slipped into the woods along a broad front, shifting past protruding branches so as not to leave any obvious sign.

"I hate to destroy it," Bakri said, indicating his pack. "But I can't use most of it."

"Then don't hate destroying it. You took it away from the terrorists. And we'll take some, too." Kyle wasn't proficient with explosives, but he could insert a detonator without blowing a finger off. And it gave them more power. "And the Aussies might want some too."

"Ah, I see value in this commodity. Perhaps I should broker." His sense of humor appealed to Kyle.

"Then we'll have to come back and hurt you," Kyle said, deadpan.

"But don't worry," Wade said. "It's not personal, just business." He smiled. Bakri returned it, not quite sure if it was a joke.

Wiesinger had his phone in hand. "I'm not sure why I'm doing this," he muttered loudly enough to be heard. He punched it, raised it, and spoke. "Stephens. Wiesinger. Shipment acquired. Employee acquired. Where do we meet you? Understood. Out." He turned back to the others.

"We're going to head south and up into the hills to meet."

"Where?" Bakri asked.

Wiesinger fumbled with a map. "Here, as near as I can tell."

"Ah . . . no, here, I think," Bakri said. "I know the place."

Chagrined, Wiesinger nodded. Kyle wondered how shaky he was on other things. His shooting was good but not sniper quality. His navigation was good but not Ranger quality. On so many things, the man was "good" rather than "exceptional." Which meant an office was the right place for him, as Kyle was tired of thinking.

"Twelve kilometers uphill," Bakri said. "Can you handle it?"

"Certainly," Kyle said, feeling as if he would die from the heat. But if two skinny little Indonesian teenagers could lug a struggling prisoner, he could manage himself and his ruck.

He was glad of the MREs, but they couldn't last much longer. The locals were eating cold rice from their packs, and fruit in plastic bags.

Cold rice. He shuddered. Rice was something he tolerated, as long as it was spiced or sauced somehow. The thought of a diet based on the stuff didn't appeal to him. Whether or not his American diet was healthy, it was what he was used to and very tasty.

They reached a clearing, almost a meadow at

1500 feet, and Bakri called a halt. They'd traveled a thousand feet vertically and several kilometers horizontally, and Kyle realized he was mixing measurements. It was amusing. Quarts for water, feet for elevation, meters for shooting, and of course everyone here used metric. Grains for bullet weight, inches for drop. He had to be tired if he was starting to laugh at the technicalities of the job.

He didn't realize how tired until he sat down harder than he expected and had trouble when he tried to get up. That let him lean back against his ruck, however. That little rest felt good. Sleep was a luxury on this mission, rations were on the low side and would get lower, and energy expenditure was outrageous, with all the walking. It wasn't the distance. It was the terrain. Between rough surfaces that took a toll on the ankles and detours around growth to avoid leaving signs, actual distance was more than double the map distance. Any break was a good thing. The others seemed to think so, too. They all packed in and set up a bivouac.

Twenty minutes later, as everyone was settling in, Stephens arrived.

"So that's him," Stephens said, indicating the trussed body.

"Yes. He hasn't said anything yet," Kyle replied. God, it was good to sit down. He'd never admit to fatigue when his hosts were so stoic, but he was drained.

"We haven't asked anything yet," Bakri said. He nodded to his henchmen.

The interrogation was ugly enough to push Kyle away. The imam kept invoking Allah, and vowing to do vile things to the children of his captors. Unfortunately, they needed his mouth intact to tell what he knew. The diatribe and invective continued. Even though it was in Bahasa and Achinese, Kyle could hear the viciousness. He wasn't going to be an easy man to break.

While they pretended not to know what was going on behind a cluster of trees, Wiesinger broached the subject.

"Kyle, we're on very shaky legal and moral ground back home if anyone hears of this."

"I don't endorse it, Mel," he said. "Officially, I asked that it not be done."

"Yeah, and that'll get you what? We could see Leavenworth for this."

"Mel . . . sir, it often happens out here that the realities go beyond the theory. There's every chance of doing one's job right, and getting courted or dying anyway. It's one of those things that just doesn't offer any good answers."

Wiesinger hesitated, his round face squinting and working. "I want it to stop. Can you tell me how?"

"The only way I can think of is for you to ask. Bakri might listen. He might move it farther away so you don't have to know about it. He might tell you to go screw. At best, you'll delay our acquisition of intel. At worst, you'll piss off our host and blow the mission. And as best as we can tell, this bastard helps blow up vacationing families and children of blue-collar workers. I detest the necessity. I can't say I'm morally bothered by the suffering. It's something I have to struggle with all the time. I don't know what the answer is."

Wiesinger was silent again.

Kyle fell asleep. If he was needed, they could wake him.

He woke refreshed. He'd slept deeply. So deeply he didn't recall hearing any more torture. He blinked and stretched.

Wiesinger was asleep next to him. He'd stripped to his T-shirt this time. Wade was on watch, talking to one of the other Aussies and two Indonesians. Two M4 carbines and two Senapan Serbu rifles pointed in different directions. That seemed safe.

Wade saw Kyle move and came over. "Wiesinger was asleep. I suggested not waking him."

"Okay. Now what?"

"Bakri suggested letting everyone rest. We've got intel."

"I'm awake. Tell me."

"We've got a story of a facility nearby that produces product for income, and configures explosives. From there, it moves to the coast. Some is shipped, some is kept for insurgency. He couldn't or wouldn't specify what, where, or how much."

"Probably didn't know," Kyle guessed. "Was it bad, the interrogation?"

"If we might get captured, I want you to shoot me," Wade said. He didn't reveal much emotion, which was a hint, also.

"Damn," Kyle said. When younger, he would have paid money to see terrorists tortured to death. Or thought he would have. Then the realities of it had disgusted him. Now, listening to it was just a job.

He wasn't sure what to think about that, either. But second-guessing himself out here was a bad idea. That could wait for return stateside. The only thing to worry about now was the impending risks to himself and civilians.

By late afternoon, everyone was awake. Stephens boiled tea. Several of the Indonesians cooked up a pot of rice with local fruits, leaves, and a couple of chickens someone had managed to swipe during the raid on Khayalan. It wasn't much, but it was hot and refreshing. The Americans passed around some MREs and a hoarded tub of Kyle's shoestring potato snacks. There was dried meat from a previous expedition. As a feast it wasn't much, especially with all the walking they were doing. But Bakri had called for his trucks again—they were needed at farms but could be broken loose for a day here or there—and said he was having them bring food, too.

Food, fuel, batteries, water, and ammo. Everything else was secondary. It took a lot of supplies to keep even a short platoon going more than a day. They had no real logistics tail to support them. That greatly impeded their operation. In Pakistan, they'd had the same problem. In Romania, they'd had cash, credit cards, and were in a modern environment. They had cash here . . . and nowhere to spend it.

"I have another report," Bakri said, and everyone moved in except the sentries. "We have a location on an explosives site. It is here." He pulled out a map. "A village once called Impian. It was abandoned after a flood in November two thousand two. Our enemy is said to be there."

"Advance as two squads, overwatch?" Stephens offered. "Encircle, observe, gives us a good position for attack or retreat? I'm happy to help if there's a big payoff in intel or damage."

"We'll get there first," Wiesinger said. "I'll do a commander's reconnaissance, then we'll see. We want to nail the people behind it, primarily. Destroying it is secondary. Further intel is an ongoing issue."

The colonel was standing far enough away not to hear what Kyle heard, which was Stephens muttering, "That presumes you're in charge, lardbum." He didn't snicker. He understood exactly how the man felt.

Stephens was lucky. He could refuse to listen to Wiesinger. Sergeant First Class Kyle Monroe didn't have that option.

No one argued about it. Really, there wasn't

much to do until they did get a look at the area. Stephens was too bright to get in a pissing contest with a foreign officer. Wiesinger assumed he was in charge. Bakri of course had his own ideas.

An hour later, the trucks arrived, four of them. It was incredibly tight with all three Americans crammed in the backseat, their gear in the rear, and an Indonesian with his gear up front. The Aussies filled a second one with another local. That left nine more shoved into the other two vehicles.

It was a ride like any other, though Kyle prayed they would not get attacked. There simply wasn't any room to swing a weapon into play. Still, between riding uncomfortably or marching forty miles, he'd take the painful ride. Wade and he kept elbowing each other in the ribs accidentally, and gouging their knees on the receivers of their rifles.

Then it was late afternoon and they arrived. With the need for stealth, Kyle was used to operating at night. The near twelve-hour days this close to the equator gave lots of dark. So he'd spend most of the time as a nocturnal hunter. Still, he was pushing the envelope this time.

"Arrived," of course, meant a solid ten kilometers away, for safety. They'd do the rest on foot, with Anda and Corporal Rod Iverson out front. They were both reputed to be the best trackers anywhere. Hopefully, their skill would be reinforced by competitive nature and they'd catch any hint of a perimeter before it knew it was being attacked.

Wiesinger was still too loud when he moved, but better at it than he had been. He might eventually shape up. In the meantime, Kyle stayed close enough to let the man follow his lead. Usually the colonel would.

Stephens crawled up close. "According to Iverson, Anda, and GPS, it's fifteen hundred meters that way." He pointed. "What now?"

"I'll do a recon and determine where we stand. Kyle, you have a notebook? I'd like it, please."

Kyle knew better than to argue. He peeled off the pages he'd used and secured them in a chest pocket, just as a security measure. He handed the book to Wiesinger, along with a pen.

"You're going in there?" Stephens asked, brow wrinkled through his camo.

"I've got to know what we're facing before planning the assault," Wiesinger said, his voice half reasonable, half condescending.

Of course, Kyle had never heard of anyone doing a "commander's reconnaissance" in that fashion after they graduated Ranger school. It was an easy way to die, as one lieutenant had learned in Grenada. He'd go along with Wiesinger and pray he wasn't going to wind up a statistic.

"It's seventeen twenty," Wiesinger announced as he looked at his watch. "I will be back by nineteen hundred. Monroe, you're with me, Curtis, take charge of U.S. material."

"Yes, Mel," they echoed. Wade didn't look unhappy. His expression was carefully neutral. Kyle looked at him just as neutrally. He wasn't sure that, if they'd been able to, they'd grin, sigh, or look disgusted. So with nothing further to say, he turned and followed his officer.

Iverson squatted nearby. He looked somewhat miffed at his recon being second-guessed by Wiesinger. Or maybe "somewhat miffed" was too mild. The man was lean, but muscled like a wrestler, and had a very dark, clenched-jaw expression. Kyle gave him a shrug and a shake of the head as he passed. *Not my decision, pal.*

11

HALF AN HOUR LATER, KYLE RECONSIDERED. *Maybe I'm getting too cynical in my old age*, he thought. Wiesinger directed him where to go and let him take the lead.

"You've got more time in the field, so I'll tell you what I want and you get it done," Wiesinger had said. Which was one part of doctrine that had been wise advice for thousands of years. Tell the NCO what you want and he'll do it for you.

So Kyle led in a crawl, fast enough to be worthwhile, slow enough for silence, around a substantial arc of the village. It had block and tin buildings, a road that dead-ended into it and electricity from what Kyle reasoned was a propane generator. On second thought, it had to be liquefied natural gas. There was enough of it here.

And the place was silent.

Khayalan had been quiet. This was dead. A

few cautious looks through night vision confirmed it. There was evidence of a fight, including bullet spalling on walls. Add in scavengers trotting through, and the smell . . .

"This is supposed to be an operations center, and I see nothing. But it's not been down for long."

"I'd say a day, tops, or we'd see more scavengers," Kyle agreed.

"So who took them out, and why?"

"Unknown. Government, other rebels are all that comes to mind."

"Okay, let's call the others," Wiesinger said. He looked scared, badly. Kyle didn't blame him, though. His own fear was more internalized, but just as real. The growing twilight didn't help.

The rest of the ersatz unit moved in quickly. The evident lack of a perimeter, the darkness, and thick air let them approach upright at a skulk instead of down at a crawl. Within an hour, they were all present.

"Talk to me," Stephens said as he came up.

"Let's wait for Bakri," Kyle suggested.

"Righto." They huddled under broad leaves and inhaled the dank air, redolent with rot and chlorophyll.

When Bakri arrived, Kyle said, "Mel and I have covered the perimeter from here to there." He pointed. "No signs of action or habitation. Spalling and other light-arms damage, including fractures suggestive of grenades, are present. It appears no one is home. Obviously, we'd like to test that theory carefully."

Wiesinger nodded. "Suggestions?"

"If you want mine," Stephens said with faint sarcasm, "I'd pull us into thirds, split around the perimeter and then have one element approach with crossed lanes of fire in case they need support. Assuming we all trust our marksmanship."

"The cover is good, the men are all adequately trained from what I can see," Kyle said. "Sounds good. Bakri?"

"I will be happy to cover fire," he said. "I would not want to tell my men to stand in the middle of the fire."

"Right," Wiesinger agreed. "We'll go in with three volunteers. You each take your teams around one hundred to one hundred twenty degrees, then we'll call for the advance."

Syarief, Rizal, Iverson, and an Aussie named Fuller, their demolitions expert, joined them. The locals were armed with AKs and were excellent in the jungle. Iverson, and Fuller each had an M4 that was almost a clone of the U.S. issue. They knew how to handle their weapons. Still, Kyle wanted the locals flanking, not behind him. Eagerness got people shot. Iverson and Fuller he was comfortable with. The SAS had a first class reputation.

Kyle had to agree with Stephens on the utility of satellite cell phones. No bulky radios for this, no codes, no worries about transmitters being located, no battery issues. Radios were often necessary, though, especially with air support. That they had no radios also meant no air and no arty. These operations were quite lonely. Even more so when fire came in.

They waited while Bakri's forces moved closer to the road, and Stephens's around a good chunk of the circle. It was twenty minutes later when Wiesinger grabbed his phone. "Roger that. We're ready." He punched it off. "Let's move." It was dark. Very dark.

They slipped in closer, weaving through the boles and vines, bushes and leaves. The silence was foreboding. Kyle's nerves stuck out like naked wires. There was something here, he was sure. He didn't believe in supernatural inputs. Fifteen years of instinct told him so. He didn't know what, but he felt the threat. He took another glance at the M4 he carried. Chambered, safety off, finger poised. He had a canister round—basically a 40mm shotgun cartridge—loaded in the grenade launcher in case he needed more oomph. It should be plenty. Wade also had a canister; Iverson and Fuller, the Aussies, had HE loads in theirs; and two of Bakri's men had RPGs. Add two machine guns, and it was actually an effective infantry platoon.

Except they were four units, really, and hadn't done more than a couple of marches together. There was plenty that could go wrong in the dark, should something spook someone.

They reached the cleared area, the ground beyond grassy and even. This place had been burned out of the jungle a long time ago. And it was empty, but had certainly been occupied since 2002. The trash and debris lying around was proof of that.

Kyle stepped out first in a low crouch, weapon shouldered and ready. Wiesinger moved in front and went prone with the SR25. Wade took one side and the Indonesians the other. They waited several seconds, ears cocked for anything beyond the cacophony of animal life.

Wade made the phone call. "Seems clear. Close in." He tucked the instrument away and resumed his guard.

Jack Stephens and two of his natives swarmed in the other side so quickly and silently they seemed to be wraiths. *Damn, but there were good troops around here*, Kyle thought. Which meant that if—when—this got nasty, Kyle would be in the midst of a battle of professionals, not a brawl of amateurs.

Well, he had wanted a challenge. Here it was. Be careful what you wish for . . .

Bakri came in from across and to the right, along the road edge. They were all through the village now. That meant they were targets from the buildings, but to hit them up close would expose the attackers to multiple shots and no backstop. That was the best they could manage.

Wiesinger said, "We need to control that large

building near the center. I assume that's an administrative center."

"Sort of," Bakri said. "Official meetings would take place there, yes."

"I want to go in fast and hard, just in case."

"Of course."

The elements recombined into two large squads, front and back. Kyle felt his phone buzz, and he checked his watch as he raised his fist. When the second hand hit 12, they'd storm this building. He coiled himself like a spring, ready to explode. He took a quick glance around that showed everyone ready, fingers twitching near but not yet on triggers.

Then it was time. As one they rose. Kyle was prepared to blow the hinges off the door, but it hung askew. Wiesinger, the largest by far, kicked the door as two of Bakri's men went in low. Kyle went in high, expecting to take some kind of defensive fire.

Nothing.

No, not nothing.

Dear God!

There were bodies galore, bloated and rotting, but that wasn't what caught his attention. He'd expected bodies. It was the apparatus and the wall decorations. For they weren't maps or charts. They'd all been desecrated, torn down or ripped, but it didn't take much to see them for what they were.

Wade came in the rear.

"Child porn studio?" he said, voice tight, disgusted, as if he might vomit at any moment. Kyle felt the same way.

"Yeah. And the terrorists . . . killed them." He looked at one of the bodies. Even before the flies and scavengers, it had been ugly.

"I never thought I'd say this, but I agree with and support the terrorists." Wade sounded a cross between revolted and amazed.

"Here," Wiesinger said, pulling a grubby sheet of paper from the wreckage. It was a color printout of . . .

"Yeah, why don't you take this, sir," Kyle said, fishing a lighter from his pocket.

"Thank you, sergeant. Much appreciated." Wiesinger struck the paper alight, dropped it, and vigorously wiped his fingers in the dirt on the floor, then on his pants.

"Man, it never ceases to amaze me how far some people can sink," Wade said. They all stared as the picture disappeared into ash, ghostly outlines still hinting at the scene on the photographic paper. The colonel stomped it with his boot and ground it to nothing.

"At least there's some places the terrorists won't go," Wiesinger said. It wasn't much comfort. It simply pointed out how far they did go, if this extreme was what they wouldn't do.

"Any evidence we can use?" Stephens asked. "Sources, ID of any kind?" He looked rather perturbed himself.

"Not without substantial digging, I'd say," Wade answered. "I'm hoping we don't have the time."

"We probably have the time," Wiesinger said. "But we're not going to take it. Let's call this a map marker and move on. If it wouldn't blow cover, I'd torch the place."

"Roger that, Mel," Kyle agreed firmly.

Stephens jogged out to go to the adjoining building where his team was. Kyle turned and ducked for the door.

It was then that a torrent of fire shattered the frame, tossing splinters of block into his face.

He dropped at once, eyes closed, and crawled back. His eyes were stinging from chips, not burning from dust. He'd have to get them clear enough to fight with, and hope the injuries didn't require more sophisticated treatment. But he was inside the door and covered, he hoped, as several crashes echoed. Outgoing fire was good. He blinked his eyes carefully, not wanting to gouge them with any sharp fragments. Then he pulled at the lids to let tears flush the dust. They still ached and itched, but he could see, even if his vision was a little blurry.

Alert again, he listened before sticking his head out. There was a lot of fire out there. Whatever the force was, they were large. Small arms. Few automatic weapons. No grenades so far. Wiesinger and Stephens were shouting back and forth between buildings.

"Force to the rear is about a squad. One RPK machine gun. Mostly AKs," Stephens called.

"In front is two support weapons," Wiesinger replied. "One RPK, one RPG not in use." That was potentially disturbing. A rocket-propelled grenade would kill everyone in the building.

"Mel, do you want any targets?" Kyle asked in a lull as his ears rang. If not, he could just shoot. But he was a precision shooter first.

"Wade, Kyle, find that RPG. Then the machine gunner."

Wade said, "Roger, Kyle, far left, second block building, rear corner, under bush."

"Sighted," Kyle said. He aimed and squeezed, but the pain and the sudden shock of rounds in an enclosed space had him shaking. His first round missed, high.

"He's relocating," Wade said. "Look for him two buildings south, same position."

"Sighted," Kyle said. The first shot winged his target, possibly a shoulder. That shook him up enough that Kyle's second shot was center of mass, just before the missileer could move. Just to make sure, he followed the body down and carefully put another sideways through the ribcage.

He shook his head. The concussion of rounds fired wasn't helping his vision or his hearing. Still, three shots wasn't bad for a valuable threat. "Where's the gunner?" he asked.

"Stand by!" Wade said. "He's gone!"

"Shit, that's bad!" Kyle said. Gone where? Behind another building? The next notice they got could be large amounts of autofire.

Wiesinger was shouting orders. "Bakri, have your RPG gunners take out those two buildings there."

"It will take a moment," Bakri yelled back. They were split up now, with part of the force inside Kyle's building, and most of the rest scattered for cover.

Wiesinger yelled into his phone, "Stephens, consolidate to the west and hold against that element. We will secure here. As soon as we are in control of our own territory, we will combine reserves to attack them . . . Yes, that sounds good. Out."

Kyle flinched momentarily as Bakri's RPG team demolished two buildings. The explosion slapped at them even here, a visible wave front tossing dirt and leaves ahead of it. It inflicted several casualties on the enemy, including one body tossed like a rag doll. But Kyle still didn't see that machine gun, and there were other support weapons out there, among troops who knew how to use them.

To highlight that point, a roar washed over him from behind. Screams and shouts, some of surprise, some of injury followed it, faint and hard to discern under the pain that meant he had hearing damage. He wasn't sure what had come in, but it was dangerous.

It was a good time to relocate. Kyle shifted

over to a crack under the window he could just see through, flopped across a chair cushion and got ready.

No, it wasn't a cushion. It was a gas-bloated corpse on the splintered wreckage of a folding chair. He grimaced in distaste. But the bastard was dead, and nothing was leaking from the body, and he'd seen worse. Screw it. He'd take his shots and then move.

"There!" Wade called. "Reference: Building to left of the one we just blew. Window on right side. Target: machine gun crew. Range five five meters."

"Sighted," Kyle agreed. There wasn't much of them visible; they were being cagey. Or maybe they were as afraid of getting blown away as he was.

They were more afraid in a moment. He fired and missed, but took splinters out of the frame. He'd been trying to peel off the top of one man's head, but he'd ducked. Still, they were both staying down for now, which meant they weren't shooting. It wasn't a win, but it didn't hurt anything.

"Roger that," Wiesinger said into his phone. "No dice. They're covered, we're covered, this could go on a long time. Might consider regrouping and retrograding under fire." He didn't sound happy.

"I advise it, Mel," Kyle said. "We're not here for a protracted battle. We're here to find a target." He gratefully hopped off the body and found another loophole to shoot through.

"Roger. We can move into the jungle in squads and cover as we go." He flipped open his phone. "Stephens . . . Yeah, that's where we're thinking. Roger that. You, us, locals. Out." He spoke again. "The Aussies are first, we're second, providing cover for Bakri."

"I am not happy being last," Bakri said. It was the first open admission that he wasn't entirely sure of his allies.

"No one would be," Kyle said. He was pretty sure it came about because Wiesinger didn't trust the locals. And, while they were better than any others he'd worked with, they still weren't a professional force, and other than Bakri, he couldn't be sure of their loyalties. So he reluctantly agreed. Besides, he had to back up his commander. That was his duty.

"Very well," Bakri said, twitching. "Be sure we get lots of support fire."

"Count on it," Wade promised him, pulling out his other C-mag. The first was likely more than half full. But the fresh one meant one hundred rounds. That was support fire. Kyle copied the gesture. He also checked for a canister load in the grenade launcher. Anything in front was the enemy, as far as he was concerned, and he'd light it the hell up at every opportunity.

Wiesinger cut into his thoughts. "Stephens is ready, our turn."

"Roger. Good luck, Bakri. See you in two minutes."

"Yes," the man said with a simple nod. He sounded a lot surer of Kyle than of the colonel.

Kyle rose and slipped back, panning across an arc in case of threats up close. It wasn't likely, but it never hurt to be sure. A grenade tossed in would end the party real quick. But if he shot the thrower beforehand, it was just more fireworks outside. He did wish he could do something about the bursts of machine-gun fire alternately beating at the blocks and slapping through the door. At least, being dark inside, the shadow would help protect him even from night vision.

Wade turned, assessed the move and followed, while Kyle took the cue and slipped out the back. That meant scrambling through a hole that had been a window and still had broken frame and glass. He tore his pants but avoided anything worse than a stinging scratch. Wiesinger was outside, squatting, back against the wall. He seemed very glad of backup. Kyle nodded and took the other side. Then Wade dropped between them.

"We're clear, fire around either side," Wiesinger said into his phone. He dialed again. "Bakri, move." Closing that, he said, "Gentlemen, that way," and pointed into the woods.

The incoming fire was much stronger. Poor Bakri was taking a beating from a substantially larger force. The Aussies and their allies dumped a few hundred angry lead hornets between the buildings, and the incoming fire slackened for several seconds. But once the enemy realized they were retreating and shooting largely blind, it picked up again.

"Dammit," Kyle said. He dodged trees and headed into the jungle, seeking cover, concealment and a good, clear field of fire. One out of three would suffice. Two would thrill him.

Wiesinger cursed. He had his phone again. "Bakri's got five men in a building with no rear exit. They'll have to come out the side into fire."

"Grenade," Kyle said at once. "One of ours." RPG rounds were too powerful.

"You can't be serious. That's—"

"Which building, and tell them to duck," Wade said. He was already closing the breech on his launcher, having swapped canister for high explosive.

"That one there," Wiesinger pointed. "But you can't really mean to—"

Wade cut him off with a *Whump!* followed by a loud bang, as a flash cracked the wall. The resulting hole was about eighteen inches at best. But it was enough for skinny, dazed Indonesians to wiggle through, after peering to be sure they were safe from further fire. The third man beat at the opening with his rifle butt to enlarge it. Bakri and his others were slipping into the dark woods. It had gone well enough, it seemed.

There was a roar overhead, that turned into a thumping, angry drone.

"Oh, shit," Kyle said as he looked up. Choppers. That meant military. Fast meant Special Forces, the Kopassus.

"Who the fuck called them?" Wiesinger asked angrily.

"Not a bad ploy," Wade shouted. "Use a porn shop to generate income. Use it as a cover. If the government captures anyone, you blow the cover, destroy it to show your good graces, then call the government and claim the kill. Icing on the cake to catch your enemies right there."

"It may be more chance than that," Bakri said. "But I do not wish association here. It is beyond sin."

"Son of a *bitch*!" Kyle said. "Fucking move, sir." The helicopters were hovering over the village. He assumed ropes and troops would follow. Wiesinger took the hint and started dodging.

The three squads broke into a ragged retreat, occasionally returning fire to threats. Kyle hoped, *hoped* the Kopassus would stick to the immediate area and not pursue further. But if they had backup on the ground or another assault, they could encircle. There was no good answer then. He was an American, an ally, but siding with rebels who were not, without diplomatic clearance. Best case, they offered a bunch of intel and got freed, while blowing the entire mission. Worst case, an Indonesian jail. And Bakri would likely wind up there either way. Indonesia jailed people for ten years for just flying the Free Acheh flag. Actually bearing arms . . .

And that assumed the Indo troops didn't just shoot them as mercs without asking any questions, which seemed the most logical and likely response.

The pursuit wasn't immediate, but Kyle wanted to put a few kilometers between them quickly. He didn't crave the headlines that might come: US CIA SNIPERS, INDONESIAN REBELS ASSOCI-ATED WITH AL QAEDA, and CHILD PORN STUDIO. Nor did he crave to get shot. Distance and dark were friends.

A long, loping time later, through tangled skeins of brush, he hunkered down and camouflaged himself. He scurried over and through a patch of thick weeds, then under them. He was far enough removed from the edge of the glade to not be visible at a glance. The spreading leaves would help deflect any heat signature, which he had to be putting out, as hard as he was breathing. He forced that breath to a slow, measured heave and listened. The rotors were steady, hovering, which meant they didn't anticipate any anti-aircraft fire from below. Under that droning, hypnotic beat . . .

Shooting and shouting, sparser now than they had been. A couple of final shots, and then the beating of rotor blades rose to a thrum. One heli-copter swept overhead, shaking the air and trees and then dopplering away.

His phone buzzed a few minutes later as he was pondering his actions. He slid it out slowly and carefully. Departure of the aircraft didn't mean all patrols were off the ground. It was a possible ploy that would easily catch the eager or untrained.

"Kyle," he whispered.

"Mel. We're going to approach and recon."

"I advise against that, Mel," he said. Dammit, no.

"Bakri is missing five men. They were in a building with no rear exit and no commo. Another building, not the one we blew."

"Shit. Understood." That was a potential disaster. He listened to Wiesinger's orders. They were pretty much from the book, and in this case, were good enough. He saw no need to quibble.

Twenty minutes later, a marathon approach by the standards involved, they were at the edge of the clearing. It didn't take much effort to count the five stripped, decapitated bodies in the middle, nor the pile of five heads, each shot through from the back.

Bakri quivered, tears in his eyes. "I suppose this is better," he said. "They could have been tortured, exposed, jailed. But they are thought part of this . . ." He waved his hands around at the smoking remains of the operation. "They are shamed."

"We know, Bakri," Kyle said. "It doesn't matter otherwise. And I think their names are safe."

The sadism of the act was that they were dead . . . That meant that any guilty parties, or any party worried about guilt by association, would be relieved at the killing of their own people. Subtle. Kyle respected that in a way. It also made him want people dead.

A quick recon revealed other bodies. Their opponents had likewise been stripped, clothes and weapons taken. It was thorough and impersonal, a revealed contempt for the capabilities of the locals.

There just weren't any good guys here, Kyle decided. Respect and compassion took energy these people used to either stay alive or kill with.

"Where to, then?" Kyle asked diffidently.

"We bury them. Then home," Bakri said. "We must think on the threats." He stared for a moment, then turned determinedly and trudged into the clearing. Kyle followed, and looked around for something to use as a shovel. The others followed.

— 12 —

FAISAL LOOKED AT THE TWO NEW HOSTAGES. The others saw them as a prize. He didn't. A Chinese woman and her half-American daughter were hardly people to boast of capturing and killing.

They'd been taking hostages and killing them, cutting off their heads, since early 2004 in Iraq. It hadn't accomplished anything. The theory, he'd been told, was that the Westerners, especially Americans, were terrified of death and of dismemberment. Their culture demanded clean bodies, even to burying them in vaults, preserved against time. A few dead as object lessons was more humane than a battle involving hundreds of casualties. And besides, they were infidel deaths, not Muslim deaths.

Only, the fear hadn't come. Outrage and disgust had come, with harsh words and threats. But as usual, those faded. If anything, it seemed the Western world didn't care if a few people, or a few hundred, were decapitated. The headlines disappeared within days. Political and military impropriety stayed in the headlines for weeks, but the death of a hostage was hardly mentioned at all, and only briefly, before attention turned back to sports, scantily clad women, and pointless pastimes. Imam Ayi and the planners said the problem was that they were not being terrifying enough, grisly enough. Sufficient violence would provoke a reaction.

It didn't seem so to Faisal. And if it did, what reaction would it elicit after so much lethargy? A minor protest? Or would the enemy come awake like a krait poked with a stick?

And why was a culture so disinterested in its own casualties an enemy? Money was the key to all dealings with Americans. In that regard, he could agree with the attack on the oil terminal. That, they'd have to pay attention to. But again, might it be in a rage that would kill millions of Muslims in retribution?

He would just as soon have these hostages released. He already knew he wasn't going to accept the "honor" of beheading them. A relationship to an executive in Mobil's employ didn't matter to him. The Chinese woman was a civilian, apolitical and absolutely not worthy of note in this battle. It couldn't be right to use her so. And certainly not her little girl.

But how to get the leaders to listen to him?

Agung was furious. Whole shipments of explosives had disappeared. Billions of rupia in bribes, finder's fees, and simple operating costs had come to nothing. More than two thousand kilograms, enough for two hundred small bombs or ten really big ones, had been intercepted by the Australian and Singapore navies, and by some damned team in the jungle. He wasn't sure if that was the Kopassus, the Australians he'd heard skulking around, or, as rumored, an American hit team. He knew of them. Several of his group's best and most powerful men had been executed by assassins, either at long range or in close engagements. He'd heard names of several of them, but the names did no good without corroboration. Some new group was operating, that wasn't SEALs and wasn't Delta, but might be U.S. Army or Marines or CIA hired thugs. Whoever they were, they managed to sneak in right under the noses of government officials. He'd never admit it in public, but it terrified him. He could get a bureaucracy to do anything, from issuing building permits to sharing classified documents. But any inquiries about this came up blank. The government didn't know. The criminal networks didn't know. These men were shadows.

So the alternative was to create a trap for them,

whereby they'd be taken care of by their own putative allies. Numbers were the strength of the enemy. But the Fist of God had a strength too. That strength was *purity*.

In the meantime, the explosives they did have should be delivered without delay. The fire and tears would cleanse at least one city, and perhaps the headlines would be enough, this time.

If not, a few true innocents would cause as much, if not more anguish. If the oil companies couldn't find employees willing to risk the wrath of Allah, then the problem would solve itself. And there was another factor . . .

Captain Hari Sutrisno looked at the reports. There was something more here than was immediately apparent. When a group of rebels was dropped into his lap with a phone call, he took the opportunity, and this source had proved reliable repeatedly.

At the same time, he didn't like being played for a fool or used as a toy in someone else's game. It was obvious in retrospect that he'd been meant to find the faction at the porn facility. Clearly, they were outsiders or mere guards, not participants. The firefight he'd interrupted had also been a side issue. So who had been running the vile operation? Who stopped it? Who found it? Who had called him in right on top of them? He had answers to none of these questions at present. But he would. No mistake about that, he would have an answer.

In the meantime, GAM was increasingly factional. That boded well for crushing it at last and maintaining a unified Indonesia. Any part he could do for his homeland he was honored to do. If promotion came with it, he wouldn't turn it down. But that wasn't his motivation. Duty was his motivation.

It was a good day for terrorism.

Pakistan was a safe place to hide, but operations there were not viable. Any disruption caused massive government response. Saudi Arabia was the same way, with Iraq becoming so. There was little to strike in Afghanistan or elsewhere in Asia. Europe had battened down tight. The current U.S. leadership had indicated a willingness to retaliate, and unless elections put in a more "sensitive" president, threats were all that could be offered, not any practical attack. Iran was Shia, not Sunni, but had a certain popularity for its hard-line leadership, even despite doctrinal differences. Turkey already had its own factions, and the Balkans were too close to Europe and had received major setbacks recently, in part due to Kyle and Wade and the CIA operations there. The African Muslim states were staunch allies of the terror networks, even if they didn't say so. That left a handful of places where attacks could be made with impunity and effect.

So it was that small bombs were detonated in Kuala Lumpur in Malaysia, Quezon City in the

Philippines, and Surabaya and Medan in Indonesia. Another in Lhokseumawe ripped through a pipeline, spilling thousands of barrels of oil before cutoffs worked to staunch the flow. Flames roared as the crude petroleum wicked through the growth and vaporized. Panic ensued as it neared an Arun gas line, but it was brought under control with a lot of effort and resources, and not a few casualties.

The Fist of God claimed credit, and vowed a much larger blast in three days, plus other unspecified actions, if several GAM prisoners were not released and money from petroleum production not directed toward Aceh.

Early the next morning, Kyle was blinking sleep from his eyes as he sat on a dirt floor. He'd been woken in a hurry.

"We've got a major fucking situation here, gentlemen," Wiesinger said. He had them in a hut, as if it were a briefing room. Stephens and his men were along, too. Still, it felt like a stateside lecture rather than a field strategy discussion. The news of the attacks and capture had come in overnight.

"Indonesia is making the correct response, which is to pour another ten thousand troops in here and shoot anything that is a threat. Unfortunately, their assessment of threats includes our allies. It's a 'if you're not with us you're against us' gesture. So we can't stick around with our allies.

"At the same time, I'm reluctant to abandon

our local help, because operating without them will be a considerable handicap."

Yeah, Kyle thought. *And utterly inhuman, crass, and rude. But don't let that bother you, sir.* At least it was a good reason to be woken up. The shit had hit the turbine.

"At least two groups are actively trying to get us nailed. Ideally, we let the government handle them while we pursue the threats to U.S. interests. But we can't get the intel we need to do that, and after the fiasco last time we tried an urban encounter"—he fixed Kyle and Wade with his glare—"it's not advisable. This has escalated beyond what we're set to handle. But if we withdraw, we admit defeat, which is something I'm not prepared to do."

No, Kyle thought. *No medals that way, sir. Got to put on a brave front. Even if we should have shared intel first and called for backup earlier.* And the urban screwup last time had still got the mission accomplished.

To be fair, much of the trouble the snipers faced was from higher up and from outside Department of Defense. But the snipers were on the spot.

Wiesinger continued, "And there's hostages. Fist of God has captured the wife and daughter of a U.S. executive. The bitch is, his wife is a Hong Kong native, meaning Chinese now. That seems to have been planned. If we wind up with dead Chinese nationals as well as American nationals, we'll have knots that will take months to deal with. The fear is that China will make incursions like ours, or even more overtly. They might deploy naval forces in these waters, for example, which is near India as well. They don't get along well, and Indonesia can't defend against a force like that and may just kill everything moving in Aceh to show they're dealing with the problem.

"So we're facing an international incident that could create a dozen wars, and has already got troops out in Indonesia and the P.I. There's a lot of diplo crap flying between China and everyone else. No one wants them here, but everyone agrees they have the right to. We're being asked for intel and action. I am open to suggestions."

"Vaseline," Stephens said. He wasn't in this chain of command and could feel free to kibitz. "Apart from that, I'm for calling my government and bailing. We've got an amnesty offer for my group and families, if we can extract them. With our casualties of the last month and a half, I can take four more people from your allies, if you can't get Washington to make the same deal."

It was sensible and fair, Kyle thought. This was a full-scale war, even if shadowy at the present. Two fireteams with local insurgents had no business trying to do more than radio out troop movements and enemy targets. And that was a job the SEALs or Air Force Combat Control or Marine Recon were much better equipped to handle than two Rangers and a desk officer. Not that it mattered worth a damn. There wasn't much to stop this. The government wouldn't be able to make a decision fast enough to matter, and Kyle didn't like the idea of abandoning civilians.

"Do the Chinese actually care about a civilian?" Australian Kevin Fuller asked. "I wouldn't imagine they care about an expat."

"Probably they don't," Wade said. "But it's a convenient excuse to bring ships down here and rattle sabers. They might also grab some more islands in the South China Sea on their way, as forward operating locations."

"Can't accuse them of being stupid," Iverson said. "Scheming, conniving, soulless, but not stupid."

"I guarantee both we and India will respond to Chinese vessels in the Straits of Malacca," Stephens said. "Wouldn't surprise me if you, the Brits, and the Japs came in, too."

Kyle said nothing about that. He agreed with what he heard and saw no reason to comment. Instead . . .

"Can we find the hostages, at least?" he asked. "If the bomb threats are urban, to hell with them, that's not our gig. I agree with you on that, Mel." *Did I just say that?* He thought. "But if we can find the hostages, we can at least report that. If they're in one of these little villes, we may be able to do something. That will take the Chinese pressure off, if we can accomplish that."

Wiesinger considered. "Good. I like it. Where do we look?"

"That's what the locals are for," Kyle admitted. "But they must be able to find something. Even if we can just localize it, it helps a rescue force."

"I'm not sure how much we should share," Wiesinger said. "Our objectives are different from theirs."

"Hell, Mel, should we put our feet in buckets of concrete? Washington isn't on the spot, they don't have the information we do. Decisions have to be made here." Wade sounded closer to an outburst than he ever had.

Wiesinger stared at him, looking as if he was about to start shouting. Obvious rage was boiling up. Stephens interrupted with, "I concur. I can call and tell my chain that I need to stay. I have that much autonomy. Stick with our locals. I'll trust yours if you trust mine. Any intel helps. I don't want to read about two dead civvies in the news."

Wiesinger closed his mouth. The comment about a mere sergeant having autonomy to make that decision obviously stuck in his craw. He'd been content so far to relay the orders from above and report back. He wasn't stupid, but he was lacking in imagination. The idea of handling the mission was obviously new to him.

"I agree," Kyle said. "I'd rather be recognized as a savior than a killer. This might do it." It wasn't much of a statement, but it might get the colonel to see the promotion potential of acting without orders. Of course, that might get him started on a path of throwing the book away. Which wasn't what Kyle and Wade did. They knew the book, they used it when applicable, and strayed only when the situation called for it. Soldiers, not grandstanders.

Wiesinger agreed to the inevitable. He was clearly struggling with authority and autonomy. He nodded acquiescence and called in Bakri and Akbar, who'd been outside and clearly weren't happy about being barred. Akbar especially had been second fiddle all the way along, with only his five men versus Bakri's nineteen, now fourteen, and the foreigners. He was older, and twitched in annoyance at the insult to his status.

The gruffness was very visible. Kyle watched as Wade tried another dose of battlefield diplomacy.

"Our government doesn't trust anyone, even us," he said. "It's not like running a unit in the field, the way it was in World War Two. Now, everything has to be passed up and certified. But we're still expected to be responsible. It's the world we live in."

The locals were slightly mollified, and more so when Wiesinger relayed the suggestion that they find intel. It wasn't his idea, but there wasn't any point in fighting about it. Let him have the credit if it got done.

Bakri nodded and grabbed his phone. "But I can only do this once," he said. "If I'm overheard, I'll be called a conspirator."

"Understood," Stephens said, twitching his moustache. "We'll back you and evac you if needed." It was probable that a phone tap existed somewhere in the chain.

Nodding again, Bakri dialed. The conversation was fast and jabberish, and switched between Bahasa, Achinese, and some other language. The Americans looked askance at Stephens and Akbar, who motioned them to retreat away.

Once in the far corner of the room in a huddle, nostrils full of mildew and sour sweat, the Australian and Akbar began translating for the others.

"He's asking about the Chinese bitch, way to strike a blow for Malays everywhere, show those Javanese bastards how things will be. But he's asking them not to blow up the oil, because it's money. It fits what his position is, and he's not a friend of the government, so no one should twig. Doesn't mean they'll tell him anything, though."

The local and the Aussie conferred, and Stephens continued, "He's really playing the 'Chink bitch' angle, because the Chinese minority runs most of the country. It's a good act. I'd believe him if I didn't know better. He's asking for a piece, asking about more hostages, and can he get some taped footage, but again, we need the oil, don't blow it up. He's offering more hostages, government officials, says he's heard of some Americans and Brits and will try to get them, wouldn't mind a few car bombs on those

American assholes. Okay, he's done, more some other time, how's the wife and kids."

Kyle almost choked to avoid laughing. It couldn't have ended quite like that, but still.

Bakri closed his phone, pulled the battery, dropped the phone to the ground, and smashed it flat with his rifle butt.

"And now the government thinks I am part of those scum," he said, his mouth tight. "Between phone calls and abandoning my crops for weeks at a time. But I know who to talk to. Of course, he may only know someone else . . ."

"Good man," Kyle said. "We'll back you up. And if we gap these assholes, you're clean anyway." Though that wasn't a guarantee, and nothing Kyle had any control over.

"Where to, then?" Stephens asked over tea. He brewed every time they might have fifteen minutes. It was good tea, too, the times Kyle had tried it.

"Almost to Lhokseumawe," Bakri said. "Long drive. Then I must ask more questions."

"So let's roll," Wade said.

It sounded to Kyle a lot like their first mission in Pakistan, where Nasima had guided them around, gaining intel by asking at places a well-bred lady should avoid. Then they'd gone there anyway. Then she'd died, shot. He didn't feel the same way about Bakri, obviously, but he still didn't want to see the man die.

Anyway, they were all soldiers this time.

"Less than a hundred kilometers?" he asked.

"Yes. We do not wish to go into the city. We seek Fiktif, south of there and inland."

Another hamlet in the jungle. "What do you know about it?" Wiesinger asked.

"I suspect it," Bakri said. "It was site to a certain situation. The army protects the government-claimed oil fields. There was rebellion and threat against surveying for more gas and oil. So they killed a number of rebels. U.S. Mobil lend bulldozers to bury the dead in a mass grave."

Kyle had seen mass graves in Bosnia. He didn't imagine they were any prettier in fetid jungle humidity. "U.S. Mobil did that?" Besides the moral considerations, that sounded diplomatically foolish.

Bakri shrugged. "I didn't see it. But it's not the first story. And bulldozers were used. Perhaps some manager allowed them to be borrowed and didn't complain. But that's why people want Mobil gone. The money doesn't help us and the Army attacks us. I'm thought crazy or criminal to want to keep it and work with Jakarta. But we could use the money here. Better that than poverty worse than we have now. The money that is supposed to be used for development is used for 'security issues,' meaning more soldiers."

"Anyway," Kyle said, uncomfortable with the situation, "you suspect the town is still involved?"

"I suspect it is largely empty, due to an attack by the Army. But it would be another good, empty place to stage from."

"So let's roll," Stephens said.

13

ONE HUNDRED KILOMETERS—SIXTY MILES—
was a trip of about four hours. That was due
in part to the narrow, rutted back roads they
took for security purposes. Not only were they in
rough shape, but they lengthened the trip by
about 30 percent. Still, despite rain, the roof
worked and the weather was warm. Itchy and
sweaty warm, in fact. But Kyle Monroe wasn't
one to be bothered by weather, after almost sixteen years of service. Wade and the Aussies were
equally reticent. Wiesinger shifted uncomfortably and swore quietly, but had the grace to not
complain any more loudly than that.

They were quite close when Kyle's musing was
interrupted by a horrific explosion.

Someone screamed. It might have been him.
He snatched at the door handle, which wasn't
working. It flopped loosely in his grip. He shoved

with his shoulder and the door flew open, letting him tumble into wet, friendly dirt. It hurt his shoulder, then his ear stung as he rolled across the butt of his M4. But he was alive and concealed. A quick self-assessment came up with minor burns that stung, a couple of scratches and a hellaciously aching foot as his injuries. At that he was lucky. A glance indicated a low-quality RPG round had torn the front off the truck, disabling the engine. It could just as easily have killed him and others. He didn't see any bodies immediately at hand, but that was just a glance. He had no idea what the tactical situation was, other than that they'd been attacked.

There was sporadic shooting. He listened for a few seconds to place the sources. There was both outgoing and incoming fire, so they'd tripped something. Likely, Fiktif was being used and there were outer sentries. Either they didn't know or like Bakri, or they'd suspected he was a threat. But that wasn't important now. What was important was coordinating with his allies and defeating or retreating from the threat. Shaking off the daze, he got to work.

Cell phones. He used a phone more than he used a rifle anymore. But it made sense. "Mel, Kyle. No reportable injuries, alone, ready to respond," he said once Wiesinger answered.

"Understood. We are grouping in two elements, five zero meters outboard from the vehicles. If you find it hot, withdraw rearward. We suspect a perimeter."

At least they were all on the same page. "Roger. Line open. Transiting." He slipped the phone into a pocket and got ready to move. At several dollars a minute, he guessed, the phone was a dirt-cheap way to keep him alive. And he better not see Wiesinger's smartass criticism of phone charges this time.

No obvious threats nearby, sources of fire some meters ahead. Giving himself the okay, Kyle picked covered locations he would use for the movement. The place in question was about thirty meters away, but he couldn't see a damned thing through this growth.

Sensing movement, he froze and tensed on the trigger. An Indonesian was ahead. Then he saw an Aussie with the man. Dammit, who the hell was who? This was getting bad in a hurry. When it was just you and the bad guys, it was easy. In uniform with professionals, it was doable. Now was a goatfuck in the woods with everyone in part uniform and part civvies. The only uniformed forces were officially allies to them and threats to their actual allies. He didn't dare hold his fire against a possible threat, and didn't dare shoot an ally.

Nor would he be distracted again.

Oh, shit, that hurt! He'd run into a limb that poked him in the cheek, right under the eye. He dropped and cringed, blinking as his eye teared up. Dammit, Kyle, get control, stop flopping like a fucking chicken! He'd twisted his left ankle slightly, too. Remember: Bad guys, good guys, and shooting. Methodical and professional.

Somehow, he made it another few meters, and was seen by someone who recognized him. They approached cautiously, leery of both pursuit and his trigger. Then he was being dragged into a hollow with a long, rotten trunk as cover. It was Haswananda, with one of the men helping her, as Kyle was near twice her weight, more with gear.

"I'm fine," he motioned. "Saya tidik apa-apa."

"Yo, buddy," Wade said softly from a few feet away. "Ready?"

"Yeah," he said. "A poke in the eye with a sharp stick."

"Ouch," Wade said without any real emotion. It was an acknowledgment rather than a commiseration. "Mel figures the village is defended."

"You don't say." It didn't take a lot of intel for that.

"Estimating the force about equal to ours. He wants to push in and capture if possible."

Kyle grabbed his phone. He wanted to hear this straight even if it was going to be the same as Wade told him. Passing orders down the line could result in "Capture France" becoming "Invade Russia in the winter."

"Mel, Kyle here, mostly functional and fully mobile. You say we're to capture?"

"Correct. If we can acquire a prisoner we'll get intel some way. Or else we overrun the position and look for what we need. If they're making this much noise, they're a target."

"Understood. Where do you want me?"

Wiesinger's basic plan wasn't too bad. An initial counterattack heavy on the ammo and light on the movement. The Aussies were to encircle one side, the north, and their locals the south. Bakri's remaining force—he'd taken another casualty—was to set a forward perimeter. Kyle and Wade were to attack designated targets. If they could get a good reversal, it was likely the enemy would rout. They didn't have highly trained Western special operations troops and Army Rangers as backup. Skulk and retreat was likely what they did anyway.

And if the village was willing to make that much noise defending against a casual intruder, they had something to hide, that was certain. Serendipitous intel, if they could handle the situation.

Bakri's men and women moved forward, slipping from tree to shrub to undergrowth. Kyle and Wade followed behind, SR25s out, with Wiesinger behind them holding both M4s. Bakri's RPG gunner had two rockets left. The RPK machine gun had one drum of seventy-five rounds. They couldn't spend ammo at U.S. rates for this.

The village was barely visible as shapes. There were figures, but no clear targets yet. And they weren't shooting. It wasn't likely they thought the threat gone, so they had to be doing something else. Kyle paused, forcing his breath into long, slow, silent heaves, and watched for clues.

Then he pulled his phone out.

Dammit, Wiesinger had closed off. Likely to save batteries or money, neither of which Kyle gave a damn about right now. Both were assets to be expended. He redialed in a hurry, and waited through three rings. While waiting, he donned the headset. Better to have it directly in his ears than trying to fumble it and a rifle.

"Mel." Weisinger finally answered.

"Explosives. I see possible crates and someone who may be capping something."

"Shit. Understood." Wiesinger clicked hold and apparently made other calls. He was back in less than a minute. "You and Wade will take targets designated by Stephens and Fuller."

"Understood and standing by. Out."

Kyle had dealt with explosives far too often to be reckless. These sideshow freaks were perfectly capable of screaming, *"Allahu akbar!"* and blowing themselves to smithereens, taking any bystanders with them. That was bad enough when the amount was in kilograms. When it was in tons . . .

He'd been there once, facing a nutcase with a suicide switch and tons of explosives in the same room as he. He wasn't eager to do so again, to put it mildly. His stomach flopped and felt acidic.

When his phone vibrated again, he clicked it as fast as a video game button. "Kyle."

"Kevin Fuller here."

"Go." He slipped the headset on, so he could keep hands free. He didn't like the wire hanging, but he could deal with it when not moving.

"Reference: central building. North side. Two men. Both targets."

"Roger, but going to take a few minutes to get into position."

"Better bloody hurry, mate. They've got what looks like a twenty-four-kilo crate."

"Understood. Tell Wade, too. He may be better placed."

"Roger."

Kyle shifted laterally a few meters, to find a thin spot in the foliage. Yes, there were two men, who appeared to be fitting detonators to blocks of TNT as they looked around furtively. And fifty pounds wasn't so much, really. If he could get it to detonate, it would solve several problems. But was it TNT, and was TNT sensitive enough to detonate if shot? Or could he hit the detonator?

Better try for the crate. If they ran, it averted the problem temporarily. If he scored a bang, it was gone, they were gone, and a message would be sent. The blast radius shouldn't be great, the effect would dissipate in the open quickly, and the jungle would buffer it. It was worth a shot.

The range was about one hundred meters. The fire had slowed to an occasional pot shot, as the attackers strove to coordinate their efforts while the defenders were hesitant to move on the offense for fear of being flanked or running into an entrenched force. Standoff.

Luckily, the new injury had been his left eye. He winced as he closed it to aim. Add in the dust damage from earlier, and his eyes felt like hardboiled eggs.

Through the scope, Kyle could see one of them place a block end-down on the crate and start twisting a detonator into it, with a fuse of some kind, probably Detcord, trailing. He took careful aim and dropped a round right through the block.

TNT *would* detonate if shot, or else he'd hit the cap. The flash caused his scope image to stutter. The bang shook the ground. His scope image returned at once and he could see lumpy red paint splashed across a wall. That was one of the two men. The crate became splinters in the air, falling, twisting lazily. The other shattered body fell several meters away, and wisps of steam arose from a hole in the loam. A few moments later, a stiff breeze swept past him in the woods. It was hot, chemical, and gusted in his ears.

All hell broke lose. He'd accomplished something, alright. He'd kicked a nest of hornets. The fire wasn't accurate, but there was a lot of it.

Fuller read off another target. "Some arsehole

just came out of the darker gray hut. RPG. Tracking . . . he's moving left." Weapons fire interrupted the conversation.

"Skulking behind a pile of rubbish and a Toyota?" Kyle asked between bangs. There was movement there.

"That's him. I'll tell Wade, too."

"Got it."

This was getting hot. There was something going down here.

The enemy grouped into two elements, with hard cover of the buildings and several prepared fighting positions. That gave them a significant advantage for defense. At the same time, they probably didn't know what size force the Americans and allies were, or where the elements were. This was where snipers, serving as designated marksmen, could be the force multiplier that would break the engagement.

Only . . . Wiesinger wasn't giving any orders, even for a frontal assault.

Kyle dialed again. "Mel, Kyle here, I recommend we take targets of opportunity, with just enough supporting fire to convince them we're still here. Press the advantage with accurate fire and we can inflict substantial casualties."

"Uh, yeah, sounds good. Not quite what I had in mind, but I approve. Stand by."

Not quite what he'd had in mind probably meant he'd frozen. The fights were getting stiffer each time. Which should give him time to adapt, but didn't seem to. And now he was de facto commander of a platoon, which he'd never done in wartime and barely done in peacetime.

So that explained the knot in Kyle's guts. Usually at this point in a fight, he was icy calm and detached, coming back to reality and shakes afterward. His unconscious knew there was a problem this time, and he was nervous. Troops needed effective orders. If not, they needed ineffective orders so they had something to do and something to bitch about while they got shot to hell. No orders meant a goatfuck.

There was a slight increase in the rate of fire. Wiesinger had apparently ordered everyone to shoot accurately, which wasn't a bad modification. If a handful of rounds came close and one hit, the psychological effect would be considerable.

Kyle sought what appeared to be an RPK machine-gun muzzle, and waited patiently. A head rose just slightly after a while, and he was able to punch a hole through the top inch. The resulting thrashing and waving of limbs indicated debilitating pain at least, maiming or death possibly. Either way, there was no more shooting.

The enemy was figuring out that they were outmatched. They fell back in a coordinated withdrawal, with suppressing fire at likely threats—a few bursts were within meters of Kyle, but far overhead. Then the fire tapered off. Kyle had no targets, and shortly, no one did. Silence reigned, part of it hearing damage from lots of shooting.

Wiesinger called through Kyle's headset. "Kyle, we're going in. Follow Stephens and cover the left, south."

"Roger that."

Kyle rose slowly and crawled forward. The silence could be a ruse or there could be a few suicidal types behind. He waited until he saw the Aussies spread on the ground at the edge of the cut growth, which was in the process of growing over the abandoned village. It was amazing how fast things grew here.

Then Kyle was easing out onto the grass, which was still eight inches deep and enough to hide him in part. Wade was a few meters over. Wiesinger wasn't in view. Either he was slightly behind or was waiting to see what happened. Under the circumstances, if he really was acting as commander, that was reasonable. Kyle couldn't help but feel it was an excuse.

But that assumed the man wasn't just behind his field of view. And that wasn't something to fret over with threats in front.

Bakri's men moved in, and shortly, it was clear the village was vacant. There might be a few wiggling wounded or someone cowering behind, and those could be threats. But the main force had retreated in the face of their fire.

Which seemed too easy to Kyle. If he had a defended position with hard cover against small arms, he'd have held it until the attackers ran low on ammo, which on foot in the jungle shouldn't take long.

But then, these groups were experienced, smart and trained, but not to the level of Rangers or the SAS. And they couldn't afford casualties. Besides losing force, they'd lose manpower for working and income.

The force regrouped in the middle, still low and covered by buildings in case of a counterattack. They put sentries in an outer perimeter, and swapped ammo around to even things out. It was getting pretty tight on ammo. Wiesinger had shot a lot. The Aussies had been frugal, but had borne the brunt of the advances thus far. Kyle and Wade wound up with fifty rounds in each drum and four thirty-round magazines apiece. It was heartbreaking to destroy the extra drum, but it wasn't realistic to expect enough ammo or time to reload a hundred rounds. Kyle stripped his empty Beta and scattered the parts. He bent up the feed lips and cracked the drum as best he could. No one would be using it now.

There wasn't time to do much cleaning, but he did open the receiver of his M4, wipe the bolt carrier down, and add some more oil. The SR25 hadn't been fired that much. He gave it a few drops of Cleaner Lubricant Preservative and grabbed an MRE to munch on. It was the last complete one he had.

The good news, he supposed, was that with ammo and food gone he had much less mass to haul.

It took less than five minutes to quarter the area, and everyone was ready to proceed.

"Time to search in detail," Wiesinger said. Bakri nodded and sent a team of five men on a patrol.

"Considering the reception, we might not want to eat anything here," Wade said.

"Good advice," Stephens agreed. "Could be anything from worm-infested dog feces to strychnine waiting for us."

A bang shook the ground. Kyle dove for cover with everyone else.

"Booby trap," Stephens reported. "Some wounded arsehole had a grenade."

"Right, let's cover this slowly," Wiesinger said.

"Not yet, Mel," Kyle cautioned.

"Why?"

"How many bodies do you see?"

Wiesinger looked around. "Four . . . five."

"We have two. We were attacking a defended position. If they have five casualties, where's the rest of them? Could be fifty, a hundred of them."

Wiesinger looked stunned. He hadn't even thought of that.

"I'll take perimeter," Stephens said. "Akbar," he called, than rattled off some local language. Kyle didn't need to catch the few words he did to grasp, *Expect a counterattack and look for bigger booby traps*.

"Mel, there could be entire buildings full of tons of explosive here." The hair on his neck was standing up as he recalled a low building in the Carpathian mountains that was on the receiving end of this logistical chain. There'd been a ton there. How much could be here near the source?

"Yes, but we need intel."

"I agree, but don't open anything without a lot of peeking."

"Understood, Kyle." Wiesinger appeared to get it about 5 percent. Hopefully, that was enough.

If not, what happened next was. There was an outhouse behind one building, on the edge of a clearing that had once been a field. It was a modern composting type with a "turd gobbler." One of the locals approached it and eased the door open. A flash, a bang, and the whole thing caved in, taking his body with it.

As the shouting died and the current bizarre state of normalcy returned, Kyle vowed to squat behind a tree if he needed to go.

But Wiesinger seemed to get it now.

"No one go into a building. Watch for wires. Scan windows first."

The search was rather brief. It wasn't that there were traps there: There weren't any buildings not trapped or mined. The personnel had departed into the jungle on foot, leaving a mess that they hoped would nail anyone who found it.

Kevin Fuller was tasked with setting charges to detonate the whole mess. He moved cautiously but quickly. He did a recon and stared through a few windows before starting. He returned muttering curses.

"Whole bloody thing's wired together," he said as he took a crate and started fixing detonators. "Looks like about a thirty-second delay. We, or whoever, was supposed to discover one, start on it, and the whole shebang goes off, taking anyone in the radius with them. Looks to be about six tons total."

"Doesn't that defeat the purpose of having it stored to send elsewhere?" Wade asked.

"No, it's not an efficient setup. Instead of fusing every charge, they've fused one crate per building. The rest will follow as at least a low order blast. There's a wired remote, a radio, and the trips and timer. Moderately competent. Anyway, we put this there and run," he said, pointing at a building that had been rather stuffed, including crates under beds. "Denies them this load, and will draw a lot of attention they don't want."

"Attention we don't want either," Wade noted.

"Right," Wiesinger said. "But we've got to take it out or wind up facing it."

"No argument, Mel. It just sucks to be us."

"Gentlemen, I've learned in the last few days that there's a lot not covered in the manuals."

"Yes," Kyle agreed. Just yes. Was the man getting a clue at long last?

Ten minutes later, they moved out in column, slowly and with lots of advance and flank. The Indonesian Army would be after them, as would the terrorists and any other groups who may have been told by either side that Bakri was a betrayer. The first time Kyle had done this in Pakistan, the risk was of a firefight with hicks. The second time, it was of arrest by non-friendly Romanian government agents with a reputation for brutality or a confrontation with a mad bomber. This time, it was pretty much three different well-trained armies who might hunt him.

No pressure.

Nor had they acquired much intel. Anything sensitive had either been taken along by their enemy or was protected by bombs. It was frustrating and creepy.

Still, they'd been accomplishing the secondary objective. A *lot* of explosives weren't going to be used for terror. Seven or more tons so far, which had to represent a big investment on someone's part. But they didn't have the key figures behind it yet, so it wasn't a solid win.

Their first two missions had been completed, even if as bloody messes. Not every mission could be perfect, but dammit, Kyle wanted to get the

people, not the tools. The people were the real
threat.

A tremendous roar announced a mass detona-
tion behind them. That felt good. Several tons of
explosive would not be used to attack civilians.
But it was all a matter of shoveling back the
ocean with a pitchfork. More would be forthcoming if they couldn't hit the people behind it.

So they had to work on that.

Stephens and his locals were making phone
calls, trying to get a few more hints. With active
cooperation four ways, they might find a lead.
Who had heard of the new hostages? Wasn't it
great? Did they need more? Who would know? Is
there a number? Yes, please leave a message. It's
regarding some further supplies I may have for
him. Yes, we both know what we're talking
about. Allah Akbar.

It wasn't too suspicious. The rumor mill was in
full swing. One source credited Bakri with taking
the hostages. Another claimed Bakri had set up
the last ambush by the Kopassus. Bakri took it in
good humor, suggesting a few other rumors to be
put out about himself. It was brave of him. He
was effectively a marked man no matter who
found them. Anda scowled. It was rather obvious
her interest in Bakri was more than professional,
and she didn't want to see him dead.

Rumors they got aplenty. Facts were far fewer,
and most were items they already knew.

Kyle noticed everyone bunching up. They were looking at something, and he headed that way, alert for any threats others might not notice. There was a break in the trees, which probably indicated a human feature. In this case, it was a road for lumber operations, well rutted, muddy and red. With tire tracks.

Fresh tire tracks. They'd either called or had vehicles waiting.

Bakri said, "I'll send a team back for vehicles."

"Yes," Wiesinger said. "We'll wait." They melted back several meters, so they could just see traffic, but should be invisible themselves as long as everyone was still and low.

"We'll take a gander a klick up or so," Stephens said. "Try to find out how many and where."

"Roger that."

Kyle and Wade covered each other while doing a better cleaning of weapons. In this humid, warm environment it was necessary. Kyle had been amazed to find mildew on the nylon strap he used to carry the M4, but it was that soggy here.

Anda and a man he didn't recall came by with fruit they'd gathered and some dried beef. The fruit was warm, obviously, but sweet even if there were some insect bites. The beef was tough and not very flavorful apart from a hint of salt. A couple of stringy bits stuck between Kyle's teeth. He knew they'd be there a day or more before he could floss or pick them out. He'd had that prob-

lem before. Still, it was fresh fruit and more pro-
tein. He was grateful.

Stephens and his scouts returned. They infil-
trated their own lines with barely a word or sound.
Once alongside the Americans, he reported.

"Looks like a dozen vehicles. Heavily laden.
Some signs of either a struggle or casualties with
limps being loaded. All have new tires. Heading
north and west, farther into rebel territory."

"So we follow and ask as we go," Wiesinger
said.

"Bakri, can you pull off being a lost member of
the party trying to catch up?" Kyle asked.

Bakri paused a moment. The idiom likely
threw him off. "I can do so. Whether they believe
I can't say."

"Do what you can," Wiesinger said. "We've
got to be close."

They didn't have to be, Kyle thought, but
likely were. Which also had its dangers when
dealing with men who knew they'd die and believed in a cause.

Bakri led one squad of his troops along the
edge of the road. The rest stayed in the trees with
Kyle and the others. They were several meters in,
where they could hide easily from vehicles and
still be close enough to provide fire. Sooner or
later—hopefully sooner—a vehicle would come
along. Anyone using these remote roads was
likely to have at least rumors.

Of course, they might also not want to stop for a group of armed men, or they might be hostile.

Kyle crawled over and under brush, thick and green and rich with rot and fungus. The jungle was an organism that sometimes seemed to move visibly as it fought to reconquer the holes people scraped in it. Down below, Bakri and his friends walked through thick, yellow mud rutted by trucks and rain. Roots and grasses were already attempting to move back into those wet depressions. It was easier, not to mention safer, to be where Kyle was.

That explained the difficulty of tracking anyone here. A single sentry with a wired phone or cell could give an innocuous signal to shut down any threatening operation, once he sighted a threat on the road. Coming through the jungle limited one to carried gear only, and posed risks of terrain and traps. Helicopters were very viable, but one had to have a suspect before using them, and could expect to take fire on approach. It would take elite troops to handle an insertion fast enough to matter. This whole area was riddled with small villages scraping out a living in crops, which was quite easy with the climate and rainfall, or providing labor for oil and timber operations. It was a wonder there wasn't more violence.

It was near dusk when a vehicle came along. Twelve hours of driving, fighting, and rucking. Kyle was as drained as his Camelbak. The only good news was that there were enough trickles and streams that they were able to filter water and refill the Camelbaks after a fashion. It took some time to pump the little filter, and twice in three days they'd had to scrape the element clean of mildew and sediment, but they did have fresh water. Far better than the cold desert of northern Pakistan. Not as nice as the hotels of Europe. Same assholes trying to kill people, including Kyle Monroe.

The incoming truck was a thirty-year-old Mercedes diesel stake-bed carrying timbers. Kyle and the others slunk into the growth so they wouldn't be seen. The temptation was always to stand and stare, but the necessity was to stay out of view. Especially when the party might be nervous.

Kyle heard voices, including Bakri's. They were loud but not antagonistic. Kyle felt his phone, wondering if Syarief with the remaining phone would call for backup, but nothing happened. Shortly, the gears clashed as the engine revved, and the truck drove on. A few minutes later, Bakri called, "Come out!"

He was past the treeline himself, barely visible in the grayness. "I think I know where," he said. "We'll need lorries. The fuel cost is starting to hurt me, too."

Wiesinger took that as a hint. As they closed up, still squatting, he drew out a thousand dollars worth of rupees. "I can issue more if need arises."

"You are gracious and I thank you," Bakri said. Unlike the Pashtun, who would only take money as a carefully offered gift because of their pride, the Achinese were far more practical. This operation was costing them in people and money, and they saw no reason not to make the U.S. help defray costs. Kyle found that a lot easier to deal with. Which was good, because Wiesinger obviously wouldn't have been able to handle Pakistan.

"Where, then?" Wiesinger asked.

"Closer to Lhokseumawe. That makes sense. They didn't take the hostages far."

"Is your source reliable?" Stephens asked.

"Yes, because they're not a source," Bakri grinned. "I just chatted, said we were patrolling for trouble, how were things? And they said they were fine, but had been ordered by members of the Movement to stay away from Impian, and we should, too. They expected a government fight soon. I can't think why else they would order that."

No, there wasn't a reason. If they suspected trouble, they'd simply be silent. Telling people to stay away indicated a fear. It also wasn't that smart to offer that information, as they had no idea of Bakri's loyalties.

Which made sense. They were simple local workers and the exact type of intel source one looked for. The captors had to know their cover would be blown eventually, so were just stalling with the warnings to stay away. Tactically, they were better off in a village they controlled than the people who'd tried similar approaches in

Iraq, where the neighborhoods were all shifting alliances and no one controlled an area.

They moved deeper into the growth and set up shop, with one third on, two thirds sleeping, and got a few hours rest. It was near midnight before the transportation arrived. Kyle awoke bleary-eyed but ready to move when Wade nudged him, and started down the slope. The trucks of their local transport element were getting to be pretty messed up. He made note to suggest to Wiesinger that any balance of cash be donated to the cause. These people had put out a lot of effort and re-sources at great personal risk already.

Once aboard the vehicle, they were served packs of rice and chicken with fruit and peppers. It was cold but filling and tasty and welcome. Rations had been very scarce for most of a day. A solid cupful of food with a good drink of water filled his belly and helped revive Kyle, but he was still groggy. He went back to a fugue state between wakefulness and dreaming. It was too rough a trip to sleep, but he was too fatigued to stay conscious. He'd passed days at a time in such states, reacting and responding as needed without actually recall-ing events until afterwards. Add in a tight position and slumped posture, and he was all aches within minutes. He knew it wasn't going to be fun.

Thirty kilometers, less than twenty miles. They scattered the four trucks with drivers along a couple of kilometers of road, and left a couple of cell phones. Two trucks were hidden well enough to not be a problem. The other two were notice-able, and ripe for questions or robbery.

Back into the woods. They hunkered down again, well hidden under brush and deadfalls with ponchos for cover. They operated in dark-ness, using red-lensed flashlights sparingly, and set sentries. Anda and Iverson slipped off to re-con the target. It was a wonder, Kyle thought, with all the skulking around, that they hadn't run into one of the other national patrols. But it was a long archipelago and the numbers involved were small. He wondered why they were having so much success at recon, but that was because all the factions were theoretically allies. They didn't fight each other. Except now they were.

He reflected now was a good time for this mis-sion. In six months it was going to be ugly, with GAM possibly fratriciding and no one trusting anyone. The end result of this operation was going to make it much easier for the government to crack down on the rebels, because all cooperation would end. They'd be picked apart and defeated in detail.

Which wasn't his concern. His concern was U.S. interests. The Indonesians needed to fix their own country. He couldn't and wasn't allowed to, and was smart enough not to get involved, even if it hurt like hell to see it coming apart. Anda, Bakri, Akbar, all the others could be dead before the winter.

He drifted into a restless sleep, not helped by the knotty root poking him in the back.

14

THE NEWS WASN'T GOOD THE NEXT MORNING. Iverson and Anda came in, wrung out, near delirious, and barely coherent. They couldn't confirm hostages, but did confirm a large armed force.

"At least one fifty, likely two hundred, bare chance of a few more," Iverson said. He accepted a cup of tea and sat back under a canopy. He was blond somewhere under the dirt, and perhaps twenty-two. But he had a maturity years beyond that. His wrestler's physique was suffering from the ordeal, but he swallowed water at a prodigious rate. He'd recover.

Anda simply curled up to sleep, her head on her pack, clutching her rifle like a teddy bear, and looking disgustingly cute. It was a natural camouflage. She was one deadly little lady, and a better infiltrator than Kyle. He respected and was amazed by her talent. And she could walk him into the ground. These people lived on foot. Cars were a tool or luxury, not something taken for granted. Thus they had a lot of early training he wished he, and especially younger recruits, had.

Kyle looked around. "We've got twenty-four now?" The odds weren't promising. No matter how good the training and the troops, numbers did matter. He leaned back against a tree and stretched.

"I can get another ten men in less than a day," Bakri said.

"We need to approach this slowly," Kyle insisted, "but I don't think we have a lot of time."

"No. The Indos are about to start shooting 'terrorists' by the thousands in retaliation for the hostages. Morally I concur, but they'll include our friends. Politically . . ." Wade tapered off.

"Yeah," Kyle agreed. There was nothing else to say. It was certain that the Indonesian military would wipe out most of the insurgents. It was certain that whatever word did leak out would be greeted largely with support, and it was certain the ringleaders and brains would use it as an excuse to escalate. With oilfields at stake here and elsewhere, and a goodly supply of suicidal fanatics, the situation would get a lot worse before it got better.

"The thing is," Wade said, "most people *will* agree with Indonesia, and if they don't do something, China and India will start operations.

Long term, I'm not sure the U.S. or Europe is going to like the direction that will take. We've got to get this fucker fast."

"I agree," Wiesinger said. "We'll have to sacrifice some stealth and supply intel to the Indonesians."

"The problem, Mel, is that the terrorists have sympathizers in the Indonesian military. This is the ongoing problem we face on these missions. Most of our allies are firmly behind us, but a handful are antagonistic or have simply been paid off."

"Yes, so we'll be picky about who we talk to," Wiesinger said with a smug look. "I'm not stupid, sergeant."

"Not implying you are, Mel," Kyle said, shaking his head. *Hell no. I'm on record as stating so.*

"So you gentlemen put together a briefing. I'll review our options regarding who to talk to."

Paperwork, Kyle thought. Yes, that's the way to win a war. Paperwork. Against an enemy, with no defined force or mission, that evaporates into the jungle at a moment's notice. Just bury them in red tape and international cooperation. You go, Colonel.

"Yes, Mel."

Wiesinger walked toward their personal lodging while hefting his laptop. He seemed incapable of handling a decision without an office, even if that office was a couple of ponchos over rucks with a square of bark as a door.

Kyle and Wade simply swapped looks of disbelief. Kyle wondered if Wade had the same churning in his stomach that Kyle did.

Stephens had been silent. "What's his story, then?" he asked now.

They gave their ally a brief rundown. It didn't appear to surprise Stephens much. "That's dealable with. As long as we know what he's like." The sergeant was cheerful enough, and had likely seen similar things.

"Actually, I think he's correct on one count," Wade said.

"Huh?" Kyle asked.

"We aren't set to try to find a ton of explosives in an industrial area, nor do we blend in. The Indonesian military has to handle it. Besides, the hostages are more our department, and we've already cost the terrorists a few tons of hardware. Really, more cooperation at the beginning, with Bakri and Jack, had we known about him," Wade nodded at their counterpart, "would have made a lot of this unnecessary."

"We might find the charges," Bakri protested.

"And if you're around when it goes off? Who will get blamed?"

Bakri chewed his lip. "Yes, that's true. But I can't contact the government. If they find out what I have done, they're not likely to respond well."

"So it's up to Wiesinger," Kyle said. "But I bet State won't listen to his theories. If he starts calling on his own authority, we can bet on a leak blowing any chance of interception. There goes our credibility, there goes the U.S. image over here, there go we, out of the country if we're lucky, jail if not, and then a week later the thing blows up anyway."

They sat for several minutes, no real ideas developing. The desired result was clear, but the path wasn't.

Wiesinger came back. "Well, that was pointless," he said. He sounded angry.

"No dice with State?" Kyle asked.

"I got treated like a beggar with his hat in hand," the colonel said.

"Mel, we concur on telling the Indonesians. We're just not set to handle this."

"That option was just taken away from me. I may be the officer on the spot, but some bureaucrat with no experience in the field gets to ride over my operation."

Kyle almost had to laugh. Wiesinger really was starting to get it. If he'd just see his own role in this, he'd snap into place and have it. Somehow, though, he didn't think that was going to happen.

"So," Wiesinger said, a thoughtful look on his face. Kyle wasn't sure he'd ever seen such concentration. Rather than quoting the book, the man was actually going to make a judgment call. "If we don't tell the government, but they find out anyway, we can deny any involvement. All we need is an incident like the last one, with the government showing up. Only we arrange it with the right people at the right time, so they nail the terrorists instead of us."

"Dangerous, Mel," Kyle said. "But I agree, for what it's worth."

Wiesinger nodded slowly. "Bakri, we need the best evidence you can find on where they're hiding or traveling. Then we arrange a brief, loud mixup and some frightened phone calls. The trick is to leave just as the cavalry arrives and not too soon or too late."

"My job is finding them." Bakri grinned. "I do not envy you yours."

Another patrol went out. Wade insisted he'd cover it. Kyle tried to argue with him.

Wade said, "Dude, you're ragged as hell. You've had less sleep than either of us, you've been handling a lot of the thinking, and you need more rest. Take it." Wiesinger wasn't in earshot. He was sleeping.

"Okay," Kyle agreed. Yeah, he was exhausted, fatigued, tired, hungry, and feeling chill in the 70-degree night. The dings and bruises didn't help. The offer was too good to pass up, and he fell back against his ruck to sleep, covered from the sky by a poncho slung over branches.

When Kyle awoke, it was to Wiesinger batting his foot. "Kyle," he snapped. "We've got too much to do to spend the day in bed."

Kyle didn't shoot him. He just rose and

grabbed his toothbrush, then snuck out to a bush to drain. He calmed down enough to deal with the prick by the time he returned.

Wade was back, too. He was out of water and grabbed the first offered canteen. It took him three gulps.

"I was impressed," Akbar said. As Stephens's local guide, he'd gone along. "It was dangerous, getting so close."

"How close?" Kyle asked.

"Thirty meters or so. I don't see any signs of them there. No food taken in, no guards. It's an armed camp and a staging area, but it's not where they're holding hostages."

"That's too close, Wade. Don't do that again," Wiesinger said.

Wade gasped. It appeared to be from the exertion of the march back, but it was probably to cover his annoyance.

"It was dark, they weren't inclined to go past the tree line, the ghillie covered me very well, and I didn't see any night vision in use. Should I write a report for you?"

He was half joking, from his tone, but didn't flinch when Wiesinger said, "Yes," and brought out his laptop. Kyle groaned silently. What a way to run a war. In fact, he had half expected and half hoped it would have failed by now. Jungle humidity and muck was rough on equipment.

Wade made no complaint. He sat down with the computer in his lap and sipped more water while he ripped out a report. He typed fast. Kyle was okay, but Wade could throw text at probably eighty words per minute. In less than ten minutes, he had a substantial statement of what he'd seen at the village, detailing persons, weapons and other equipment, supplies, and events. It was almost certainly a rebel training and operations site. There didn't appear to be anything that would suggest hostages. Dead end.

They all gathered for a strategy session.

"Okay, let's look at the map," Kyle said. "They were captured here, and were taken south. We have rumors of them here . . ."

"And here," Bakri said. He pointed.

"So what people are offering definitely places them within a few miles of us," Stephens said.

"Drive and do it again?" Bakri asked.

"Slow, but I don't see a better way. Where else does this particular group operate?" Kyle frowned.

"Tolol. But they . . . might be there," Bakri said. Obviously, he had thought of something.

"Oh?"

"It's a setup near an oil field. Not an actual village, but people shelter there. There was a killing there of an employee protest." He paused over the awkward phrase. "They shot the protestors. It might appeal to their odd sense of justice to do the same thing back."

"I'd say you're right." Hell, yes. That was very likely it.

"Why?" Wiesinger asked.

"Just how they think, sir. Revenge. Blood for blood. Lots of these groups. It's certainly worth looking at. And we might just find our head asshole there. And pull off the original plan, too."

"It's here," Bakri said.

"Not far."

"No, ten kilometers. Walk?"

"Better drive," Kyle said, grimacing. "How close is safe?"

"Three kilometers."

"Doable. How?"

"Access road here, along the edge of the oil field."

Kyle looked at the map. It wasn't much of a "field." It was more clearings in jungle and brush. Roads were typical industrial access, graveled.

"Won't they notice us?"

"If we're seen as a group, yes. Weapons hidden, and in one vehicle at a time. Luckily, you won't be remarkable as Americans."

"Good."

Kyle and Wade had traveled in all kinds of disreputable vehicles. The Land Cruiser was actually one of the choicer ones. It even had working air conditioning. So of course, Murphy had to compensate with a spine-grinding ride over a "road" that was rutted, rooted, and full of sinkholes in the soft loam. Kyle was glad to be in front. Wade was stuffed in with Wiesinger's bulk and two rucks, and Anda and another were squeezed in the back. The "gravel" road was not in great shape. But that seemed to mean it wasn't used much. There were few signs of even temporary repairs. If this was an important path, it would have been paved.

It didn't take long to reach the location they'd set for their staging area. Bakri slowed and drew over to the roadside. Kyle eased the door open and slid his feet out, then sank slowly into the mud. The door creaked slightly as he pressed it gently closed. Wade was behind him, and a splash indicated Wiesinger stepping in a puddle. Kyle swore under his breath. It probably wasn't loud enough to attract attention, and no one was around, but dammit, the man was an increasing liability.

Shortly, their squad was hunkered together in the woods beside the road. The humidity was palpable, but that would help damp out sound, too. Small advantages added up to victory, and Kyle would take them.

"Which way from here?" Wiesinger asked.

"Three kilometers that way," Bakri said.

"How long?"

"An hour if we move well."

"What's our plan?" Kyle asked.

"We need an evac route first," Wiesinger said. "Stand by." He wandered off a few feet and messed with his phone.

"I would truly like to be kept in the loop on

these discussions with HQ," Kyle muttered to Wade.

"But that would compromise secrecy."

"Maybe. Or else he's just a self-centered asshole who doesn't think enlisted people matter."

They stopped, not wanting to drag their allies into the discussion. Stephens had expressed his position, and Bakri said volumes with his silence on the matter.

Wiesinger came back. "Okay, we have extraction in process. It will take a few hours. So we should use that time to patrol. Not too closely, but I recommend three recons. Two on this side, one on the far side of the road."

"Growth is thinner over there," Bakri said.

"Right. Who do you recommend?"

"Anda of course."

The slight woman smiled and nodded, then grabbed another by his arm and slipped away in just her clothes, no ruck. A single look back let Kyle focus on her calm eyes, pouty lips, and clear skin. She really wasn't bad-looking at all, even out here. Cleaned up, she was probably very pretty. He wasn't sure if she'd ever attended a dance or dinner. Probably not.

"Kyle, you and I should make one patrol. Mister Stephens, will you go with us?"

"Right," Stephens agreed with a nod. "Send Wade and Kevin? Iverson can cover here."

"Okay. Bakri, we'll be back in . . ." Wiesinger stopped to think.

Kyle did the math in his head instantly. Three kilometers of rough terrain each way, an additional hour for margin, two hours of recon. Nine hours in this growth, you moron. You've read the books.

"Eight to nine hours," the colonel finally concluded. It must have been thirty seconds.

"Permission to leave rifles with Mister Iverson, Mel?"

"Why?"

"We're recon, don't need to carry weapons. If it gets to that we'll want to run more than fight. That's what sidearms are for." He slapped his Ed Brown, which was in the standard issue holster on his right hip, where it had been since just after they landed. He would even have bathed with it on, if they'd been able to bathe. A few minutes of rain dancing had been the limit of external hygiene, plus a few diaper wipes to sanitize hands. They were all pretty rank.

"I'll take an M four," Wiesinger said. "If you wish to take just a sidearm, I'll allow the choice. Wade?"

"Just the Beretta, Mel. Rifles can stay here."

"Right. Let's decide who goes where."

As they each chose a direction to approach the facility from, Kyle reflected on the irony that the officer whose standard-duty weapon was a sidearm wanted a rifle, while the two rifle-toting grunts wanted to travel light.

Kyle didn't need much for this. He had his water, his pistol, and four extra eight-round magazines and his tactical load-bearing harness. He removed the rifle magazines from it and filled the pouches with a few spare MRE packages, mostly fruit and crackers, with GPS and cell phone. He took the ghillie, rolled up, to don when needed. Fresh camo paint, brown, just to darken his skin against notice. Most people used way too much green. Nature was brown, when it came down to it.

Stephens was waiting, wearing a dun T-shirt and carrying a little day pack. His web gear was hung with full pouches. He had a Browning Hi-Power in a thigh rig. His equivalent to the ghillie was a camouflage nylon fishnet with burlap braided in. It was a cover rather than a garment, but should work fine. All were wearing nearly identical "boonie" hats, broad brimmed and soft.

Wade and Fuller were already out of sight. "Time to walk," Stephens said, looking plucky and cheerful. Kyle fell in behind him, with Wiesinger bringing up the rear.

The first kilometer was easy, at a relaxed crouch, simply alert for anything obvious. There were no signs of human passage and the animal noises were typical. It took about twenty minutes to cover the distance, or the speed of a slow stroll. They ducked from tree to bush to hollow, avoiding standing tall or crashing through brush. The key, even when in safe terrain, was to not draw attention.

The second kilometer was slower. They dropped to low crouches alternating with hands and knees. They dispersed across a front a hundred meters wide and ten deep, each taking his own route. Discovery of one should not mean discovery of the rest. That allowed at least a chance for the other two to escape discovery or exfiltrate, while the one who was sighted would be very loud and aggressive once escape was impossible. If the enemy was busy, they might not notice non-threats, like two other troops departing.

It took about an hour to cover that kilometer, which left almost two in their timetable, plus a spare, to cover the last few hundred meters before commencing recon proper.

Kyle stopped about two hundred meters back, in mid-afternoon light. He found a nice elevated spot with a thick tangle of greenery, which he hoped wasn't poisonous in some fashion, and got ready to work.

His first task was to draw a map of the facility, using GPS, a parallax range finder, and a terrain map. From there, he scaled his own sketch on grid paper with a protractor and scale.

There was a pipeline running through about 100 meters beyond the buildings, and off in the distance, across a field that had been burned clear and was partly regrown with scrub, was an oil well capped with a boom-type pump. He estimated it at 525 meters.

There were four buildings, low, block with

metal roofs. One had windows on the back side, which faced them. The others did not. One had a small vent window on the side. He kept making notes and drawing. They'd compare all three later.

While scanning with the M49 spotting scope, he kept watch for Anda. Nothing indicated her presence, and he knew she was there. Nothing. Excellent.

He did see sentries. Three of them, carrying rifles. They were squatting in shade and watching the road, totally bored. That made sense. There was no real threat. But why sentries? Obviously they feared something.

His phone buzzed and he clicked it to answer while digging for his headset. "Kyle."

"Jack here. Stand by." There was a click.

"Mel here."

"Good, we're conferenced," Stephens said. "And should be clear of any interference."

"I've got a map. Windows on the second building from the left, south, are facing us. They raise. Can't see inside well. There's stuff in there, but the shadows make it hard to discern."

"Understood. Assume the sentries are trained well," Stephens said. Kyle nodded. He'd been suspicious anyway, but now he saw the threat.

"Oh?" Wiesinger asked.

"That's a soldier, an Army deserter, I would guess."

"Oh?" Again.

"He has most of a uniform, a fairly military bearing, and an SS carbine," Stephens patiently explained, saving Kyle more aggravation.

"Agreed," Wiesinger said. Kyle tried not to groan. It had been fairly obvious to him what they were looking at. Likely, all Indonesians looked the same to Wiesinger. He really wasn't that observant. They swapped intel for ten minutes, or more accurately, Kyle and Stephens did. Wiesinger did at least confirm a lot of what they saw, but offered little additional insight. He even complained about the cost of a conference call by satellite. Kyle clicked off and then sighed.

Two hours of observation gave good, refined maps and not much else. There wasn't much activity. What there was was hard to pin down. Kyle positively identified a dozen people in addition to the three guards. But there were signs of habitation elsewhere—clothes hanging out a window to dry, fresh trash, other indications. There could be a large force here.

Kyle's phone buzzed again. It was Wiesinger. "I'm calling this done. Let's head back."

"Roger."

It was important to make the exfiltration as smooth and silent as the infiltration. Being done didn't mean the threat level changed. Kyle was half afraid Wiesinger would stand up and walk out, as he had a few days earlier. But he showed decent aptitude. Though Kyle did spot him from fifty meters away when they were a good kilometer out. He almost tripped over Stephens, who was within ten meters when he whistled and stood.

The three headed back in the same skulking crouch they'd used on the way in. Kyle felt . . . odd. Sometimes he felt lighter afterward, threat diminished. Sometimes he felt more burdened from fatigue. This time, he didn't feel much of anything, which was bothersome. He was either too fatigued or too mentally strained to care. That was dangerous.

Anda had different intel when she returned. "I saw through the door. Looked like a child."

"Child," Kyle muttered.

"How sure are you?" Wiesinger asked.

"Quite sure. Small height. Long hair. White socks and short skirt or trousers."

Kyle said, "Probably. I can't think why else we'd find someone of that description."

"I count twenty-three men." She gave descriptions and locations.

"Hell, I counted five more, allowing for the ones that positively compare," Kyle said. Wade counted two others, and Stephens another. There were almost certainly more than that, asleep, on patrol, or out running chores.

"What's our approach then, gentlemen?" Wiesinger asked.

"Backup," Stephens said. "Tell the Kopassus where it is. Let Indonesia take the bite. They're competent, they'll have troops trained for hostage rescue specifically, and can overwhelm this group."

"I agree," Wade said, after swapping a glance with Kyle.

"I am not happy with the government," Bakri said. "But if I am not associated with this group, my position is better. I agree it should be done."

Wiesinger looked anguished. He was being advised to throw the book away and violate policy, procedure and State Department regs. But this was Defense, not State, and Kyle frankly didn't care what some suit with a theory thought. It took several seconds, but the man came to a decision.

"I'll call," he said. "Who do I call?"

Everyone looked askance.

"I'll search online," Wade said. Once connected, it took ten minutes for him to find an Indonesian government Web site with links to the Aceh province. A bit more digging turned up a phone number to the regional police office.

Wiesinger dialed the number. "Do you speak English?" he said. "Yes. I know the location of the two hostages, the woman and her daughter. Yes. My name is . . . Robert Richardson." He hadn't paused much. Kyle grudgingly gave him credit. "Yes, they are in the facility at Tolol. There are more than twenty men armed with rifles. I saw others to the west—" They were actually to the east—"but they seemed to be a different group. When I spoke to them, they said they were scouting timber. That is all I can tell you, but they are definitely there right now." He clicked off.

"So we wait," Stephens said.

"Shall we back away, boss?" Kevin Fuller asked.

"We might want to. Assume they'll use the road or aircraft."

"Why stay at all?" Wiesinger asked.

"Because someone will escape, no doubt, and we want to get that person for more intel. Meantime, we're surveillance."

Another night in the dark, but they did have food that had been brought by the now departed trucks. There was no reason to have anything within several kilometers that could be seen by infrared or visually from the air.

It wasn't very satisfying, Kyle thought, to travel halfway around the world and do recon the locals were capable of doing, just so Uncle Sam could have an official report, and then hand the task off locally. But really, this was a bigger event than they were trained or equipped for. The second round of hostages and the second bomb were too sensitive. But they'd intercepted several tons of explosive and tracked a source, as well as taking out one sizeable cell. It might seem like nothing but days of hiking in rain forest and watching state-built villages, but it had been worthwhile. The action of the last two missions had spoiled him.

"That's what it's like, mate," Iverson had said, while Fuller and Stephens nodded. "We spend weeks or months creeping around in the crud, calling back reports, and they tell us we did a fine job. Half the time we don't know why."

Kyle couldn't see them in the dark. They were just vague shadows. It was really dark when the moon was down, with canopy above them and growth all around. That did mean they should be well hidden from anything passing by.

They ate cold rice with water buffalo, veggies, and peppers. It was a bit slimy here and there where fat had congealed, but it beat the Chicken with Noodles MRE all to hell. The Chicken with Noodles was flat, tasteless, bland slop. With that at the bottom end, and some very tedious unseasoned rice in other parts of the world, the local cuisine was quite respectable.

Everything was in their rucks, and they sat back wearing them. They might have to move on a second's notice. Besides the risk of losing gear was the risk of leaving evidence. Even if it didn't trace back to the troops, it left suspicion, and it was sloppy. So they all sat geared up and ready to move. The Americans had their helmets back on, in case of fire. It was easier to wear them than carry them. Kyle's had been in his ruck since they landed, the soft headgear preferable for what they'd been doing. But if they were to move fast or take possible fire, he was going to wear it. He and Wade also had thin, police body armor that would stop many pistol rounds or slow rifle bullets. It couldn't hurt and might help, especially against fragments.

There wasn't a safe way to play cards without risking losing some of them. Talking was contraindicated. Dozing wasn't approved of, but was hard to avoid. At least the weather was clear and warm, and it was easy and comfortable to drift off. Kyle did so, trusting the active sentries and enough of the rest to be alert. It wouldn't take much of a hint to wake him, anyway.

Some hours passed. The military could respond within minutes by helicopter, as they had done many times before. They could respond on the ground within an hour or so. It might take time to confirm the story or marshal troops, but the response itself should be quick.

Or it could be that they were infiltrating already. It was near midnight. The infiltration might be silent, but once the shooting started, everyone should know. Still, the delay was frustrating.

"Where the hell are the government troops?" Wiesinger called in a harsh whisper. He was obviously agitated.

"I doubt they're operating on our schedule, sir," Kyle replied. Every time you added a variable, things got more screwed up. Relying on any government to be there when you needed it was foolish.

Now it was possible the target would bail out again. Enough well-placed attacks and they'd figure out, if they hadn't already, that someone was closing in. In which case, they'd either disappear, go on the offensive against the much smaller unit, or pull some kind of fuck-you gesture that would kill a lot of people.

Really, this mission had been badly set up, and it was probably no one's fault. State didn't want foreign troops with U.S. intel, neither did CIA or NSA. There wasn't any way to field a large enough U.S. force. The choice of troops was wrong. Just like operations that required stealth, where the first reaction of the President or Congress was to toss in the Marines, who were first class shock troops, but not the kind for a subtle approach. Here, snipers for intel and precision shooting were being used as deep roving scouts and in a position that really required a suit with connections. Last time they'd had that, they'd just provided the shooting. This time . . .

The whole point of using snipers was to avoid a face to face. In Pakistan, even when things went to hell, the al Qaeda target had had no idea what was happening until Kyle put two bullets through him. A face to face here was inevitable.

"Right," Wiesinger said, "I'm going to make a close patrol to get better intel. Bakri, I need one good man to go with me. Kyle, Wade, you provide overwatch from here. Stephens, can two men follow for backup against patrols, in case I need to exfil?"

"Yes, Mel," he agreed. "Though I recommend extreme caution. Any discovery at this point could be bad." He was trying to hint that the idea was insane. If the military showed up on the ground while he was patrolling, Wiesinger would be a target himself.

"I concur, Mel," Kyle said. "I advise against it. Very strongly. But I'll give you all the backup I can if you go ahead."

"I am," Wiesinger said. He didn't get the hints. He didn't sound scared, either. Either he was a lot braver than Kyle had figured him for, or he really had no clue what he was doing. The first was bad—it indicated recklessness. The second was potentially lethal.

"I will go," Anda said. She looked scared but determined, which Kyle thought was a good combination.

"Ah . . . why you?" Wiesinger asked, and the question was obviously posed because she was female.

"I know the area and are small enough to hide. Scout is what I do," she said.

Bakri just nodded. "Hati hati," he said. *Be careful.*

"Okay," Wiesinger agreed, looking unsure. "How long do you need to get ready?"

She checked her weapon, unslung her pack, downed most of a canteen in a few gulps, and said, "Ready." She had the SS1 she'd acquired as booty from some battle across her chest and extra magazines filling her pockets and disrupting her slim figure.

It was almost amusing to see big, bulky Colonel Wiesinger confused and unable to handle a woman half his age and size.

"I'll call with reports," he said. "Expect us back in six hours." He shouldered his patrol pack and ported the M4 he held.

"Mel, if you can't talk for stealth reasons, blow Morse Code into the mouthpiece," Wade said.

"Uh . . . I don't know Morse," he admitted.

"Well then, blow SOS if you're in trouble, wait five minutes and fire a burst if needed. We'll find you," Stephens said reasonably.

"Right." He stood for a moment, nodded at Anda, turned and walked off.

Everyone held the tableau until he was safely distant. Stephens snickered tightly. While his advice was workable, the intent had clearly been to shake the man up.

"I think he missed the whole point of being a sniper," Kyle muttered.

"Actually, Wiesinger's almost like a sniper," Wade said. "Except that he does it up close, without a lot of thinking, and doesn't aim much."

"Funny. I notice you tell more jokes when you get scared. How funny are you feeling right now?"

"Like Robin Williams, only darker and younger," Wade replied, glibly and without pause.

"Shit."

15

FAISAL WAS DISTRAUGHT. AT SOME POINT, they'd crossed a line into sin. He didn't know where that line was, but he was quite sure they were past it.

Killing infidels and using them as object lessons for others was something he'd learned to accept.

However, the current events struck him as very wrong. Imam Ayi said that they were not to rape or torture the new hostages, and expected that to satisfy Faisal's reservations. The group would hold them safely until the West succumbed to logic and faith and removed itself from Islamic affairs. Or, as seemed likely with the recalcitrant dogs, the hostages would be quickly and mercifully killed to reinforce the demand. Their bodies would hang for all to see.

Except, no matter the scripture and Ayi's interpretation, Faisal couldn't accept the killing of a little girl and a woman as justified. At every prayer he begged Allah to intercede and to show him what was right. By Muslim law, these were innocents. By Western law, both were merely family members and not active participants. No matter the shock value that would be gained, some things were unacceptable to God and man.

Only, God was silent.

He needed the advice of the imam, but couldn't admit why. That was disturbing in itself. But if he asked gently, wisdom might reveal itself bit by bit. He rose and left the hut, grabbing his rifle on the way. The walk would help him phrase his questions.

The foremost question was why he could get no answers. That was innocuous enough. He had that ready to ask when he reached the long, low building that served as the mosque, and also as Agung's headquarters.

The imam had tea steeping, and invited him in. Faisal studied him. His eyes seemed to be both at peace and driven. An intensity of peace. Faisal longed for that feeling himself, rather than shadows of doubt. He wouldn't mind a beard, either, rather than the scraggly growth he wore.

He accepted a cup of tea, and inhaled the aroma. It was sweet and fresh and fragrant. By itself, it cleared the mind. A sip teased his taste buds, adding another sensation added to all that he felt.

"You are troubled," Imam Ayi said. "Tell me and I will see what I can offer."

Faisal hesitated, then blurted out, "What does it mean when God is silent?"

"God is never silent. One simply has to look for Him and His message. What is your question?" he probed.

"I am not sure, Pak Hajji." Pak Hajji, father of the Haj, the pilgrimage to Mecca. Would Faisal be able to make that trip someday? "There are issues of rightness in my thoughts that I must find answers for. Issues I can't properly put into words." He was leery of discussing his qualms. They might get him removed from the cause, his loyalty questioned. He was totally loyal and wished to serve, so he saw no point in suggesting otherwise. He held the cup tightly, not realizing it.

"Then pray as you do. Sooner or later, when Allah sees fit, He will show you your questions and answer them. You will know."

"Thank you, Pak Hajji." The wisdom was beyond his comprehension. He'd have to think it over for a while.

"In the meantime, drink tea and think. I find it clears the mind."

Faisal hoped something would.

Kyle was woken from a restless sleep at dawn. "What?" he asked, snapping awake and raising his rifle.

"Easy," Wade said. "Wiesinger got captured."

"Oh, fuck me." No, it wasn't a nightmare. It was all too real.

"Yeah. Anda came back, said they got close and he insisted on going in closer. Someone saw him and they gave chase. Firefight, which Stephens heard an hour ago, and they seemed to want him alive."

"Right." Something occurred to him, and he asked very softly, "How sure are we of Anda?" Ripples were running up his spine. She had suggested going, was trying to charm Bakri, and he might not be catching hints of . . .

"She is in tears, sobbing and hyperventilating. Poor girl thinks she's created an international incident by 'losing' the American colonel."

"Good. I mean, not good but . . ."

"I understand you."

"Right," Kyle said. He was still waking up, eyes gritty even without the abuse of previous battles. Damn, they were taking serious fire this time. Worse than Bosnia. He was starting to get a grasp of what an earlier generation had dealt with in Vietnam. They had his increasing respect and sympathy. This crap sucked.

"So we need to figure out what to do," Wade hinted.

Kyle woke up the rest of the way. He was the ranking American. Non-Americans couldn't decide on this mission, so he had the job.

His buzzing phone saved him from an immediate answer.

He fumbled it out of his pocket. "Kyle," he answered.

"Kyle, Gilpin here. You heard about the colonel?" Mister Gilpin was the civilian executive for General Robash. He had a hellacious GS something pay grade and was retired military himself.

"Yes, sir. Working on it now. I'm guessing you got a call from the enemy?"

"Yes. What the hell happened?" The man might be a civilian, but he had the decision-making authority that General Robash did. This was no time for bullshit, and Kyle wasn't the party on the spot—the colonel had made the decision himself.

"He was on a patrol and got captured. The other element returned and told us."

"Right. Well, they want a million dollars into an account, they want Indonesia to release a number of prisoners, and they're adding him to the bargaining over the 'imperialistic venture between American corporate whores and the Javanese occupiers known as Pertamina.'"

"Sounds about right. What time frame?"

"Twenty hours from now. Frankly, we won't miss a colonel, or even you guys. No offense, it's just the situation."

"I understand perfectly, sir. That's why we're here. But you need those civilians."

"At the very least. And any leads on the explosives for the oil terminal. We concur on that threat, and that's now the priority."

"That one's a bitch, sir. Could be a truck, a plane, lots of people with crates. Really nothing we can do about it. Which is why I concurred with the colonel's decision to tell Jakarta." He was sticking his neck out here.

"Yes, so did I," Gilpin said. "And State are a bunch of assholes who can't make a decision without a formal meal and a five-star hotel. General Robash is trying to take over again, and I'm insisting he rest, so if you can offer any good news, it'll help him, too."

"Best reason of all, sir. How is he?"

"On his feet most of the time, sitting some, a bit short of breath, some pain, bitching about not being able to smoke cigars again, and threatening to kick someone's ass if he's not given a sitrep."

"Damn! That's good news." He smiled. "But we'll do everything we can, especially if it'll keep the general calm."

"Good man. I know you can't give me nightly briefings to tuck me in the way Wiesinger does—" it was the first Kyle had heard of that, but hardly surprising—"but do keep me in the loop."

"Will do, sir. What do we do about exfiltration?"

"From where you are, we're going to get you to the north coast. Any advance notice appreciated. You'll be met by mammals."

Mammals. SEALs. It wasn't a code per se, it was just away to avoid using a word that would excite anyone overhearing it at either end. "Understood. Can you get a satellite map of this facility . . ." He grabbed a map and read off coordinates. "Those are as close as I can get."

"I downloaded those to Wiesinger's laptop earlier."

"Dammit, he didn't tell me or make a backup."

"I'll send them again. Which account?"

Kyle spelled out his address and said, "So let's get it done."

"Good luck."

Kyle clicked off. "The general's bitching up a storm about not being in charge," he said.

"Hot damn, he's going to make it," Wade said with a grin.

"Yeah. And we're in danger of losing a colonel."

"Good news all around," Stephens joked as he came up behind. Kyle and Wade might think that, but would never say so out loud except in very secure quarters between themselves.

"But we've got twenty hours, and those two civilians are at stake, too. Suggestions?"

"Only one," Stephens said. "But I don't think you'll like it."

"What?"

"You get into the building where they are, off any threats, and shoot anything that moves."

"If we can get in there, I'm all in favor," Kyle said. "If the government shows up then, we're in a much better bargaining position, even if we have to relay by phone. They don't dare risk the hostages." He got the laptop plugged into the phone and dialed the server. A large file was waiting for him.

"I dunno," Wade said. "Jakarta knows that. Does their local commander know that?"

"Well, a frontal assault is out," Kyle said. "I'd want ten times the force we have to consider it."

"How about a frontal diversion?" Stephens asked. "Make a lot of noise, draw them out, subject them to fire from as many directions as possible while another group goes in to get the hostages? We are trained for that."

"Good, but are the three of you enough?" Kyle asked.

"Dunno. There aren't really any good options here."

"Or else we try to nail them through windows. Then the distraction, then the assault."

"Problem is," Kyle said, "we need more troops trained on sniping and hostages than we have, plus a good infantry commander as well. I hate to say it, but we could really use Mel here."

"That just tells me how much things suck," Wade said.

"Yeah, well, we knew that. Let's talk to Anda."

The woman arrived at once. "Yes?" she asked as she slipped into their shelter.

"Tell us everything you can." Kyle laid out the map he'd sketched and the satellite map. The latter was more accurate, the former probably easier for an amateur to read.

Nodding, she began. "We approach, low and slow. Then we crawl. We come in this way here," she indicated on Kyle's sketched map. "There is large tree with big roots. Good to hide, but causes trips. Then we move over here. We see backs of buildings like you did, but not more. We walk all the way south around to here, where I was earlier. Mel say he want to get closer. I tell him two hundred meter! Two hundred meter safe, closer are plants cut. He point to high area of ground, say he stay behind it and look. I move back by pipe, keep small. He crawl out, low. Did good, but patrol come between us. They see and move in. He try to shoot, get one, only wound. They circle him. He try to move back, but they move in closer. He did kill one, but rifle snatched and he beaten to ground. I wanted to help, but would have meant catched."

"Yes it would. You did the right thing by coming back," Kyle said. Son of a bitch. The asshole had been too eager on low ground, hadn't waited to ascertain patrols, and probably wanted to show up the local girl, if not Wade, by moving closer to prove something. Moron.

And they'd taken him without shooting him. So they might want intel, too. Would they kill him for publicity, or keep him and torture him? The deadline was much more important now.

"Sorry. I want to help," Anda said.

"Anda, you did a good job, really. This isn't your fault. Mel should know better. But you say he was alive?"

"Yes, beaten down, dragged along, then marched on feet. They took his things."

"Well, boys and girls," Kyle said, "that gives us an additional complication, seeing as we're bound to rescue Mel."

Jack gave a wry chuckle and said, "Better you than me, mate. Better you than me."

"And they know he's American, since they called our contact. That makes him much more valuable to them as someone to threaten. At least as they see it."

"Well, we can't leave him behind," Wade said. He didn't need to add *much as I'd like to*. "So we'll take him into the calculations. And the gear he lost."

"Right. Which included some grenades. Wonderful."

Faisal stared at the American. The man was *huge*, bigger than Wismo, and most of it wasn't fat. Certainly he was overweight a little, but he was not far from two meters tall, possibly a hundred and ninety centimeters. He had to break one hundred kilos. His shoulders were almost twice as broad as Faisal's.

And his gear was all military—rifle with grenade launcher, ammunition, knife, water bladder. It was nice gear, too. Faisal lusted after it, and they'd said he could have his choice of an item after they beheaded him or if he was ransomed. The men who'd caught him had already demanded the rifle and backpack. Faisal thought that back-mounted canteen a marvelous creation. Or the GPS unit.

He tried not to be nervous as he eyed the new bargaining chip. The man was blindfolded and tied to a chair. He should look terrified, but didn't. That was a disturbing sign.

Or was that a tremor? Yes, it was. He was scared, and that was reassuring. Faisal caught his courage again. Yes, the man should be afraid. He was helpless.

"Untie me and fight me like a man," the American said. Faisal spoke English and understood him. The tone was arrogant and demanding. Even tied, there was no submission.

"Guess you don't speak English," his soon-to-be victim said. "But if you're expecting me to beg, fuck you."

Faisal didn't catch the obscenity exactly. He'd heard it around the oil crews and knew it was rude. Still, this man was not acknowledging his position and didn't seem remorseful over the political situation. He was conceited, smug. It made Faisal furious.

At another level, he wondered what killing this man would accomplish. He left, silently, as he'd been told. Silence was intimidating. Actions, not words. He glanced at the Chinese woman, stoic and silent in her terror, and the little girl, wrung of all emotion. She was too young to grasp what was actually going to happen. All she knew was, she was scared. Days of tears were gone. All she did now was sit.

He really wasn't sure where this was to go. Part of him wanted revenge for his brother, dead because of a fight at the oil refinery. But the actual killing had been by government troops. The Americans were mostly making a living, like the Indonesians they hired. A damned good living, especially the executives, but they weren't hateful. This was a soldier sent to fight their war, so he was a fair target. But he was also a soldier like Faisal, and he could see himself in a similar position. The Quran spoke of mercy, but was that mercy misplaced on enemies who'd show none? And what of a man's wife and daughter? Yes, it would pain that man, but was it really necessary for innocents to die?

It was a quandary he'd needed to consider for some time. Except . . . he hadn't discussed his quandary with Imam Ayi. He'd been afraid to mention the real issue. Why was that?

It was because he knew what reaction that would get: He would be disgraced and driven away, mistrusted and sneered at. Just for questioning. Yet did not the Quran tell them to test their faith? It shouldn't be a sin to ask for guidance.

Unless the matter at hand was a sin, in which case none would speak of it.

Faisal opened his eyes and sat back. A sudden surge flowed through him. Despite their differences, Ayi had been correct. He had spoken the truth. Through an object of sin, a message had come regarding rightness.

It was time, and Allah had made his wishes known. God is great, all praise be to God.

And now he knew what he had to do. It might mean death or disgrace, but it was Allah's wish. I am but a slave of Allah, he thought as he stood. There was no fear within him, despite the dangers to his body and reputation. There was no fear, because his soul was ready to do Allah's bidding and await His justice.

The tiny platoon slipped closer. Kyle was quite impressed. This group knew the jungle, knew patience and stealth. They didn't move without orders, and didn't stop without them. A few weeks of professional polish and they'd be a first-class infantry unit. If there was any way to get the Indonesian government . . .

No, politics wasn't his venue. Stick to the military side. Though he didn't crave to read about Bakri, Anda, and the others in some newspaper.

They'd spent all day approaching from two different directions. It was afternoon again. Kyle was starting to hope for some kind of ending. He hadn't dared take his boots off in the last three days, and his feet were itching, stinking, and hurting. He worried about athlete's foot or other fungoids, rot or rash or infected blisters. People died from foot problems. While that wasn't likely, he didn't crave long hospitalization or surgery, either.

With this many people, twenty-three without the colonel, they were creeping. They were paired or in threes, watching each other, watching behind, watching ahead, trying to close in on a facility that had to know of their presence. It was a wonder everything hadn't been loaded into vehicles and taken away, but there were no vehicles on-site—probably due to the risk of discovery. The captors apparently didn't crave to walk out on foot with two distinctive hostages who might be seen by aircraft. That actually was a slim risk. Visibility from altitude while moving wouldn't be clear. But without troops experienced in aviation, they probably didn't know that. Clearly, they were reluctant to enter the jungle where other forces might be.

So the good news was that the bad guys were bottled up for now. The bad news was that they were cowardly, sociopathic little fucks to start with, and might panic. Kyle had heard this called "Murphy's Law of Thermodynamics." Things got worse under pressure.

He ate scraps as they moved. Leftover apple jelly from the MREs, some hard candy, cracker sections. Likely they'd see no more food until this was over.

It was near dark, and he was losing track of

days and time. It was never really light down there. But in twelve hours at most, the hostages would be killed. It didn't get much darker than that. The Straits of Malacca and the surrounding waters would be full of Chinese, Indian, Singaporean, American, and Indonesian vessels, and everyone would want a piece of GAM and any other rebels. The low-intensity civil war would turn into a slaughter. It could even become major.

Kyle was still musing, awaiting a report from the advance scouts. They were within a few hundred meters of their target, just over a kilometer, choosing every meter before moving, relaying messages by crawling and delivering them in whispers, or by hand signs.

A hiss ahead alerted him to an approach. He looked up to see Anda, Syarief, and someone who seemed to be their prisoner.

"We bring him to you," Anda said. "As my commander order. I would kill him."

"Well, let's see what he says," Kyle said, looking him over. Skinny, young, dressed in cheap clothes. Anda might really want him dead, or just be playing bad cop. He'd see where it went.

"My name is Faisal and I know where the hostages are, and also an American soldier."

"Shit. This is either Lady Luck rolling a seven, or painting us with a huge target," Wade said as he shimmied up.

Kyle nodded. "Fairy Godmother or Practical Joke Department. Guess it's my call."

"He says. I don't trust him," Anda said.

"What can you tell us?" Kyle asked.

"Will you give me your word you will not harm me? Or let the government?"

"Son, I can't speak for the Indonesian government. I won't harm you. I can ask our State Department to help you if you help us. But I won't promise something I can't deliver." He noticed the boy—man—didn't ask for protection from the locals. Either he thought that fruitless, or he was willing to take his chances. That meant something. But what?

"That is fair," the boy agreed. He was in turmoil over something. "I must tell you something bad."

"I'm sure we've heard worse," Wade said.

"It is I who cut the head off Keller. I know now it was wrong and not Allah's way." The words were out in a rush.

"Jeeeeezus," Kyle burst out. Rage gripped him, and he gripped his rifle. But he didn't raise it. Anda swore quietly but brightly in Achinese and reached for a knife. Wade waved her down.

"I was to do it again tonight, to the woman and child. But I cannot. It cannot be right, it cannot be just. So I disobeyed and came here." He seemed very small and helpless, terrified of dying on the spot. But he stood and waited, eyes wide.

"Son, in this, your God and mine agree. You've done the right thing, and we'll do anything we can to help you." Kyle forced his hand to unclench. The kid had fucked up on a global scale, and in a way that Kyle was morally and legally bound to kill him for. But he'd admitted his mistake and wanted to make amends.

If he could help them bring down this gang of scum, that just might do it. Especially since he was facing death from his own people at this point.

"Can you draw a map and give us names and numbers?" he asked.

"I can."

Kyle wasn't inclined to trust the boy. He could still be a ruse. He wasn't saying anything yet, but there was no way this boy was leaving before Kyle was sure of his loyalties. Otherwise . . . well, he wasn't going to say anything. But shooting a spy was legally and morally safe, and far less bothersome than things Kyle had witnessed on this and other missions. He clutched at his knife briefly, because he didn't have a suppressor for the pistol, and would need a quiet kill.

Once provided a pen and paper, the boy began to draw. The map fit what they had on download and from recon, and the layout described was reasonable. So far, so good. The kid almost certainly didn't know there was a satellite providing data. Nor was he likely to know the limits of its resolution, so he could be challenged with the magic power of the satellite if need be, "magic" defined as "technology the boy couldn't explain and didn't understand." As to their own patrols, he could probably guess. He seemed to realize things were about to explode.

"How many people?"

"I'm not sure. It changes. More than one hundred today, I think. Many came in from an attack on the place where bombs are built. Kopassus, they said."

Kyle avoided grinning. That his group was being mistaken for the feared Indonesian elite was good for PR. Wait until the word got out that it was six Westerners and a handful of locals.

"We heard about that attack," he said. "You're sure this is where the hostages are?"

"Yes. A Chinese woman and her child and a large American man who speaks rudely."

"That would be him. Windows and doors on that building?"

"Windows are glass, but usually raised. Doors are wood."

That was useful. "Okay, we'll talk this over. Anda, don't kill him. Just keep him here."

"I understand." She switched to local dialect and said what had to be "Come here, boy."

Kyle liked her. She took no shit. She shot well. She was quiet and soldierly. There were some women like that in the U.S. military, but not nearly enough. Political Correctness had devalued soldiering in favor of a sensitive image. That called for cute uniforms, makeup, and press releases, and no harsh language. Anda probably didn't own makeup or heels and swore like any other soldier, in a very crude, personal fashion. She was all business.

As the locals left, he turned to Wade. "Right, so what do we do?" Kyle asked. He was running out of ideas.

"First thing is to get around to where Mel is," Wade said. "And then we need a large force to raid. In addition to a large diversion while we snatch him."

"Or," Kyle said, "what they *think* is a large raiding force. How much ammo do we have?"

"Close to a thousand rounds for all three weapons."

"That should be enough."

"What do you think?"

"I think we have the locals go in the front, led by Stephens. They stop short of actually entering. They fire the place up loud. We're in place to shoot through the windows at anyone we see. Requires us to be spread slightly, and we'll need our phones open. Thank God Wiesinger let us all bring phones. One phone would be as useless as tits on a boar."

"Right," Wade said. "Call the Aussies and Bakri? And we need to get a bit more on our informant. He showed up too soon."

"Have him call Jakarta and report it just before we attack?"

"Good. Very good," Wade agreed, grinning a yard of teeth.

Kyle called Stephens in and explained the situation. Stephens agreed.

"Sure, I can make noise. I also have no authority to throw my command away. Much as I want to help, noise is it, then we have to skedaddle. If I wind up dead, command will kill me. If I don't wind up dead and create an incident, command will kill me. I was advised today in no uncertain terms that unless I have a reasonable prospect of acquiring more intel, I'm to sever ties and continue my mission, which is recon and intel for my government."

"Understood, and I'm sorry for taking you for granted," Kyle said. He realized he had been. The Aussies were not part of his command.

"Hey, glad to help. Wish I could stick around. Sounds like a bit of a bash."

"That's the idea. Anyway, you lead the locals, get a good amount of attention and fire, and we'll shoot from the back. If we can break loose or secure our objective early, count on us to drop quite a few." Kyle figured they could each drop a man every five seconds if they weren't seen. That was conservative. If no one tracked their fire, one minute would be twenty-four out of the hundred dead. But that assumed they secured their objective. Likely, they'd be extracting under fire. Which was going to suck.

"Now, who's carrying the hostages?"

"I'll carry the adult," Wade said. "You lead. If

Wiesinger's healthy, he can carry her. That leaves you or I to take the child."

"And if Wiesinger's injured, we toss him a weapon and bid him good day."

"Nice thought, isn't it?" Stephens smiled under his moustache.

"Oh, I'm serious," Kyle said. "Our mission is the civilians first. Wiesinger's expendable, and I was told so on the phone. If he can't walk, I toss him a spare weapon—" other than his Ed Brown, which he wasn't parting with—"and he can cover the rear until backup arrives, either Indonesian or American. But I can't and won't jeopardize the mission for a commander who got himself captured."

"You sound so upset by that," Wade said.

"Maybe. I do hope we all come out. It's a pride and professionalism thing." He'd lost two people on these ops. He didn't want to lose a third. Disliking the man made it harder, if anything. Kyle didn't like being a judge of worth. Too much like playing God.

"Right. Let's get the details down further. We know they'll get fucked up anyway," Stephens said.

"Explosives," Wade said. "Bakri has that TNT."

"We use it?" Bakri asked.

"Some of it," Wade said.

"Good. We need detonators," Kyle said.

"I can spare some," Stephens said. "Fuller has a few. I can get resupplied."

"It also detonates when shot," Kyle said.

"Frequently," Stephens agreed. "But you can't bet on that. Use detonators. We should have some fuse you can light with a flame. We usually use a firing device, though."

"God, I'd hope so. Wish there was some way to put timers on them."

"I can do that," Fuller said as he arrived to Stephens's wave. "I have some. Usually they're for minutes or hours, but they'll dial down to seconds."

"How hard to activate?"

"How much risk can you face? If they're preset for time and mounted to the charge, press the button. But there's no safety."

The skin on the back of Kyle's neck crawled. A backpack full of HE and await a button to get pressed on something.

"Okay, with an M four, an SR25 and a spare for use on arrival, plus grenades, extra explosives and shock factor, we should be able to make a good entrance. I want small charges I can toss outside to keep threats at bay once we're in. I want something small enough to toss inside as a flashbang, even if it might cause minor injury. And I want a couple of large ones, a couple of pounds, that we can toss as ersatz artillery."

"Doable. Boss?" Fuller asked.

"Go ahead. I'll account for the fuses and detonators."

"Understood. Give me a few minutes." He nodded and slipped away.

"So," Stephens said, "we make a lot of noise, kill as many as we can?"

"By all means," Kyle said with a mock bow. "Thank you, Sergeant. Most appreciated."

"My pleasure."

"Mine, actually. But lots of noise and body counts. You use the distraction to rescue the damsels and the ogre. Let me know as soon as you've done that, because I need to didi mao like no one has ever maoed before."

"Yeah, it would be embarrassing if you got caught."

"It would bugger all. You yanks have a huge government, a corporate interest here and a lot of firepower. No one will fuck with you much. We live in these parts and have to deal with Indonesian refugees and smugglers, pirates and politicians. We dare not get caught."

"I understand," Kyle said. "I'll see that it's mentioned in the appropriate places that you not be thanked for the risks you aren't about to take since you aren't here."

"Good, as long as we all understand that."

"Okay, that's the rough plan. Now, for finer details . . ."

16

FAISAL MADE THE CALL AS REQUESTED. KYLE got the number from Gilpin, after a brief debate. Wiesinger probably could have had more authority if he'd just demanded it as necessary, rather than being a toady. Kyle called directly to the local military district this time—though "directly" was subjective. He had it patched through the military to a civilian line and back to Indonesia through some other cutout so it couldn't be traced.

After two rings, a male answered, "Malam." *Good evening.* Kyle handed the phone over to Faisal as soon as he confirmed contact.

"My name is Faisal Rachmat. I am reporting the location of the Chinese hostages, and an additional hostage who works for the oil company," he said. They'd decided not to admit to American military presence just yet. Stephens and Akbar were listening to his prepared speech, ensuring he followed the plan. So far, Akbar was nervous but agreeable. Like Bakri, he hated the government, but knew there wasn't much choice in this case.

"Yes, a woman named Lei Ling Park, now Madden, and her daughter Suzanne Kii Madden. The American I don't know the name of. The head of the camp is Agung, and Imam Ayi is advising them. The explosives for the oil terminal are to go off at noon. They left here aboard a lorry, gray, thirty-five-hundred-kilogram capacity, Mercedes . . ." He rattled off all he knew. It shouldn't take more than a few minutes for a military operator to realize this was real intel, not a hoax. It might be a setup, but it wasn't a fraud.

"I am doing it because I know it is wrong to kill women and children. The Achinese do not need this kind of reputation. Please stop the terrorists, they are enemies of us both." A moment later he handed the phone over to Stephens.

Stephens spoke briefly. "That's what we have. Hope the information is useful, mate. We're departing now. Goodbye." He handed the phone over to Kyle. The Aussie's voice would confuse the government further as to who and what was involved.

Kyle stared at the phone as he clicked it off. "Well, that's that. Well done, son. You've just become a good guy."

"What must I do now?" He looked nervous, excited, and a bit bothered.

"You stay with us," Kyle said. "We may need more information." He also wanted the kid where he could watch him, and might need to shoot him. It was a cold thought. Meantime, he'd have to deal with fighting with one foot in a bucket.

The platoon split for the last time. "Don't forget to call," Stephens said, grinning and batting his eyelashes. Kyle snickered. With that, the locals and the Aussies disappeared like ghosts. The local contingent was already on its way to the staging area. The Americans' gear was with Bakri, who had detoured away to provide vehicles for exfiltration.

Kyle felt very alone then. It was hard to find a more hostile area. At this point, anyone they met was an enemy. And some were putatively on the same side, which meant shooting at them was undesirable.

Kyle sucked down water. He was going to be expending a lot of energy shortly. It was hot already. He'd be soaked in sweat, and wanted extra liquid on hand. Other than that, he had weapons, ammo, body armor, and technical gear totaling fifty pounds or so. There was nothing light about infantry work. He would feel much more secure in the armor and helmet. It was familiar, so it was psychologically protective, too. But he couldn't wear the helmet and reach the scope properly. Given a choice between better defense and better offense, he chose offense. It was what he did, after all. But there was no point in lugging the helmet for later, so Bakri had it. Kyle would just have to be exposed for the duration.

"Okay," he said, and pointed. Wade slipped forward as point man. He walked carefully, lest his ghillie tangle in the brush.

They slipped into a position from which they could cover the building where the hostages were supposed to be. The "supposed" was key. They might have been moved, if anyone noticed Faisal gone. They might have been killed. Or they might be there with a battalion around them. But doing nothing definitely meant they'd die.

At a nod, Faisal moved out between them. He was painted with camo and covered in burlap rags that hung loosely. It wasn't as good as a ghillie, but it was easier to move in, had been fabricated in a few minutes and still broke up his silhouette. Kyle had the suppressor on the SR25 and was prepared to dump a match round through his brain if there was any sign of dissemblance. The kid might be remorseful, but he'd also sawed somebody's fucking head off. That wasn't easy to forgive.

Kyle followed along. He took tall steps to avoid kicking low growth, watching and feeling for his foot placement. He used no night vision equipment at present, relying on his natural sight. Once close enough to shoot, he had the night capabilities of the AN/PVS-10 scope.

Ahead, Wade sunk back down into the growth.

Faisal moved in behind and to his left. Kyle liked that position, and sat back a couple of meters, where he had a clear right-handed shot at the boy without risking Wade.

"Lie down flat," he told Faisal. That would put him in a position where a few seconds reaction time would be available, and he couldn't reach both soldiers in that time, though he might reach one.

"How's the view?"

"I've got a window, and an armed man," Wade said. "Nothing else yet. Let me relocate a few meters." He squirmed across the ground like a sidewinder, disturbing very little foliage.

Once settled in, he took another look. Through the phone he said, "Chair, legs. Hold on." One more move and he said, "Mel. Got him."

Faisal said, "The woman is to left, and the girl left of her."

"He's right so far," Wade said when Kyle relayed that.

Kyle said nothing. It was reassuring, though. The boy had ratted out the scumbags, had given correct data and was doing as he was told. It seemed he was what he said.

Kyle appreciated that. Given the choice between an unrepentant coward he'd have to kill and a kid who had a conscience and the guts to stand up when he knew things were wrong, the latter was a much better companion. No one said doing the right thing was easy. But it was often the judge of character.

"We need to get closer," Kyle said.

"We've got about ten hours," Wade said. "How close do you want to cut it?"

"I want at least two hours leeway, in case they get eager or spooked. Sooner is better. Exfiltrating in daylight would suck rocks. Then there's the government, who may just get out of bed and show up."

"I think I can get within one hundred meters in this growth. The problem is finding a good, clear field of fire I can move from in a hurry. Trees are handy, but these monsters are hard to climb and I'd be limited on field of view."

"Right. Any high ground? How much elevation do you need?"

"Three meters would do it. I see a rise over to our right. Might work. There's a downed tree with a root ball, too. If the angle is good . . ."

"Right, do it."

It took an hour of maneuvering to get good positions. Wade was standing, leaning through a root bulb and prepared to do so for hours if need be. He was effectively invisible from any direction, from more than a few meters away. Faisal was lying down where he wasn't visible and couldn't move fast. That was the lot of turncoats—no one ever trusted them completely. He seemed mature enough to know this and didn't complain. Kyle was on the rise, in a bush, carefully picking leaves off to clear his field of view slightly without letting the bare patch show.

Kyle phoned Stephens and gave him an update. "We're in position, we're checking objectives. Information is correct so far, say again, correct. We have visual contact."

"Roger. Say when. We're standing by, close and ready."

"Roger, out." He clicked back on to Wade, ten meters away on land and 48,000 miles away by phone, to avoid talking above a whisper. "Any time we decide, we're on."

"Roger. What are we looking for?"

"Fewest threats in the building. You have the door?"

"I can see the door. Anything coming through dies."

"Roger. I can cover right front approach. That leaves a blind left."

"So we've got at least a fifty-percent reduction in threat."

"Yeah, but we need one hundred."

"I know."

They really needed an entry team as well. They also needed satellite TV, couches, and hot dogs. They weren't getting those, either. The rule was to use the resources at hand.

"I don't think the conditions are going to get better," he said. "So let's wait and see if the traffic level drops."

"Roger. Right now there's six people in there. They're setting up the video and making sure the victims know."

"Cocksuckers. Just fucking cocksuckers." Kyle trembled with rage. He wasn't sure words existed for his state of mind.

Faisal started crawling. Kyle waved him over.

"Yes?" he asked.

"They will set up camera and lights, then count down the time, praying for Allah's help. They will shoot through the heart and then dress in clean clothes to hide blood. Then they cut heads with large knife."

"Understood. Tell Wade," he said. He handed over the headset. He was nauseous. This was worse than the corpses under Castle Bran, almost as bad as watching Nasima get shot in Pakistan.

Faisal spoke through the phone to Wade, then nodded. "He knows."

"Good. Wait some more. We do a lot of waiting in this business."

"I understand. I hope you can save them."

"We'll do everything we can." Though he wasn't sure what that could be.

"It's not going to get better that I can see," Wade said. "They come and go. Averaging six assholes in the latrine."

"Another distraction would be nice. A quiet one. Sports? A bar fight?"

"I can distract them," Faisal said.

"What?"

"I can distract them? Draw attention?"

"Oh, I heard you," Kyle said. "Are you sure?" He realized he'd let the boy get right up behind him. Then he realized he wasn't concerned.

"I can walk down and distract them. They know me."

"They're going to be very suspicious about you leaving and showing up."

"If I can get any outside, you have less inside. If I'm in the way . . . just shoot me, too. Save the girl."

"Son," Kyle said, "I can pick a fly off a cup. You'll be fine. You get them out, I'll nail them. Do it."

"Then I go now."

"Clean up first." Kyle soaked a bandage in water and handed it over. Faisal scrubbed his face, and dumped the ersatz ghillie. He was still dirty and grubby, but might pass.

"Clean enough?"

"Your face is, yes."

Faisal nodded faintly and stepped forward, an aura of calm around him.

"Allah be with you, son," Kyle said to his back.

"Thank you." He nodded again and slipped away.

"Brave kid," Kyle said into his phone.

"Yeah, I heard your side of it. I hope he can do it. A few seconds will make the difference."

"Yup."

Kyle watched as the boy picked his way through the growth. Kyle mostly trusted him. At the same time, the kid might, just might turn his coat again, now that everyone was brought in. It wouldn't make sense to blow cover like this . . . but at the same time, these weren't sensible people. And if they knew they were going to get nailed, they might decide to hold ready on the hostages and invite a firefight. If they could kill a bunch of troops and the hostages and pin the blame on "overeager soldiers" they just might. It was the kind of complex plan that appealed to amateurs, and did sometimes work.

But Kyle didn't believe it. The boy—man— seemed honest, and had given far too much intel for something like that.

But there was still a chance of fear taking him, once he was face to face again. Impressionable age.

Kyle was willing to take the risk. Even if the kid did waffle back like a second-rate politician, he'd still be a momentary distraction, and Kyle had trained for years to exploit those. That would be all the time he needed to start blowing away any threats inside.

Faisal reached the edge of the clearing, far back from the road, and stepped onto the ground. He wasn't seen at once.

"He's down," Kyle reported to Wade. Then he called Stephens.

There was a tension in the air. It was eagerness, fear and alertness, seasoned with a little bit of hate and cynicism. *No matter what happens, you gutless fucks aren't getting out alive*, Kyle thought.

"So let's do it. Ready?"

"Ready."

"Ready," Kyle lied, and called Stephens. "Commence in exactly three minutes. One eight zero seconds from . . . mark!"

"Three minutes, one eight zero seconds, understood. Six, seven, eight . . ."

"Confirmed. Out." He redialed. "Wade, in one six five seconds, one six four, one six three . . ."

"Roger. I will commence fire two seconds prior. Two seconds."

"Two seconds roger. Rangers' Bullets Lead The Way."

"Amen to that."

They stopped talking and got ready to shoot. Kyle wanted to peer inside, but Wade had that. He'd chosen to cover any approaching targets from outside. That meant faster but less-precise shots, so Wade would have fewer incoming threats. They had to hope for some slight confusion inside to keep the hostages alive for a few seconds. Once threats were minimized, they were storming the building and shooting everything except the hostages, with the explosives as distraction to give the impression of overwhelming force.

Wade's first shot was a muffled bang from back where Kyle had paused earlier. Kyle thought he heard a second one, but it was lost in a cacophonous roar from the front of the compound, diagonally from both sides of the road. It was nicely done, and four figures dropped.

"Three down," Wade reported. "Two more not in range."

"Damn. Get them." Kyle rose and moved. Wade was hidden and wouldn't be traced. So Kyle was now acting as a decoy for him, should anyone follow the shots back. He was also getting closer so he could pour out some fire.

"I think they're ready to do it," Wade said. "Oh, sonofabitch. We've got a roomful of scum and three hostages. That frontal assault has convinced them to do it now as a fuck-you gesture."

"Plan fast," Kyle said. "Save the girl first, mother second, Wiesinger third. I wish I could say it was personal, but he is a soldier on a mission. He's last." Dammit, they'd come from off to the left. He'd had no shots.

"Roger," Wade said from behind his scope. "I count eight targets. Cameraman should be last. The new knifeman is wearing khakis and a ball cap.

"Yeah, got it. Can we get closer?" He took a

careful look through his own scope as he snuggled up to a tree for cover and support.

"I don't think so. Better angle here, unless we get right up close or inside. If you shift a few meters left, I think we can create a fire zone around the hostages and just shoot anything that steps into view."

"Roger that. Anyone with a firearm has to be first. Once we have them down, we need to leapfrog in." He started moving in a crouch, quickly but stealthily.

"Yeah. Going to be rough."

"Faisal is out front," Wade added a few moments later. "I damned near bagged him by accident. He was talking to one of them."

"Dammit, why did he have to wait until now to choose the right side?" Kyle asked softly while he waited. He didn't realize it was aloud until Wade answered.

"Young, idealistic. The problem is there's no challenge and no army for kids like that. They imprint on the first powerful figure they meet, and in much of the world, it's a self-serving asshole. Get them to a recruiter and they turn into something else."

"Me," Kyle said. He recalled having the exact same thought a few days before.

"And me."

"Roger," Kyle said. "Get forward." Wade was a few meters closer. But Kyle couldn't move from his position until he knew there were no threats to his charges, or until Wade had a good, clear field of fire from a different angle. The lights went out in the building, which was a good sign. He clicked the scope to night vision and let his eye adapt to the monochrome.

Once they'd killed the lights, it took a few seconds to get reoriented. People were scrabbling about on hands and knees, slowly rising. Kyle chose one and put a bullet straight through the top of his head.

I know what the last thing to enter your mind was, asshole, he thought with a grin. He scanned for another and settled on an exposed hand that was just visible at the edge of the window. His shot shattered metacarpals and blew through the wrist. Now if he could find another wrist and the ankles, he'd crucify this motherfucker twenty-first century style.

I've got to calm down, he realized. He was taking too much pleasure. One should enjoy one's work, but not to this level under these conditions.

Maybe some of it was just relief over being able to shoot at last. He hoped so.

"I'm good," Wade said. "Move."

"Roger." He came off the scope and slipped forward again. He couldn't see Wade, which was good.

The noise up front continued. Rifle fire in two calibers was joined by machine-gun bursts and the occasional slam of explosives. He picked out an RPG round and what was probably an Australian grenade. Then there was the sound of TNT in small charges. Good. They should think the entire Indonesian Army was down on them.

"If you see a threat on the hostages, shoot ASAP," Kyle said. "And if I think you can get one of them through Faisal, I'll do it. I hate like hell to say it."

"He knows the risk."

"Yeah. So did Nasima. Doesn't mean I like it." Though Faisal had his own crimes that Nasima hadn't. Still, he was taking a big risk to do the right thing, and it always sucked to watch good people die.

"I know."

"We've got to advance. Cover them. I'm moving twenty meters. You follow."

"Roger."

Kyle stood and rushed.

It was a very unsniperlike tactic, but it was an infantry tactic. He took distance off with meter-long strides and slipped up behind a tree, leaning as high and far forward as he could to get some kind of field of view.

He really should ask about police work, executive protection, or Secret Service when he retired, he decided. This was exactly the type of work they did. The muzzle of his rifle was describing little circles. But the little circles here equaled large circles at one hundred meters, circles that encompassed the hostages. A figure stepped into the path of the circle, and Kyle didn't jerk or twitch. He simply let the muzzle drift around on its orbit, not forcing it, and snapped the trigger as it passed the appropriate part of the arc. He'd led just enough, and the bullet smashed through the back and shoulderblade of the threat.

There. Movement, and it wasn't female or Caucasian. He snapped off a shot and watched to make sure he'd hit. "Go, Wade!" he said.

Moments later, a bush with a rifle sprinted past. Wade took up position lower and closer. But they were losing angle while they gained proximity. A mucky depression behind the buildings was for runoff or sewage and would make advance and shooting awkward.

Kyle started his next run and caught a glimpse of movement just as he lowered the weapon and began to sprint.

There was no time to try to recover. He had the headset on and said, "Shoot now!" in a whisper.

Wade took the shot. Kyle didn't know how it worked, but he was momentarily in his next position, barely forty meters away. Wade would take another twenty on his next advance, probably to that corner there. Then they'd go around.

And he could just see a man with a raised pistol, chambering a round. His intent was obvious.

He shifted imperceptibly, bringing the reticle over the man's head. A squeeze of the finger and the window imploded in an instant before the man's brains blew out, scrambled by a 180-grain boattail match .308 bullet. The report clapped

Kyle's ears, followed at once by another report from Wade's weapon as he came past at a run. The muzzle blast was contained, but these were still supersonic bullets with a healthy crack. It wasn't deafening, but there was enough noise to be obvious.

Kyle sought another target, saw only a shadow against the wall thrown by stray illumination. There was no time for a good shot—the man was moving fast—but he put a bullet into the wall hopefully only a few inches away. If he could get someone to flinch, that gained seconds. Wade fired again. Kyle sprinted past and came right up to the tree line.

No one else had rushed the hostages as he lost sight of them. Wiesinger should have tried to throw himself on the civilians to give them cover with his ample bulk. He hadn't, that Kyle had seen. Kyle would give him the benefit of the doubt that he was either surprised or holding still to avoid spoiling a shot, rather than being paralyzed with fear. He was blindfolded, too. And holding still did make targeting easier. Wade should be in a much better position now.

In front and to the sides, he'd seen a huge mob forming. Everyone was bent on killing those hostages. Brave men. Big, strong, powerful men. There were three Aussies and a dozen Indonesians out front, and they'd show the world their manhood by killing a little girl, a woman, and a man tied to a chair.

Kyle wanted to puke.

Still, a mob of cowards might be easier to handle when he went charging in among them. He'd drop the SR25 and unsling the M4 banging against his ass. That would give him one hundred rounds and a 40mm canister, which in his line of work they jokingly called a nice helping of Have a Shitty Day. He was two buildings away and on flat ground. One hundred meters and a bit. Easy range for him.

Faisal slipped back into camp. He'd been gone eight hours, which wasn't too suspicious, unless someone had gone looking for him. In that case, he was about to die. Allah be praised. He'd trust Allah to show him where he must go.

"Faisal! There you are!" Wismo called. "Where have you been? You're a mess!"

"Sleeping. And toilet. Then I took a walk and fell." He showed a muddy streak on his trousers. "I had to wash and, and then it was time to pray. Breakfast. It's been a really busy night. Are we ready?"

"Ready, yes. You're late! Ayi is looking for you. They're going to start the killing soon, and film before dawn."

"I'm sorry. I'll hurry right over. They didn't agree to our terms, then."

"No," Wismo sounded disappointed. "But you wait! The Chinese are sending warships, and the Americans, and the bloody Hindu Indians. It's a sea full of impotent infidels, trembling at our word!"

"Very nice." He didn't think so anymore. Would the Chinese use nuclear weapons? American cruise missiles? The Army send a million troops to burn the jungle clean? Would the entire Asian sphere invade? This wasn't a game to be played at this level. "Have you a few moments? We can talk."

"I suppose. You didn't get the news when you woke up?"

"No, I was praying on what I am to do. Allah is favoring us. That many nations and ships brings hope for a war of scriptural size. Isn't it grand?"

"Indeed."

It was reasonable that he head toward the hostages. He just couldn't appear too eager or too reluctant. That, of course, put him closer to the fight. He realized now he wasn't in a hurry to die. If need be, yes, but not as an assumed course.

It was troubling, all the changes he was feeling. He'd been secure in his place. Now he wasn't.

The trick now was to get close to the building, but not yet inside. He was needed out here, to distract people. To kill them. He'd killed before, or helped, and it had been heady and exciting. This was harder.

Harder . . . because they'd fight back. But he couldn't admit that. That was a sign of cowardice. Allah had given him this test. Could he kill when there was threat to his own life? That is what he had to face. He was loitering in front, speaking softly so Ayi didn't look for him at once. There was a rack right outside with rifles. He couldn't pick one up yet, because there was no reason to.

"Hey, Faisal, where's your pedang?" Wismo asked. He'd noticed at last. The knife had been taken when he surrendered.

"Oh, I'll have to get it. Thanks for reminding me." Where were those shots? It had to be time.

He was saved from further stalling by the bullets he was hoping for and dreading. As the shooting commenced, with two simultaneous bangs, Faisal said, "It's an attack! Give me a weapon!"

Wismo had been frozen. He nodded stupidly and grabbed an AK from the rack.

"Come! Let's get them!" Faisal shouted, waving his arm and running for the door and the rack. He paused and turned, making sure Wismo followed him. "God is great! We fight!"

With that he jogged a few yards back from the door.

"Kyle, Faisal has an AK. I'm still worried about trusting him."

"Kill him if you have to. I hate to say it, but we can't risk it."

"Yeah. He's not an immediate threat yet."

"Roger," Kyle said. The man could be trying to play the act, or provide cover, or just defend himself. He could also be a threat. It was hard to know where his loyalty lay at this juncture. Dammit, he'd been an enemy, a turncoat, an ally and now was a threat again.

Kyle sprinted up the side of the adjoining building in a sideways crab that kept his back to the wall. A few more seconds . . .

All Faisal could do now was what he felt to be right. Allah would guide his hand. If he was to live or die, he would know soon enough. He'd been prepared to give his life to kill others. He felt a sudden thrill that his life might save others. He didn't know Kyle Monroe's musings on the subject, but at that moment he understood the principle exactly. This was what a man died for.

No. This was what a man *lived* for.

Yet the irony was that he would have to kill so others might live. There was so much in this world to consider, so many things he'd never had time for. His emotions were cascading through him, thoughts flashing. He realized his devotion had been to blindness. The leaders didn't want him to see the world outside of a narrow scope. There were so many ways to look at events, depending on viewpoint, so many things that one could never hope to learn them all. *That* was the greatness of Allah—that he could create a universe so grand it was beyond comprehension.

That, too, was worth living for.

In a euphoric haze of revelation, adrenaline,

and fear, he spun. Bambang was out the door, the others bunched up just inside. He waited as they staggered and shoved, firing one shot high into the jungle to make it look as if he was doing something. A deceit, yet for right. He'd decided that wasn't possible. Now he was doing it again. So gray, this world. How to decide right and wrong?

The AK kicked into his shoulder as he fired. Half the magazine, about a second and a half burst, went into the group coming out of the doorway. He was amazed at his own accuracy. He'd started low on purpose, knowing it would kick high and right. But it was the best burst he'd ever fired.

A crowd was gathering, some coming out, some in, some rushing in to see what the problem was. Releasing the trigger, he swung toward Wismo. Wismo had already deduced what was happening and had his own weapon raised, a murderous, hateful glare on his face. He fired first.

Faisal felt the freezing burn of bullets entering his body and tried to gasp. Then he felt a horrific pain in his face.

17

"HE'S DEAD," WADE SAID.

"Damn," Kyle muttered. He tried not to let it affect him, to take it in stride. Hell, the man had sawed Keller's head off! But he'd figured out it was wrong, come around at considerable risk to himself, and died. Kyle felt more anguish over losing him than he would have over Wiesinger, who had theoretically always been an ally.

But Wiesinger was still alive, along with two civilians, and it was his duty to see them free. He put the matter behind him and resumed shooting.

"Ready," Wade said, and Kyle slapped his left hand down to help push off the ground. He drew the SR25 closer to his side, like a football, and came up at forty-five degrees, like a sprinter off the blocks. He heard Wade fire at some threat or other as he crabbed sideways, ran two long steps, shifted past the corner of the building, and could see the building front at last. He'd have to shoot off hand now, standing. But the range was eighty meters and that was very easy shooting for him. He could see a side window that had dim back-light from the moon and operations up front. So he could provide more cover. They might pull this off yet.

He brought the rifle up to his shoulder, snugged into the sling with his left elbow on his harness, tight behind the pocket on his vest, and took one deep, measured breath to slow his pulse.

"Ready," he announced.

Movement! It was inside, but just under the window where he couldn't see or shoot. All he saw was the top of someone in a crouch.

The problem with suicidal nuts, he reflected, was that they didn't care if you killed them. When their purpose was to kill hostages, there was nothing you could offer or threaten them with. Only now one was about to kill Wiesinger or a little girl. He hoped it was Wiesinger, and it really wasn't personal.

His mind, experienced in dozens of firefights, honed by years of study and practice, whipped through an intuitive calculation no computer could ever match.

Those walls won't stop 7.62, he thought to himself.

All he had to do now was figure out where the crawling body was. Or at least, where the child was not. It wasn't efficient to simply fill the space with bullets, but it might be the only option.

Then Wiesinger appeared in his sights, apparently kicking out at something.

Kyle dropped his aim and fired three rounds, rapid.

Ba-ba-bang! It was almost fast enough for automatic fire, and his skill, the improved grip, and the weapon's mass allowed him to put all three in a very tight group. Dust blew up inside and out from the block shattering. Yes, hard-ball 7.62 ammo would punch through block. There was a substantial fan of gray in front and a hole through. If anyone had been behind that, he wasn't going to move soon enough to be a problem.

There was a definite gaggle of people outside the door. The rest were all tied up with the assault up front. But they'd have to sneak out or do some massive damage to disperse the enemy. This wasn't over yet. But first, they had to get to the hostages.

"I'm down," Wade said.

"Down how?" In the area, covered, wounded? The statement wasn't clear.

"Ready to roll."

"Understood. Fifty meters and closing."

"Roger. Give me five seconds."

A loud explosion was a bomb landing in front of the building. Wade's throwing arm was as good as his shooting. There were no friendlies there now, Kyle recalled. Damned shame. "Dying like a man" wasn't a bad thing, but living was far better. He'd say a prayer for Faisal's soul when he had time.

He was seen now, and badly aimed fire came his way. He couldn't plan on that to last; these people had proven competent. He was at extreme range for a canister load, but he needed something fast. He slung the SR25, letting it bang against his legs, and replaced it with the M4. He reached forward, aimed coarsely and triggered the canister load in the grenade launcher, the recoil thumping his wrist. He followed it at once by raising the carbine to his shoulder and rapping off quick shots into the mass. He dropped to one knee, then the other, then to his left elbow, getting low so he could pour out more accurate fire with a lower profile. Also, Wade would be on the other side, doing likewise. They could shoot over each other.

Between grenade, canister, and bullets the locals were disrupted. They scattered for cover. Now was when it got dangerous.

In a moment, Kyle was on his feet, calling into the phone, "Running!" as he did. It wouldn't do to have Wade shoot him.

"Likewise!" was the reply.

Weapons low, they sprinted toward the building. Kyle would twitch his arm now and then, to pan the muzzle across someone on the ground. Alive, wounded, dead, it didn't matter. He was paying insurance with bullets. He wanted them all down before he made it in, so he wouldn't have to face them on the way out.

He saw Wade skipping and crabbing for the door. "I've got the right," he said. He was better left handed than Wade was. They'd cross over as they entered. Kyle reached into a pouch and pulled out a three-ounce piece of TNT with a jury-rigged timed detonator built from a stopwatch. The timer was set for three seconds. The start button was protected by a thick piece of tape. He peeled that back, cautious of where his thumb went.

"Roger."

"On three. One, two, threeee," he grunted as he piled on the power. Two seconds later, they crashed into the thin door, Kyle having a flashback to a hut in the Carpathian mountains, where he'd done that and come face to face with a ton of explosives and a loon with a suicide switch. He lobbed the improv flashbang and stepped aside. A moment later, it exploded and shook leaves off the roof.

He spun through the doorframe and swung right, Wade swung left a half step behind him. Three bodies were on the floor, and he paid the insurance with three bullets, the sound echoing loudly and hollowly despite the suppressor. A rifle with 36 dB of reduction was still louder than a shouted conversation.

"Clear!" Wade announced.

"Clear!" Kyle agreed. "Glad to see you alive, sir," he added.

Wade went back to the door, got low, and resumed shooting. That left it to Kyle to get the hostages unbound. The dimness was occasionally lit by explosions from outside. Kyle needed some light, and had his Mini Maglite ready. With an amber lens it wasn't quite as obvious, but gave enough light to work by. There was another faint source behind him. A laptop.

Both Wiesinger and Suzanne, the child, had wet themselves. It might have been fear, stress, or simply the long wait. It wasn't something Kyle would hold against the man, except it was so representative of the mission so far.

They hadn't blindfolded the girl, and she stared at him with huge eyes. Her head swiveled like an owl's as he stepped deliberately behind the chair she was lashed to. She didn't cry or utter a sound, but when he cut the bonds and the pressure slipped off her wrists, she stumbled out of the chair and ran for the corner, curling up in a ball, back to the wall and arms over her face. Then she started bawling with huge, wracking sobs.

"Good," he said, to no one in particular. "She needs to get the stress out."

Lei Ling, her mother, was apparently conscious of being rescued, but still stiff and frightened behind her blindfold. Her daughter's distress didn't help. Kyle realized he probably should have freed her first. He'd been sentimental.

He pulled the hood off her head, and she blinked, head darting around to see what was hàppening. She recognized them as Western and soldiers, deduced they weren't terrorists, and that she was safe. Her eyes teared up from both the light Kyle was shining, and from relief. Kyle cut her hands free, then reached down for her feet, laying the rifle within inches of his hand as he did. He wanted it close by just in case of another altercation.

As he pulled the shredded rope away and stood, she pointed at her daughter. "Please?" she asked. He nodded, and she gave an almost smile as she staggered, stumbled, and finally crawled over that way. Her legs were likely numb from hours or days of inaction. But she gathered her daughter up in her arms and cuddled her, leaning back against the wall. The expression on her face might be grateful, under the sunken eyes that had seen too much fear.

Kyle wondered if he'd looked like that last time, as he'd faced down a lunatic with a back-pack full of explosive and a trigger in his hand.

"Gentlemen," Wiesinger said, panting slightly. It was hard to blame him. "That was some very, very fine shooting." He appeared about to say something else, but just sat while Kyle cut the ropes and removed his hood.

"Thank you, sir," he said. "As long as it's a happy ending, who cares if it's by the book?" He shoved another grenade—canister again, into the launcher.

"There is something to that, Sergeant Monroe."

Wade had gotten his cell phone out. "Contact made with Mel. All elements intact and movement capable. Last two referenced persons accounted for, alive and able to travel with transport. Need transport to Point X-ray . . . waiting."

Wiesinger was rubbing his wrists to restore circulation. They were badly abraded. Presumably, he'd been fighting the rope. He twisted his ankles and stomped his feet a few times.

"I think I'm able to move. Are my boots around?"

"Don't think so, sir," Kyle said, taking in the rubble in a sweep of his eyes. And the corpses. Some rail-thin little imam in a hat and prayer shawl. That had been who Kyle had hit through the block wall. He'd been disabled but hadn't died fast with that gutshot. Pity. Not. That was the freak who'd told Faisal it was holy to chop the heads off people. Even second hand, that information made Kyle quiver in disgust. One of the other bodies had a shattered wrist.

"You might have to barefoot it a bit," he said to Wiesinger.

"If I have to, I have to. Is there any reason to stick around?"

"Not that I can think of," Kyle said. "This way." He indicated the door.

Wiesinger accepted the SR25 and checked the load, limping badly. The battle was mostly at the front still, long bursts, short ones, individual shots, occasional explosions. With both sides dug in, it could last hours. Kyle only wanted it to last a few more minutes while he got everyone into the brush. After that, they should be fine.

Kyle stopped for just a moment. The cameras, two of them, were feeding into a laptop. They had been recording. They were still recording. They looked to be modern models that might shoot infrared, or be able to be processed to show dim features.

That was not only prime intelligence either way—of who the snipers were and how they accomplished the recovery, and of who the terrorists were—it was potentially a propaganda bomb that would scare many more of these assholes into quitting the game.

Kyle checked the screen. They were still filming.

"Wade, light the bodies!" he said. He pointed as he swung a camera across. Wade shone his Surefire in blinding momentary bursts while kicking the faces toward the lens.

"Thanks." Kyle pressed STOP, typed a new filename of KYLE and saved and closed. He shut the laptop down, pulled the cord and reached behind to cram it into his patrol pack. Some things were too convenient to let go.

Lei Ling carried her daughter. The girl wouldn't let anyone else near her, and clutched tightly. Wade took point, Kyle took rear, with his better-rate-of-fire weapon, and Wiesinger stumbled along in the middle with the spare SR25, feet hurting from poor circulation and lack of shoes. He'd been bound tighter. Apparently, they'd perceived him as a threat. He seemed to be recovering somewhat, and increased his pace.

The obvious problem was that any notice they got would make them a major target. At this point, there was no reason for the enemy not to kill the hostages. Kyle was dripping sweat, more than the water he'd drunk earlier. If things just held off another minute . . .

Someone shouted and a bullet snapped past. Lei Ling howled and ran faster, which was probably the best reaction to have.

More fire came, and Kyle spun. He fired two sustained bursts and the canister, then reached back and grabbed a hand grenade, heaving it in a long lob. He wasn't sure of a particular target, he just wanted lots of noise to keep heads down. Once in the woods, he'd have the advantage against any reasonable number of opponents.

The weapon was hot and jammed on the next round. He cleared it instinctively and latched the bolt back. A few seconds of cool air couldn't hurt. Meantime, he grabbed his Ed Brown. It would make noise, and anyone close would find out just how hard 230 grains of lead hit, like that guy running to intercept and raising a fucking shotgun. Kyle clicked the safety, squeezed, rode the recoil, and squeezed again. The two heavy bullets crashed into the man, who stumbled and staggered. He might or might not die, but he was no longer a threat.

Then they were heading into the trees, Wiesinger cursing loudly as he winced and danced, feet getting poked and toes getting jammed.

Kyle speed-dialed. "Stephens, we're clear, and thanks, buddy. 'Go SAS!' or whatever you say."

"We've been gone. They've been shooting at each other for five minutes, mate, with an occasional encouragement from our allies. 'Who Dares, Wins.'"

"Damn, sweet. And nice phrase. I've got to run. Later."

"Ciao."

"Bakri," Kyle said, as the next number answered. "We're in the woods at the south, you say there's a road?"

"Four kilometers ahead. You should hurry."

"Dammit, that's a long hike. You can meet us?"

"We can. Talk more as you close."

"Roger." He was panting hard, putting distance between him and possible pursuit. There was a lesser deadline now—making sure everyone knew the hostages were alive. He dialed Gilpin. "We have them, we're on foot, we're departing. Awaiting local transport."

"Outstanding. Bring it on home and I'll put the word out." The civilian exec sounded thrilled.

"We're not clear yet. Possible pursuit, possible government risks. An hour to transport, another to the coast, then we have to get clear."

"That leg will be waiting. You just put distance on." Kyle could hear Gilpin talking into another line, a landline. The word was going out.

"Yes, sir."

They stopped for about a minute, Wade pulling spare pants from his ruck and ripping them to strips that Wiesinger could wear on his feet. Kyle dropped the bolt on the M4 again, and reholstered his pistol. Lei Ling was gasping and dry heaving, but showed no intention of stopping if she didn't have to. "Three more kilometers," Kyle said slowly, not knowing her grasp of English.

"I can make it," she said. Her voice was a raspy contralto with an obvious accent. "I won't stop until we're away from those sick fucks." Apparently, she spoke English well enough.

Kyle shared water all around. Suzanne wouldn't drink, shaking her head and tucking into her mother's shoulder. Wiesinger and Wade each gulped enough for Kyle to feel the load lighten. Then they were moving again, Wiesinger managing a slightly better pace in his improvised slippers.

"We're out," Wiesinger muttered.

Kyle wasn't sure. It would be quite obvious to the enemy that they'd head for the city or the coast. Bakri's cover was blown for certain.

Putting that together, pursuit wouldn't be far away. These people weren't rational, were bent on killing, and they weren't going to let their sacrifices escape easily. Random death in the street was one thing, but this was a picked target. They were determined to get Lei Ling and her daughter, and getting the Americans was gravy—it would prove they were a force to be taken seriously. As the U.S. couldn't operate openly in Indonesia, and not on a large-enough scale clandestinely—probably not at all after this—it would be a net win.

The whole solution, Kyle reflected morbidly, was best solved with large bombs.

That was post-battle depression hitting him. He was shaky, jittery, and scared. He always was. It was part of doing the job. Then would come euphoria, and a desire to get drunk and screw. He didn't drink anymore, and Janie was half a world away. He'd deliberately not been thinking about her, because he didn't need anything holding him back or distracting him.

He kept on, ducking leaves, dodging trunks, ignoring the birds and ground animals. None of the larger forms were present, which was good, as spooked herds could be a giveaway. He had to assume their enemy was smart, cunning, and right behind. He made periodic pauses and watched for signs of pursuit before hurrying to catch up. The dark didn't scare him. The dark was his friend.

"We're about there," Wade said. "Perhaps two zero zero meters."

"Roger. Stand by." He dialed Bakri. "We're there."

"There will be a car along shortly. Lights will blink twice."

"Better yet, blink them some other number and I'll confirm."

"Very well, I think I understand."

It was an old trick. While Kyle didn't think any faction could have a tap on the cell phones, it was possible the government did. If they knew any signs or passwords . . .

Shortly, they all pulled up into a ditch. It was wet and cool and wonderful, even with slimy rotten things pooling in it. A car was far to the north, several minutes away. It was traveling perhaps thirty-five miles per hour.

The lights flashed three times.

"I see three flashes," Kyle said.

"Yes," Bakri said.

"Everyone up," Kyle hissed.　　　　　　　　　•

It was the worn, ugly Land Cruiser, and Kyle was delighted to see it. Fatigue was hitting him hard now. It stopped, and four of Bakri's men debarked and spread out, acting as a rearguard. That was awfully nice of him, Kyle thought.

Lei Ling and her daughter were ushered gently into the cargo compartment of the Toyota, the little girl hiding her face from the men with guns. It was understandable. To her, virtually any armed man, and certainly any Indonesian, was a threat. They were cramped because the rest of the Americans' gear was back there. Amazing. They were going to exfil with all their gear except what they'd expended. That might be a first.

Wade stood to at the rear, weapon raised and ready. Kyle ran to the front. After the civilians were bundled in, Wiesinger climbed in the back. Wade ducked around and leaped feetfirst in next to him. Kyle swung around and took shotgun, as the four troops jumped onto the bumpers and fenders and Bakri revved up and popped the clutch. They juggled weapons around and he got an SR25 while Wade got the M4. He wasn't going to worry about it. He checked the magazine and then reached a hand back. Wade dropped two more magazines into it. Easier to swap them than the rifles.

Kyle didn't remember much of the trip. Fatigue and stress had finally overwhelmed him. He knew he was conscious, and once shot at a threat that turned out to be merely shifting shadows of leaves looking like a human outline. But he recalled neither the twenty kilometers of road nor how he acquired the dozens of bruises and scrapes that came from the rough track they drove on. There had to be several generous samples of his DNA in the truck, though.

Then they jounced hard and slewed left out of the woods to race along a shore road that was in good repair. It had to be an oil-company access.

Whatever had happened to cause Kyle to zone in the woods was over. He was alert enough to continue, even if ragged and worn as hell. But he'd been there before; he'd trained for that for fourteen of his sixteen years of service.

Captain Sutrisno watched silently. Next to him, Murizal, his exec, growled.

"Easy, soldier," he cautioned. "There are rebels and there are rebels. If they kill these filth, let us not complain. At the same time, if any of them die in the process, that is Allah's will. Bakri is smart and honest. We'll watch him more closely. But there is no need to shoot him or arrest him yet."

Indeed. It was Napoleon who had cautioned never to interrupt an enemy when he was making a mistake. If the factions could kill each other, then the ones who survived would either be more reasonable or less of a threat. Though there was still the issue of Americans and Australians operating in Indonesia without permission. That made Sutrisno far angrier than any dispute between GAM groups and Jemaah Islamiyah. The presumption and arrogance was insufferable, no matter the motives. Sutrisno's people were quite capable of handling these missions. That his unit, and apparently their own government, had been kept in the dark was a grievous insult. But that was for the politicians.

He forced calm upon himself, and let it radiate

out to the others. Nothing should be done yet. The Americans had run away, Bakri's men had departed, the Aussies has long since ducked, showing a canniness he had to respect. They were men not afraid to retreat, and who made a game of it.

The faction here had suffered a huge loss. They'd taken perhaps twenty-five casualties in the fight, and some survivors were scattered widely. Others were pursuing the Americans. They'd be dealt with shortly. For now, the stillness returned. It was a patient twenty-minute wait before movement picked up again.

First came two rebels, lightly wounded and terrified. They stared in despair at the wreckage and corpses. Sutrisno grudgingly admitted the foreigners were good troops. It was an impressive ratio of damage. These two simply huddled in shock, ignoring the occasional moan from a dying comrade. A dozen more wandered back from the road, confused at the disappearance of their attackers. Then someone figured out the hostages were gone. There were shouts and accusations.

An hour later, an advance party of three arrived, scared and suddenly in a standoff with two of their wounded allies. That was most amusing, but no shots were fired. An hour after that, a larger force came in at the prompting of the scouts: sixty-seven GAM rebels, skinny and underfed and bearded, indicating strict Muslim beliefs. All had weapons. All wore fatigues of some kind. The combination marked them as a threat to the nation, and with the hostages gone, there was no reason to show any mercy, except for some few who might provide intelligence if motivated. The rest could be an object lesson.

Sutrisno checked his kit. The flag was ready. It was a large, new Indonesian flag, which these people hated to see. Sometimes the Kopassus would attack with miniature flags hanging from their rifles. Today, they'd leave no survivors, but they would leave a full-size flag as a slap. This was Indonesia. It would stay Indonesia unless and until the government decided otherwise, and rebels, especially terrorists, were not going to change that schedule.

Sutrisno whistled, and his company of Kopassus rose from the growth to bloom into a swath of death.

18

THE TRIP OUT SHOULD HAVE BEEN A CHANCE
to relax, but they weren't free yet. Not until
they were on the deck of a U.S. ship, and even
then, they needed to get into friendly waters. Kyle
was a Ranger. He could go a long time under
stress, underfed, and without sleep. But he was
groggy after moving so far, so fast in this climate.

He was still hyperaware, too, and that took a
toll. He listened to the chorus of insects as they
drove, shifting with the greenery. The road noise
and engine sounds changed. Occasional other
noises were natural enough. Then . . .

"Coming car, everyone down and weapons
hidden," Bakri said.

The headlights grew and illuminated the inside
of the roof as Kyle scrunched into the footwell.
He drew the SR25 in tight, the muzzle past his
ear. The lights swept across as what sounded like

a truck roared past. He counted two and started to shimmy back up.

Bakri swore in Achinese. "They are turning around. Coming in pursuit. It's a security vehicle."

"Wade, make it go away," Kyle said. He was having flashbacks to Romania and one of their too many car chases.

"Roger," Wade said. He leaned out the window, bracing a leg across Wiesinger's lap, ignoring his momentary protest. He raised the M4, clicked the safety and squeezed. Four shots rang out, four empty cases *tinged* as they ricocheted inside, and then the lights swerved.

"Tire and three radiator shots. That should slow them down."

"Yeah," Kyle said. He already had his cell phone out.

It answered. He'd known it would, but ever since the snatch, he'd been nervous. "Gilpin."

"Yeah, Monroe here. Is our transport ready?"

"They're hidden. Do you need backup?"

"Not at this moment. We may any minute. I'll keep the line open."

"Don't. I'll have them call you directly."

"Roger that, Monroe out." He clicked off.

Thirty seconds later, the phone vibrated in his hand.

"Monroe," he answered.

"McLaren. We didn't meet on the Black Sea, I'm told." It was an American voice, and it was coming from very nearby. That helped Kyle steady out.

"Good to not meet you again, McLaren." He kept looking over his shoulder anyway. Nothing else at present.

"Well, we'll meet in about three minutes, according to my math. Unless I dropped a decimal and you're actually in San Jose."

"I wish."

"Okay, you'll come to a bend to the left in the road," McLaren said.

"Bend to the left, roger," he spoke aloud for Bakri's benefit.

"Continue straight ahead on foot."

"Straight ahead on foot, roger." They'd have to carry gear and the girl.

"Distance is two zero zero meters."

"Two zero zero meters, roger."

"I'll find you."

"You'll find us. Roger." He hoped so. Fumbling in the dark on the coast would suck.

"I'll be wearing a black trenchcoat and fedora."

"Black trenchcoat and fedora you say." He had to grin at that.

"Would you settle for black camo over a wetsuit and boonie hat?"

"McLaren, I'll settle for you wearing a pink fucking tutu, as long as you get us out of here." Hot damn, they were going to make it.

"Tutu not an option. I'll note choice for next

task. I see headlights," McLaren said, serious again. "Flash them."

Kyle cupped the phone low and said, "Flash headlights twice."

"I count two flashes," McLaren said a moment later.

"Confirm two flashes. That's us."

The road curved sharply just ahead. Bakri leaned into the brakes steadily, and they stopped right at the curve. The civilians necessitated a full stop, or Kyle would have risked bailing out on a roll. There was no additional pursuit from either oil-terminal security or terrorists yet, and hopefully there wouldn't be. But the sooner they were gone, the better.

Kyle rolled out to his feet, facing rearward. Wade sprang out and sprinted around back. He threw open the hatch and motioned for Lei Ling to pass her daughter up. Kyle was past and scanning for potential threats.

Then Suzanne started screaming.

There was no way she was going to let a soldier take her again. Wade returned Kyle's inquisitive glance with a shrug and a look of helplessness.

They were both saved when Lei Ling jumped out, staggering slightly, and let her daughter clutch her around the neck. "I do it," she said.

"Run," Kyle said, pointing, with his rifle held ready in the other hand. Wade grabbed his ruck in one hand and Lei Ling's arm in the other. They bounded forward, off the road, and down a rocky beach that turned sandy, dark from occasional oil spills.

Wiesinger, already out, followed along, grunting in pain in his bare feet. The man lumbered and had an obvious silhouette, Kyle groused to himself after a moment's glance back. But at least he wasn't complaining anymore. And he was making respectable time on feet that had to resemble hamburger. The man wasn't entirely a coward. He was more a self-centered ass.

Then it was Kyle's turn. He ran past the driver's side. Bakri had his arm out and was looking as casual as one could under the circumstances. "For all of us, Bakri, thanks. This has been our smoothest mission so far."

"If that's so, you are a brave man. Good luck, and *salemat jalan*." Good travel.

"And you." He shook the offered hand.

That was as much as there was time for. Bakri coaxed the truck forward as Kyle picked up two rucks. They had been packed in a hurry and were quite bulky, even with food and water depleted. They tangled on his back as he slung one on each shoulder, but it wasn't a long trip; he could manage. He picked his way down the beach at a run.

As the Toyota pulled around the curve, Kyle tripped. He threw the butt of the SR25 out and broke his fall. But he caught his right boot toe between two rocks, banged his knee, and skinned an elbow.

Wincing, he stood and resumed his path, limping. It felt as if he'd torn the boot open, though a quick glance didn't show any obvious rips in the leather. His foot was squelching, but that could be sweat as much as blood. But it burned like hell, and was sharply painful. His right knee had either loose skin or sharp pebbles embedded in the skin, and stung with every movement. His elbow lit up with every shift of fabric or breath of air over the open wound.

He saw the boat, and a young American in an odd camo pattern with a flattop haircut and some godawful variant of an M4 Kyle wasn't familiar with, with rails all over the receiver and barrel, a bulky suppressor, some kind of night vision, and other gadgets. But it helped prove he was an American, and was likely devastatingly effective.

"Monroe?"

"Yeah, injured, rocks," he said through clenched teeth. "Teach *me* to hurry."

"McLaren. Here." The SEAL reached out a hand and heaved, taking the weight off Kyle's injured foot. Kyle dropped the rucks and then they were swinging their legs over the gunwale of a rigid inflatable boat. McLaren stepped back and grabbed a ruck in each hand, barely straining.

"Anything fragile?"

"No," Kyle said, as the two packs sailed over the inflated tube. He chuckled. The question had been an irrelevant formality.

The boat had a cockpit of sorts, enough for

two crewmen to stand in. One stood there now. Another man crouched forward at a Browning M2HB .50 caliber machine gun. Kyle's foot sent streaks of pain up his leg as McLaren piled in.

"Go," the SEAL said. It wasn't much above a whisper, but it was enough.

Then they were moving, slowly, as the heavily muffled diesels rumbled.

McLaren was speaking into an encrypted radio. "Got all three items, and two supplemental. Both female. Request female medical support who look as nonthreatening as possible, over . . ."

Kyle sank back and let the gunwale take his weight. Damn, that felt good. He was on a friendly vessel and didn't have to worry about his command or about taking charge himself.

"You realize I *am* going to puke," Wade said. He sounded cheerful about it, though.

"Red, white, and blue?"

"Or Army green. Something patriotic. Goddam, my man, we did it again. Busted up, worn out, but we saved a little girl. Dunno about you, but I feel pretty goddamned good!"

"Yeah," Kyle said noncommittally. He really did feel good, but the exhaustion and tension were fighting inside him. He could feel a thrill of victory later. Right now, it was the agony of the feet.

But he did have to smile at the pun.

19

KYLE WAS LEANING BACK, LIMP, WHEN THEY hit deep water minutes later. Whether it was wave pattern, or shelter from formations, Kyle didn't know. But the motion changed from a light rocking to a heavy tilting. He understood why Wade got sick. He felt none too good himself. Though only part of it was the ocean. It was his medical state. He wasn't sure how bad his foot was, but it was screaming at him. Surgery for certain, though he thought he had it all there. But hell, that meant they couldn't use him for a couple of months. He snickered to himself.

"So, we meet at last, Sergeant Monroe," McLaren said. He cleared all three rifles and stowed them in an open crate. Made sense. Random holes in the tubes would be a bad thing. The boat was metal hulled, but required the inflated gunwales to support it.

"I think we're meeting at first," Kyle replied. Dammit, Wade's humor was catching.

"Right. Anyway, what I've heard impresses me. Both you and Wade."

"Thanks," Kyle said. Wow. Yes, they were all on the same team and all good at what they did, but the SEALs were about as overall best as you got. For one of them to say he was impressed was praise indeed.

"What's the camo?" Kyle asked. He looked his host over again. Young, bulky but lean, no nonsense about him.

"Standard BDU pattern in gray and blue. Civilian purchase, but great for beaches at night. Or nightclubs."

"Good. I wonder if the Army would approve them."

"Not likely, Monroe," Wiesinger said.

It was annoying. He'd been making a joke and chatting to unwind, while being friendly with a man who was saving their lives, and the asshole had to prove he had no sense of humor.

"Ah, shit," McLaren said, cutting off further conversation. Kyle shifted and looked astern, following the SEAL's gaze. He couldn't see much from this low level.

"What is it?"

"Some kind of small craft. But bigger and better armed than this one." He stared a bit longer. "Looks like a fifteen to twenty meter patrol craft. Same kind that's involved in quite a bit of piracy."

"Define 'better armed'?" Wade asked. He looked a bit queasy, but it wasn't the enemy. He'd looked like that the whole way out.

"Oh, probably a twenty-three millimeter Russian. Enough to blow the hell out of us before we do more than love taps with the fifty." He turned to the bow and shouted, "Mike, bring the fifty!" Turning back, he said for no one's benefit, though they all heard him, "But we'll damned sure try."

Kabongo had been largely invisible up front. He was a massive black man, with shoulders that looked to be carved rock. The defined shape of them could be seen right through his wetsuit. He carried the dismounted .50 Browning at port arms as he came surefootedly astern.

In moments, the two SEALs had it mounted to a rear pintle that had obviously been retrofitted. The welds on it were crude but sturdy. Apparently, it was intended that the heavy firepower be used forward. That was a limitation they obviously didn't approve of.

"Piracy?" Kyle asked.

"I dunno. Fifty attacks in this area this year. That were reported. Plus tramps who went missing in unknown conditions that might not be storms. Or it could be contracted to the companies. Or it could be your friends. They might have seen us come in and then waited for us to leave. I don't think they're government."

Kyle's phone buzzed. He started in surprise, and grabbed it.

"Kyle."

"Bakri here."

"Yes, Bakri?"

"I was just called and threatened with death."

"Damn. There's nothing we can do at this point."

"That is not why I called. Our friends had observers. They said they would hunt you down at sea."

"That explains the boat behind us." He stared at the dot on the waves.

"I'm sorry."

"No, thanks much. You protect yourself." Damn.

"I will do so. It is to get violent here. Very."

"Good luck. I'll call with my home number if I get a chance."

"I hope to be here. I may change phones."

"If that happens, I won't try to find you. Not safe."

"I agree. Good luck and God be with you."

"And also with you."

He clicked off and turned to the others, painfully. "That explains that. Assholes aren't willing to let go."

"Didn't we do that a couple of shows back?" Wade asked. They'd been chased from Pakistan into Afghanistan.

"That group wanted revenge," Kyle said. "This group is still trying to bag the target and win points. They kill the Maddens, they get a war started."

"Well, maybe they'll turn away," Kabongo mused. "It's not as if they've got good odds."

"We've dealt with these assholes before," Kyle said. "They won't turn away. A bloody nose won't do it. You have to knock teeth out before they get the hint. And some of them never do."

"Well, we're not that easy to hit," McLaren said. "We're small, moving fast, have a very low radar profile, and a head start. That might be enough. On the other hand, we're not going to make thirty knots in these seas with all this extra gear."

"Should we jettison?" Wiesinger asked, coming from the front. He'd been talking to the civilians, or at least trying to.

"Don't think it'll make that much difference, sir," McLaren said. "And truthfully, the mass is holding us deep enough for better propulsion. I don't want to start tossing stuff around. Especially as we may need ammo. Call me a miser, but I hate to throw away even government property if I can avoid it."

"Same here. Thought I'd offer."

"I appreciate it."

"What about the Indonesian coast guard?"

"They're a long way away, might not believe us and would be royally pissed. We'd all be in jail and on the news. Your call, it's your mission."

"Sir?" Kyle asked.

Wiesinger shook his head. "Let's outrun them. I really don't want that kind of attention drawn to us."

Or to your next promotion, Kyle thought.

"Right. Do you want to call Gilpin or should I?"

"I will," Wiesinger insisted. Kyle handed over his phone at once. The colonel dialed. "Wiesinger here. Yes, sir, injured but recovered . . . Thank you, sir . . . We're aboard the boat and being pursued, last-ditch effort to get a kill, we think."

Lei Ling cringed. Kyle thought, *Nice going, asshole. Scare the civvies.* But he should have been expecting it.

"Yes, sir," Wiesinger said. "Understood. We are at sea, hope to call with better news soon. Out."

"Oh, shit, they're firing!" Kabongo said.

The blob on the horizon flashed occasionally from reflected moonlight. That was a silver light. This was redder, uglier. And it had a tempo that only comes from mechanical equipment.

The first burst was nowhere near the U.S. boat; Kyle didn't see any splashes or hear anything. But it would be used to range them. By halving the difference every time, it would take less than five bursts to get the distance. After that, it was simply a case of pouring enough fire out to get lucky as the boat tossed on the waves.

The second burst was a lot closer. It splashed behind them.

"Can't you stop them with the fifty?" Wiesinger asked before the next burst. He'd missed the earlier conversation.

"Not that easy," McLaren said with a shake. "We can blow it full of holes, but it won't sink at once. If they've got the pilothouse armored, they can keep closing. And they must have backup to recover them if they do sink. Closer than ours."

"Time to call a chopper?"

"No, sir. Not while we're in Indonesian waters. The twelve-mile limit is the minimum. We're at an oblique course to clear various underwater obstacles. So it'll be a half hour or so, and I'm saving the chopper. Would suck to have them show up, then leave because of fuel issues. We may need them a lot. Besides, we're forty-five minutes from the *Juneau*, the Amphibious Transport Dock ship picking us up," he elucidated.

"Will some precision fire help?" Wade asked.

"Hell, if you think you can tag something, go for it." McLaren shrugged. "Far be it from me to stop an ally from killing a bad guy. And fire downrange never hurts."

Wade grabbed both of the long rifles from the locker and made sure he grabbed magazines of match grade. He tossed one to Kyle. Both snipers loaded and shouldered the SR25s and sat down, Kyle wincing in pain.

He hunkered low to rest the handguard over the tubular gunwale. This was going to be tough shooting. It wasn't helped by the odd angle he had to keep to stop his foot from being squeezed, and hence sending sharp pain shooting up to his testicles.

McLaren started popping off bursts every time the shifting waves brought the two boats into line. The .50 BMG is a big cartridge, verging on being a light cannon shell, but half inch holes in a boat with good pumps aren't an immediate threat. And he'd have to hit it first. But a single 23mm hit on the smaller craft could cripple it. The engines were exposed to incoming fire, and there was no protection for the occupants. Nor could the multiple compartments of the tube take too many hits from explosive or even solid projectiles before the boat would founder. Both craft had low radar signatures and manually aimed weapons, making it a game of visual chase and shoot in the growing dawn.

Kyle winced as he shifted his seat. Cold seawater swirled around his ass and testicles. His stance had his foot braced against the gunwale and it hurt. Whenever another slop of water rushed over the boot, it would sting again, coldly, then slowly warm back up. While he wasn't getting seasick, the shifting waves were disorienting him. Every swell caused the boat to sway, and the gray horizon blended into the black sky and gray mist. And it was dawn again, dammit. He needed some serious sleep once the threats were diminished.

A snapping, ripping, popping sound was a 23mm projectile through the air nearby. That got Kyle's undivided attention, until he forced himself into his shooting trance. Nothing he could do would stop the incoming fire, except to hit it at the source. No panic, no shakes, just take the fire and make the shot count. A swell slopped over and soaked his sleeve, burning the raw patch on his elbow. He squinted for just a moment and got it under control.

He brought the rifle into plane and caught the pursuit in the scope. Now he had to find a worthwhile target, and he wasn't that familiar with even U.S. military boats, much less foreign ones. He could see a lit pilot house, a gun mount up front with two men crewing it, and some assorted spidery equipment of no real interest. The best targets were the gun and the gunners.

This would work out to simply be a shot at a moving target, he figured. Or not "simply," as the target was moving, he was moving, and the platform under him was subject to sudden direction changes.

"Range?" he asked Wade.

"I'd say one four hundred meters," Wade replied.

"Long ass shot. But okay. Guns and gunner."

"Roger tha—" Wade replied, drowned out by another burst from McLaren and a wave breaking over them. They were now soaked through, eyes stinging from the salt and chilling quickly.

Kyle put that out of his mind. The shot was what mattered. He closed his eyes for a second to clear salt and let his mind refocus, then opened them again.

The swells were fairly steady, and the boat was moving with *that* motion. The other boat was moving with *that* motion, so he should lead about *there*. And how high to compensate for range? Could he recall the chart? He was zeroed for five hundred meters, and velocity at that range was about 1548 feet per second, figure the additional range and . . . He relaxed and steadied the rifle. It didn't do any good to fight motion, in fact it made things worse. He'd have to squeeze the trigger quickly, losing some small accuracy in exchange for meeting the window he had.

There . . . and there . . . and *BANG!*

Wade's shot was a bare fraction of a second after his, and an empty case smacked Kyle in the head. It stung for just a second, but didn't burn through the sheath of cold water.

By scope, both shots had missed, because nothing happened. But Kyle had caught a glimpse of what might have been a ricochet. It was the only evidence to work from, so lead *there* and . . . BANG! as another burst crashed overhead.

Miss, but it was the best he could do. So shoot again. Breathe, relax, squeeze . . . BANG! Another of Wade's ejected cases caught him. He should move, but it was a minor annoyance and he had work to do.

One of the gun crew spun and tumbled. Good. It might have been his shot or Wade's. It didn't matter. Kyle knew how good he was, and how good Wade was, and they didn't need to compete. That was the right lead, and he fired again as it came by, and again. The remaining man tugged frantically at the gun. Perhaps one of the shots had damaged it? Or it could have just jammed. And shoot. And shoot.

Then the gunner staggered back, ducking a round. He seemed to crash against the pilothouse and fall over as the boat swayed. He scrabbled to his knees and disappeared inside. At this range by starlight it was a tough call, even with a night scope.

"Score two," Wade said.

"Yup. More targets." They were in good shooting position, comfortable enough and able to stay here for hours, with range and windage for the target. There was no hurry to move.

"Looking," Wade said. "Nothing. Want to try for the pilot house?"

"I have an idea. Get the scope," Kyle said. An idea that was goofy, except that it might work.

"Stand by," Wade agreed. He fumbled with the rucks until he found his, then inside until he found the spotting scope.

"Mr. McLaren, I have an idea," he said. McLaren looked at him. "I need to borrow your shoulder."

"Show me," McLaren said, looking quizzical.

Kyle cleared the SR25 and laid it down, rose and took the grips on the .50. "You stand in front, facing me, gripping the mount. I'm going to steady over your shoulder. You're a strong man?"

"Strong enough. I got ya. How the hell are you going to aim, though?" he asked as he squatted and wrapped himself around the mount.

"I'm not. Wade is. Wade?"

"Ready!" Wade agreed.

Wiesinger said, "Monroe, you're a fucking nut. But good luck." He was wincing from saltwater on his feet.

"Thanks," he replied shortly, as he lowered the gun back down over McLaren's shoulder. The SEAL reached up and wrapped an arm around the heat shield. "Perfect," Kyle agreed.

He fell back into trance, closing his eyes, opening them, judging the combined motions, picking a lead. "Shooting!" he announced, and gave the paddle a press.

The .50 fired and slammed. A single round banged out. McLaren shouted, "OW!" from the noise so close to him and the recoil. The empty case whipped out and over the side, a flash of slightly heat-crazed brass.

"Need me to stop?" Kyle asked.

"High and right, several meters," Wade called.

"Your ass! Keep shooting!" McLaren said. "I'll deal!"

Kyle nodded and shifted just slightly. McLaren was inhumanly strong; even with a good part of the 85 pounds of the .50 balanced against his shoulder, it took effort for Kyle to move him. Which was good. He chose his new point of aim and settled back in. With no scope, the boat was just a toy on the horizon.

"Shooting!" The Fifty crashed, McLaren shouted, Wade called, "Roof, left, one point five meters."

"Dammit, it's not steady enough. Going to take a lot of luck."

"More mass!" McLaren shouted. "Kabongo, time to make your swim buddy smile!"

"Will do, Dan. Stand by." Kabongo had been gently offering water to the civilians and Wiesinger. He came running over like a boulder with legs. He got behind McLaren, reached around him and grabbed two of the three struts on the pintle mount. He strained until his arms bulged and hugged tight. Then he straightened up.

The end result was two shoulders under the receiver, braced with four feet and the metal structure.

"I'll need to move it," Kyle cautioned.

"You move, we'll move. Shoot, damn you!" McLaren said.

"Roger. Targeting. Shooting!" Another round of crashing and yelling. He was off the mark from the shifting, but that couldn't be helped.

The 23mm mount was working again. Several hornets on steroids and rocket fuel ripped through the air. Three voices yelled, "Shit!" simultaneously. Then they had to not laugh, because it *was* hysterical.

"High, right, about three meters," Wade called. He was able to track the rounds by heat trace and by disruption of the dense, humid air.

"Roger," Kyle agreed, and depressed ever so slightly. Both SEALs were bleeding from the side of the head. At least he hoped it was scalp and that he hadn't blown their eardrums out. They were about three feet from the muzzle and facing the other way, but it couldn't be pleasant.

Hell, he wasn't enjoying the swells, the spray, or the incoming fire. These guys were just nuts. But a good kind of nuts.

A burst came in, and the pilot, who hadn't been introduced, swore in a shout. Kyle glanced back. A round had blown through one of his instruments. One of the tubes had been hit, too, but in an oblique crease along the top. If they didn't ship too much water, they should stay afloat. But there was no way to bail.

There was nothing to do about that. Kyle came back to his weapon and reacquired his position from muscle memory.

And fire. "Shit!" McLaren shouted.

"Glass gone!" Wade shouted triumphantly. "Nail him again!"

"Shooting!" Kyle said, and waited for the waves to match up again.

BANG! "OW, goddammit!" "Son of a *bitch*!" "Hit inside the pilot house. They're turning!"

McLaren slumped. "Holy shit, that was a workout. Wish I could have seen the shooting!" He turned to observe. "And they are leaving. Nice." He heaved a deep breath. "My ears thank you for finishing." He was greased with blood on the right side of his face.

"Kick ass, brother," Kabongo said with a nod as he dropped to the other gunwale. "Call me officially impressed." His face was abraded along the jaw line and under the ear. That was what the bleeding was. But he still might have suffered hearing loss.

"Yeah," was all Kyle could say. It had been an athletic workout for him, too, and a mental drain. But he'd made the shot. Several shots.

Even Wiesinger said, "Monroe, I retract any doubts I had about your shooting ability. That was fucking amazing."

"Thank you, sir." Yeah, the man wasn't a total waste. Another couple of field ops and he might turn into a respectable officer. The problem, Kyle realized, was that he had a second lieutenant's manners, experience, and ego, and a colonel's service time. No one had done him any favors by keeping him in administrative slots.

Far off were the lights of another boat. A bigger one. Presumably official from somebody.

"Is it time to call the chopper yet, Mister McLaren?" Kyle asked, his voice high and tight.

"It's time!" McLaren agreed. "By the time it gets here, we'll be in good water."

"Use your left ear," Kabongo said. "We can bandage each other while you call."

The chopper flew escort in the graying dawn. It would have been a faster trip aboard the aircraft, but would mean two winching operations. Kyle was happy enough to wait the extra two hours. The helo also flew interference when the Indonesian patrol boat came to inquire. It landed on the tail of the boat and someone debarked. After a few minutes of face to face, he reboarded. It was impossible to tell through the scope what the details were, but Kyle gathered another "training exercise" was being stretched until it could be seen through. But that wasn't Kyle's problem, and the intel could be freely shared, now. A few extra kills for the local forces always sweetened relations. The overhead cover was also welcome as the boat started listing. Water was slowly but steadily filling the compartments of the starboard tube.

It took a subjectively long time to reach the *Juneau*. Kyle wasn't up to date on ships. He knew an Amphibious Transport was designed for Marines and helicopters, and was a moderately large craft, but seeing it was substantially different.

"How big is that?" he asked.

"The Mighty J, LPD Ten, displaces seventeen thousand, five hundred tons full load, is five hundred sixty-nine feet long. She carries eight hundred thirty-five Marines full load, plus a crew of about four hundred, plus flag crew for amphibious landing operations." McLaren rattled off the specs. That helped Kyle see it for what it was.

"That's the size of a small aircraft carrier," Kyle said.

"Pretty much. The Wasp class are carriers, for practical purposes, with Harriers as well as helos. But *Juneau* is plenty big enough for this."

"How do we get aboard?" Wiesinger asked.

"We steer right into the well deck at the stern. Slip this sausage right up her . . . ah," he looked around at the two huddled civilians, who were wrapped in a blanket, wide-eyed and silent. "Well, in the stern. Nice and safe."

"You've all saved our lives," Lei Ling said. "Go ahead and swear. It can't be worse than engineers."

"Thank you, ma'am, but we should learn to use proper punctuation anyway," McLaren replied.

The helo made another pass and Kabongo waved them off. It was past dawn now, and the ship was filling the northeast view. Kyle had never dealt with ships, though he had seen a bunch in port here and there, including the Black Sea. Being in this position to a major warship was a new experience.

The flight deck of the *Juneau* was crowded with running people as they approached. Then the crowd shifted as the chopper landed.

It really wasn't long, according to his watch, but it seemed to take forever to approach the dark cave of the well deck. *Juneau* was sunk at the stern so they could guide the craft right in. A rail on the left, port side, was crowded with people, and cranes and winches stood ready. The pilot of the boat, a Petty Officer Murphy, was busy with controls and wheels. He hadn't said much for the trip, but had stuck to the cabin area. Navigating a tiny boat in deep water had to be a difficult task, Kyle thought. Every time he ran into other military careers, he was amazed at how much was involved. There weren't any dumb grunts, as certain frothing web posters and "reporters" implied. These people were all technical professionals.

Then they were inside, the bright morning light doused and replaced with the yellow-tinged glow of large spotlights. The smell of the sea mingled with machine oil and metal. The noise was a steady hum with mechanical clatters and bangs interspersed. They drew up to the rail and Kyle felt like a bug as people stared down. He was too tired to care, and these were all friendlies. It was damned good to see nothing but U.S. uniforms.

Two female medics, as McLaren had specified, wearing very feminine-looking makeup, and civilian clothes with no insignia other than ID packs on their arms, came to escort Lei Ling and her daughter. They were smiling and cheerful to reassure the little girl, and whisked them up the ladder and away to sick bay for observation. Suzanne looked suspicious but didn't complain. There were running Marines in MARPAT camo with rifles, maintenance crews in color-coded uniforms, crewmen in dungarees, and the SEALs and their support staff in wetsuits.

"Who're they?" someone asked, pointing at the shaggy, filthy soldiers, as three sets of hands helped Kyle scramble one-footed up a ladder. Kyle had to wonder just how bad he looked. Death warmed over? Or totally roasted?

"Army Delta or something. Rescued hostages, my man! U.S.A! U.S.A!"

There was no need to correct the error, and Kyle was too damned tired. He assumed Wiesinger would say something, but even he was quiet.

A medic came over and knelt down next to Kyle. "What's wrong?"

"Superficials on knee and elbow," he said. "My foot may be worse."

"No problem. Sit here and lie back." The man nodded as he inspected the injuries, and had a relaxed confidence that came only from knowing he could handle the situation. Even though the injuries couldn't possibly be critical, and Kyle had seen, experienced, and inflicted worse, it still helped him relax. He lay back as they gurneyed him to sick bay through echoey metal corridors. Passageways? Companionways? Whatever the

Navy called them. He was in a daze and didn't even notice when he arrived.

He came alert again because his foot twinged as they cut the boot away. He risked a look down as they snipped and peeled the sock.

At first it was hard to recognize it as a foot. It was gray and wrinkled from days in the jungle and the water, curled and cramped from the cold. But it resolved to its proper shape, and the swelling and discoloration at the toes wasn't bad. A slight encrustation of blood was under the nail of his big toe.

"Don't even think it's broken," the medic said. Kyle could see the three stripes of a petty officer first class printed on his sleeve. "Got to hurt like hell, but we can drain the hematoma and you should be fine. We'll X-ray anyway, of course."

"Bring it on," Kyle agreed. "I'm not going to complain. But I would like something warm to drink and eat if you can."

"Not supposed to until after treatment. But you're hungry?"

"Yeah, and cold. I'll even eat Navy food," he joked with a smile and a wink.

"Then I'll have them bring you some Navy food, and you can tell the cooks what you think personally." The medic grinned back.

"Done deal."

He was unconscious before it arrived.

Four hours later, bandaged up, showered, fed

excellent food, and wearing borrowed USMC utilities, Kyle felt human again. Dammit, it had been a good mission, even with that pusillanimous Wiesinger along. And they were heading for Singapore and ready to fly home. He dozed again, and the painkillers had nothing to do with it.

The next morning he rose early. He was having trouble getting back to a diurnal schedule, and Wiesinger's order that he be up and about pissed him off. The allegation of "malingering"—while he tried to eat and drink enough to cover the ten pounds he'd lost in a week, plus the painkillers keeping him from screaming when he put weight on his foot—didn't sit well. But he said, "Yes, sir," and got up. He shaved and trimmed his hair back to Army specs, cleaned up and met the others on deck.

The three soldiers were finally back together, watching the sun rise somewhere over the Philippines as they stood at the starboard forward railing. The monstrous port of Singapore was ahead and around them. Ships and docks stretched literally for miles—everything from wooden sailing boats to supertankers and freighters. There were islands all around. A large percentage of the world's ocean traffic came through here. It was the nautical equivalent of Chicago's O'Hare Airport. The lanes were crowded in every direction.

Wiesinger said, "Good news: the Indonesian military stormed the site, finally. They found enough evidence to convince them, I assume, because they did raid Lhokseumawe. They shot the hell out of a bunch of people, but they did intercept a truck with bombs disguised as welding tanks and toolboxes. The target was one of the main tanks at the terminal. Could have taken the whole damned place up."

"Yeah, good, sir," Kyle agreed. "They don't have security around that place?"

"Apparently it has holes. But the Australians have offered an intel brief about sources for explosives. Pisses me off that State won't do it."

"Yeah, that always sucks," Kyle said diplomatically. Frankly, he preferred anonymity, and Robash was the man who could bump his career. What the rest of the world thought wasn't that critical. "One more thing to deal with."

"I'm glad we're leaving," Wade said. "I expect more bombs, and more fragmentation of the rebels. Bakri may be in for an even rougher ride."

"Good luck to him," Kyle said.

"Sergeant Monroe," Wiesinger said after a few seconds of quiet.

"Yes, sir?" he replied.

"You are an insubordinate, impudent, rude little jackass."

Kyle said nothing. It was all true, though "little" was only in comparison to Wiesinger's bulk. The laundry list of complaints he had about the colonel would take a book.

"But you did do a respectable job. I'm going to

ignore a lot of what happened the last few days," the colonel finished.

"I appreciate it, sir. And I'm glad we were able to get the job done."

"I will expect a full after action review on events, specifying what you did against my orders and Army regulations, and why. While I won't charge you, I want you aware of what you did."

"I am aware, sir, and I'll give you that report." *And I'd do it again in a second, you pencil-pushing clown.*

"Very good. If there are any areas where you feel changes are needed, write them up as suggestions and I will forward them. That's how it is done. Sergeant Curtis, you also."

"Yes, sir."

"Will do, sir."

So Kyle was going to get buried in paperwork for his sins. He realized he was just happy to have it over and done with, and would go along with the program without feeling disgruntled.

Besides, he thought, it was just barely possible his recommendations would be accepted.

He let the issue drop. They were all on the same side anyway.

20

A WEEK LATER, THEY WERE BACK IN THEIR small, unassuming shop/office in a sixty-year-old building. It felt good, Kyle thought. Be it ever so decrepit, there's no place like home. Far better than cargo aircraft, decks of ships, trucks in jungles, huts in jungles, or bare skies in jungles.

On the other hand, to be stuck here every day would be a sentence in hell. It was the contrast and variety that kept Kyle sane. You had to leave to know how good home was.

The stop in Germany had been far too brief. Besides, he'd stayed in hospital for follow-up tests that showed nothing. That was the military. Afraid he'd develop something lasting they'd have to pay for. They'd concluded it was minor, would heal quickly, and posed no long-term threat. So he didn't get any German beer or sausage. They weren't popular with Janie, either. She'd spent half the night snuggled up to him in her waterbed, sobbing in relief and clinging. The other half, she'd been incredibly passionate. He could still feel her hair and skin touching him, her hands. It was good to be missed, and to be welcome home. But he wasn't about to credit the Army with that.

He sat at his desk, perfectly arranged with the pile of magazines and tech manuals on the left, phone on the right, miscellaneous junk on the shelf above the monitor and sick, twisted jokes printed out from the Schlock Mercenary comic strip on the wall. It looked like a mess to anyone else, but everything he needed was at arm's reach. That was helpful. His foot throbbed even when elevated and despite lots of Motrin. He wouldn't be walking much for the next week.

The in-box was stuffed, of course. Between receipts for all the material and paperwork they'd handled so far, and routine memoranda, the stack was inches high. Same for email. Some soldiers could never get over the amateur habit of replying-all to acknowledge a letter. Some people felt compelled to report every minor event. Still others sent out jokes that were appreciated by most but triggered a wave of responses. Kyle groaned and started deleting, reading, filing, sorting, and signing. Wade followed suit at his desk, which was much neater, even obsessively so. Neither spoke much, though the occasional sharp tap on a keyboard indicated satisfaction or frustration with the load.

"Wiesinger returned most of the cash upon reporting back," Wade said.

"Figures. So Bakri got his trucks repaired in exchange for hospitality, food, lots of hours, risk to self, seven of his men dead, and a price on his head. Such a deal."

"Nothing we can do now, man."

"No," Kyle agreed. It sucked. Get over it.

He received an email from someone in intel. He read it.

"They think they got him!" he announced to Wade.

"Who?"

"Some scumbag who goes—went—by 'Agung,' who was the probable party behind the explosive shipments was probably one of the ones the Kopassus killed in the raid. And we got the imam . . . so we may have batted a thousand."

"Will we ever know for sure?" Wade asked.

"Probably not. It's all extracted data."

"So don't sweat it, Kyle. We did our job, we came back in one piece, we saved a lot of people. Let the intel wienies worry about it."

"I guess so," Kyle agreed. It made sense. But, dammit, he wanted to know. That was the point of the scope to him; to be sure he got the kill.

But that was a rare situation. Guys in Iraq and 'Nam had swapped fire daily and never known if they hit anything. So he'd take the probable and be happy.

It was 1530, a half hour from the end of the duty day, when Wade snagged another document from the box and stared for a moment.

"Hey, check this out," he said. He waved two sheets of unit stationery.

"Whatcha got?" Kyle asked.

"We are each getting an Arcom for 'supporting the operation,' per Wiesinger."

Both of the last missions had been Bronze Stars with Combat V for valor. For this one, they were credited with "support," and getting an Army Commendation Medal, akin to that given to people who volunteered for deployments to Germany or Turkey to support the war.

Kyle was a professional. He didn't really care about the medals save as markers to point to his record. The acts spoke for themselves. Nevertheless, to see Wade and himself credited with so little was a slap in the face.

"So what did Weaselface put himself in for?" Kyle asked.

"A Silver Star."

"Shit."

"Yeah. Asshole." Wade's usual relaxed demeanor was dark.

"Well, we're still alive, the mission's a success, and we saved some civilians including a little girl. I say we call it even."

"You don't really believe that."

"No. But Robash is healthy again and we'll

have things back to as normal as they ever get next time. Meanwhile, he might sort this out. You and I know what we did."

"Yeah." Wade sounded more than a bit disgruntled. Kyle knew it wasn't the Arcom that bothered him. It was the Silver Star for Wiesinger.

"Hey, buddy," Kyle said, standing and coming to attention, facing Wade. Wade stood and faced him, looking curious.

"You're the finest spotter and shooter I could ever be teamed with. Wiesinger may not say it, but I will. You rock." And he raised his hand in salute.

Wade snapped to attention that would credit him on parade and popped his own arm up. "Means more from you than any medal he can ever award, buddy. Thanks." The look in his eyes was probably a match for Kyle's own.

They both dropped back to attention, then relaxed again. It was a close moment, but also an embarrassing one, with the circumstances behind it.

"Screw it. Let's get my girlfriend and go watch civilian chicks dance without any fear of being blown up." He indicated the door.

"Sounds good. You're buying," Wade agreed, cheerful again.

"How come I always wind up buying?"

"If you don't know . . ."

It turned to friendly shoves as they headed out the door.

Author's Note

NDONESIA IS A FASCINATING NATION, AND I
hope I've presented it well. It has a chaotic past
and its own current problems, but has some of
the friendliest people and most beautiful scenery
on Earth. It's always hard to be critical of places
one isn't familiar with, and my Indonesian
friends deserve thanks for helping me build this
story with some liberties on the political situation for sake of entertainment value. There have
to be bad guys and there have to be heroes, but in
the real world, things are not so black and white.